WA

Jamie Smith ... ...m and studied histo..., ... journalism at the University of Wales, Bangor. He spent several years moving around the UK and Australia before landing in Thame, Oxfordshire where he was living with his wife, Anne, and their two children at the time of writing this book. Since then they have been joined by a third child and moved their life to Donegal on the North West coast of Ireland. He is also the author of the acclaimed spy thriller, The Soviet Comeback, and the fantasy novel, Where Giants Walk.

BY THE SAME AUTHOR:

Nikita Allochka Series
The Soviet Comeback

Många Världar Series
Where Giants Walk (T. S. J. Smith)

Jamie Smith

WALL OF SPIES

JimJam Press

© 2025 Jamie Smith

All rights reserved.

No part of this ebook may be reproduced or transmitted in any form or by any means, electronic or mechanical, without the prior written permission of the author.

This is a work of fiction. Names, characters, places, and incidents are products of the author's imagination or are used fictitiously. Any resemblance to actual persons, living or dead, or actual events is purely coincidental.

ISBN: 978-1-9193789-0-9

Cover design by Kieran Stanislaw Mace

First published in 2025 by JimJam Press.

For Mammaji and Pops

PROLOGUE

East Berlin, November 4th, 1989. 8 a.m.

The hooded woman was clad entirely in black. She strode purposefully along Schadowstrasse, keeping to the darkness in the early morning gloom. As she reached the end of the road and turned left onto Unter den Linden, the central boulevard running through the heart of the city, she melted into the crowds that were gradually filling the street. The atmosphere was one of growing excitement and nervousness. She glanced over her shoulder and saw the Grenztruppen sentries in the watchtowers in front of the wall, weapons scanning the crowd nervously. Behind them, she could just see the top of the Brandenburg Gate, the entrance to a world forbidden to those on this side of the city and to the entire Soviet Bloc for the past twenty-eight years.

As she moved swiftly along the road, the crowd swelled, hundreds spilling out of side streets to join the march. Banners fluttered above them, daubed with angry calls for change. In recent weeks, brutal violence had been carried out against protestors by the East German government and its ruthless Ministry for State Security - better known around the world as the Stasi. Yet still the people marched on.

But the woman in black did not join the calls or raise a banner, instead increasing her pace. She kept one hand inside her black winter jacket, fingers tightly wrapped around the butt of her Makarov PM semi-automatic pistol. As the throng approached Alexanderplatz, the noise became deafening, with over 500,000 people squeezed into the square for the protest against the German Democratic Republic. She didn't allow herself to be carried by the crowd and instead turned against the tide, crossing to Karl-Liebknecht-Strasse and darting down a cul-de-sac running alongside the looming concrete Galeria Kaufhof department store building. She cast her eyes from side to side before withdrawing a key from inside her jacket and then letting herself into the side door of the old building.

She unzipped her coat and pulled back her hood, revealing a tumbling mass of brown curls and a black shirt with a name badge indicating she worked on the perfume counter. She smiled benignly at people as she passed them in the corridor, but instead of heading towards the shopfront, she entered the stairwell and began climbing, not stopping until she reached the emergency door to the roof. Removing the alarm connection, she pushed down the barrier and let herself onto the roof. The cold November air bit at her face, and she pulled the hood back over her head, zipping the coat and making her way to the low edge of the building. She removed a metal grid from the top of a large pipe running along the edge of the roof and pulled out a package wrapped in plastic bags attached to a piece of string. From it, she withdrew the pieces of a sniper rifle, which she swiftly and expertly assembled. She knew she must act quickly, while her contact in the Volkspolizei had briefly distracted the patrols from this roof. She propped it on the ledge of the building, lay flat against the rooftop, and began scanning the building opposite through the scope.

She soon found what she was looking for in the Hotel Stadt Berlin opposite. The hotel, the tallest building in Berlin, rose forty-one floors into the frigid November air, but it was the twenty-eighth floor on which the woman's gaze was fixed. Through the window, she could see Ernst Schleicher, the head of the Stasi, gazing down at the crowds with a look of great distaste on his usually expressionless face. He was a very small man with beady eyes and a hairline receding high onto his head but remaining thick at the back and sides, and, despite such an unimpressive physique, even from this distance, he oozed cold authority. He then swiftly turned and disappeared from view, but the shooter remained motionless, keeping the scope trained on the window, her finger curled around the trigger. Further back in the room, another man came into view, and unlike the grey-suited Schleicher, he was more conspicuous in full Volkspolizei uniform. He was a blocky, rigid man whose face was hidden in shadow, and he was rolling his shoulders as if in preparation for a battle. The shooter swiftly moved her line of sight away from the room and scanned the neighbouring windows and rooftops, quickly identifying other police uniforms half-concealed behind curtains. All were armed with automatic weapons, which were trained on the crowd below, ready to unleash more violence on the peaceful demonstrators. The order to crush the demonstration could not be given. Berlin was ready for change.

She swung the scope back onto the room on the twenty-eighth floor and saw that Schleicher had come back into view through the window. He gave what was clearly an instruction to the policeman, who walked towards the phone sitting on a table to the side of the room. When his face came out of shadow, the shooter recognised him as Julian Rausch, the East Berlin Volkspolizei Chief, and the second his hand touched the receiver, the woman exhaled slowly and pulled the trigger.

Rausch toppled, a small red hole in the centre of his forehead. Schleicher looked on in apparent disgust at the blood splattered across the wall behind where his police chief had stood. The woman refocused her weapon swiftly and pulled the trigger once more. But as she took the shot, her arm jolted and turned the gun sharply upwards as, without warning, a knife embedded itself in her arm. She rolled away as what would have been a killer blow came down towards her. A second knife clattered into the concrete floor as the man wielding it fell expertly into a roll, pushing himself up and propelling himself towards the woman. In a crouch, she tugged the knife out of her arm and slashed as her attacker jetted towards her. She sliced across his face, but his momentum carried into her, and they both crashed into the raised ledge at the edge of the building. She was pinned, and he began to furiously rain punches into her ribcage, and she felt at least two ribs crack as the wind was driven out of her and the knife fell from her hand.

The man pushed himself to his feet. Blood was seeping heavily from the deep cut she had left from one cheek to the other across his upper lip like a gruesome second smile, dripping onto his black leather bomber jacket and onto his faded jeans. He may have been in plain clothes, but everything about the way he held himself screamed Stasi. He was a large, muscled man with a squared-off jaw, and he wiped a hand across the cut, which only served to smear it across his crazed face, and brought up a heavy boot to stamp her head back onto the lip of the building. He brought it down with such force that, had it made contact, it would have completely crushed her skull against the wall, but again, she rolled to the side and, with a swivel, grabbed the knife and jammed it into the back of his knee. He cried out, the sound lost in the swirling wind and noise from the crowds, and fell to the ground as she collapsed, wheezing and holding her broken ribs tenderly. As both lay on the floor, their eyes fell on the sniper rifle still propped near the ledge. The man yanked the knife from his leg with a grunt and tried to pull himself to his feet using the ledge. The woman crawled past him, still wheezing, and he grabbed hold of her coat, pulling her back and clawing desperately at her mouth. She felt the corner of her lip tear and swung an elbow backwards that connected with his head. He fell away but tried to grab her feet or grab a purchase on her. Just clipping her ankle, she stumbled and fell forward, unable to stifle a scream as she landed on her broken ribs and the wind was again driven out of her, causing her to retch.

She heard footsteps and saw another Stasi agent appearing from the other side of the roof, previously blocked from sight by the raised central block where the door to the roof stood. The rifle was just yards away, and she desperately tried to claw herself towards it through the excruciating pain in her side and felt her foot again pulled back by the injured man. She kicked out and used his head to push herself forward. The newcomer was closing in fast and shouting, 'Nicht bewegen!' *Don't move.*

With a last superhuman roar, she drove herself forward and, grabbing the rifle, rolled onto her back and shot the running man from point-blank range through the torso. Without pausing, she ejected the shell from the weapon, snapping another cartridge onto the chamber and squeezing the trigger, the bullet exploding the face of the man she had fought, whose hand stayed aloft for a moment in either a grab or a plea for mercy before it slumped to the ground. She reloaded the weapon and shot the running man once more. *Always make sure.*

She slumped down onto her back and allowed herself a moment to gaze up at the swirling grey November sky. She pushed herself gingerly to her knees and looked through the scope to the window opposite. The room was full of chaos as officers and medics surrounded a body on the floor, which was being covered by a sheet.

The woman used the edge of her coat sleeve to dab gently at her damaged face, hoping to remove as much evidence of her bleeding lip as possible. Then she dropped the rifle back into the drain; she would have to dispose of it properly later and left the rooftop. She melted back into the crowds as their chanting reached a fever pitch.

'Freiheit! Freiheit! Die Mauer einreißen. FREIHEIT!' *Freedom! Freedom! Tear down the wall. FREEDOM!*

CHAPTER 1

ONE DAY EARLIER.

Spīn Ghar Mountains, Eastern Afghanistan.

There were bodies, debris and dying fires all around, flickering in and out of shadow as the waxing moon passed behind the clouds. All was silent, punctuated only by an occasional distant crash, but Nikita Allochka did not flinch as he sat at the mouth of a cave looking out over the Khyber Pass and beyond to Pakistan.

He looked down at the notepad he was holding and at the telegram he was drafting to send to Maxim Denisov, the head of the KGB.

ONGOING GUERILLA DISRUPTION. UNSUITABLE LOCATION. CONSIDER NEW STRATEGY.

He'd written and rewritten the telegram multiple times, trying to say it all without saying very much, trying to find a way to get out of the hell he had found himself in. For almost two years, Nikita, the KGB agent known as the 'Black Russian', had been based in the infamous Tora Bora caves of the Spīn Ghar mountains on the direct orders of Denisov. He had been sent there to oversee a highly classified mission to turn the caves under the mountain into a secret storage facility for the Soviet's mid-range nuclear weapons. The same nuclear weapons they had agreed to relinquish in a landmark treaty with their Cold War opponents, the USA. But all he had overseen was failure.

The Soviet Union had been engaged in a long and arduous war in Afghanistan, and, keen to turn their withdrawal into a success, all military might had been thrown at the cave complex to flush out the remaining Afghan guerrilla forces. But the caves went deeper and further than they had ever imagined, and every night, pockets of resistance would creep from holes deep underground that they had been hiding in throughout the day and collapse key passages, cutting off supply lines and power, ruthlessly cutting down soldiers as they slept, and making the even vaguely safe storage of missiles alarmingly dangerous. In the beginning, it had seemed straightforward. The Afghans were rudderless, leaderless and defeated, and the plan seemed like it might even work. But in recent months, the tide had turned. Out of nowhere, the resistance had become organised; they worked in groups and had a clear strategy, and now it was the Soviet forces that were beleaguered and deflated, feeling their way in the dark and fighting shadows.

Nikita's melancholy musing was interrupted by the sound of someone clearing their throat behind him. He turned to see General Pavel Lipovsky standing at attention. Lipovsky was the Red Army officer in charge of the military operation in the region, but because of the nature of the operation and what was at stake, the KGB had oversight and control of it, meaning that Nikita, who now occupied the KGB rank of major - a title he rarely had any use for - had a general reporting to him.

'What is it, comrade?' Nikita asked wearily.

Lipovsky's mouth tightened noticeably, verging on a sneer, but he quickly collected himself.

'We have managed to capture one of the enemy, sir,' he said. 'A cave militant.'

Nikita leapt to his feet. 'What? How? Speak quickly.'

'One of their men got caught on the wrong side of a rock fall after they collapsed one of the transport tunnels. He is wounded but alive and has been made secure.'

'Lead the way, General,' Nikita stated. They walked briskly in silence through the rabbit warren of caves, lit by loosely wired lights dangling along the sides, which cast long shadows over the frequent fissures and alcoves in the rock. Nikita had lost many men to Mujahideen guerrillas hiding in such holes, and any journey under the mountains was fraught with fear. He could feel an ember of hope burning inside him now, after months of fighting against shadows, that they might finally have a lead. There had been no shortage of firefights leading to deaths on both sides, but capturing an enemy soldier had proven impossible. The Mujahideen were proud men, and they found glory in falling on their swords rather than being captured.

I'm still searching for a place in the world where there's a glory I can believe in, he thought to himself bitterly. There would certainly be no glory in what was coming.

Lipovsky led him deep into the mountain, where the air grew stale and frigid, temperatures a long way from the relentless heat of the world outside, and to a cave that was manned by armed soldiers. A steel door had been driven into the rock, and, on the general's signal, a guard opened the door.

Inside the dimly lit room, a young Afghan man sat propped up against the rear wall, faced by another two soldiers. There was no question of his escaping, as his right leg and arm had clearly been crushed in the rock fall that led to his capture and was a bloody, mangled mess. Despite the cold, his face was pallid, dripping with sweat, and his eyes darted from one face to another, unable to hide the fear within them.

'Time may not be on our side here, General,' Nikita whispered to Lipovsky, who nodded slightly but said nothing.

'Has he told us anything so far?'

'He does not speak Russian, sir, so we have been unable to get anything from him.'

Nikita sighed and sat down on the rocky floor opposite the man.

'Salaam alaikum,' he said softly.

The man said nothing, beginning to look very tired.

'I am Nikita. What is your name, soldier?' Nikita asked, continuing to speak in faltering Pashto.

'Naseefa,' he shrugged, then winced.

'Is the pain very great, Naseefa?' Nikita asked.

Naseefa nodded. 'Yes, it is very bad.'

'I can help you with that. But I will also need you to help me.'

'That is something I will never do.'

'I understand. You have your honour, and whether you live or die, I will not take that from you. Some of my comrades, however, are not men of honour. They know only brutality, and I will not be able to prevent them from making this pain you feel now seem like little more than a scratch if you do not speak to me. Do you understand?'

'I understand. You are not my friend. You are with them and so have no honour. You work to steal the land from my family, to turn these holy mountains into a laboratory. If I am to die, so be it. I will find my peace long before you ever do.'

Nikita turned to Lipovsky.

'Do we have any translators available?'

'No, the only two translators are both out on missions close to the border. You are the only Pashto speaker here at present.'

Nikita grimaced. It meant he had to be present for what was about to happen, and it would not be pleasant.

'Soldier, I am going to ask again for you to help me. I only want some information, nothing more. You do not need to die.'

Naseefa was getting closer to unconsciousness and just let out a short, dry laugh and said simply, 'God is great.'

'Very well,' Nikita said to himself in Russian.

He turned to Lipovsky. 'He will not talk. We must make him. I do not need to tell you the importance of the information he has.'

The corner of the general's mouth curled in a smirk, and he beckoned to the two privates who had been watching from the corners of the room.

'Assist Major Allochka in helping our guest to become more talkative.'

They didn't smile but also didn't flinch.

***

It was sometime later that Nikita found himself sitting back in his favoured spot at the mouth of the cave, looking over the Khyber Pass as dawn just began to touch the horizon. Often, he found himself imagining it back in its Silk Road heyday, stretching all the way to the east of China and the Yellow Sea beyond. Other times, he would gaze into the distance and imagine crossing the land to reach his father and sister, now safely stationed in Cuba, or Elysia, the woman in Baltimore he loved but might never see again. Right now, however, his mind was on more immediate matters.

Once again, his thoughts were interrupted by General Lipovsky, who walked out and came to a stop next to Nikita.

'The view looks a little less like we are on the precipice of hell in the cold light of day, sir,' he said, his tone less frosty than usual.

'Looks can be deceiving, General,' Nikita replied sourly.

'The interrogation did not go well?'

'Not for our friend. For us... it told us a great deal.'

'Oh?'

Nikita sighed and pushed himself to his feet to face the general.

'It goes a lot bigger than we could have imagined, Pavel,' Nikita said, his face a picture of concern. If Lipovsky minded Nikita using such familiarity, he did not show it. Instead, he was thirsty for the information they had been so desperately needing.

'They have a new leader, one named Bedar Al-Zalmay,' Nikita added.

'It is as we suspected then,' Lipovsky said, nodding. 'Did he reveal much about the man?'

'Very little, he was fading by that point. Only that he has risen fast and is a fundamentalist. Promising to bring strict Sharia law to the country once they have ousted us.'

'That's almost enough to make the rest of Afghanistan want us to stay,' Lipovsky said with a grim chuckle.

'With the things we have done to this country, they have had to endure much. When times get hard, extremism becomes all the more appealing.'

Lipovsky looked like he was chewing on something unpleasant and clearly had to make an enormous effort not to strike Nikita for speaking ill of the Soviet Union.

Ignoring him, Nikita continued. 'But it goes much further than an extremist man taking charge of the Mujahideen. He has formed a new organisation that they call Kulu Alqasas, and it sounds like they have big plans. How realistic they are, it's impossible to say just from Naseefa.'

'Naseefa?'

'Our unfortunate friend. I do not think he was senior in Kulu Alqasas circles,' Nikita replied.

Lipovsky shrugged. 'Then he did not tell us much that we had not already guessed. They have a new leader and are more organised. He has merely confirmed things.'

'There is more, General. This Al-Zalmay appears to be very well funded, and he means to strike at the heart of the Soviet Union in ways far beyond collapsing caves. I need to speak to Denisov immediately.'

'What is it that he is planning?' Lipovsky asked eagerly.

'That, General, is a KGB matter, I'm afraid. I need a chopper to the communication centre at Dushanbe immediately.'

The general looked like he had been slapped, and again, it seemed as if his teeth were chewing on the inside of his cheeks to stop him from open insubordination. He just nodded curtly, turning on his heel.

***

It was three hours later when Nikita touched down in Dushanbe, the capital of Soviet Tajikistan, some 450 miles from the Spīn Ghar warzone he had called home for the past twenty-two months. Wide boulevards and grand buildings were set in a fertile valley where two rivers met against the backdrop of snow-capped mountains. The stunning city came as something of a culture shock to Nikita, who now felt the exhaustion of the seemingly endless months of blood, dust, and bombs weigh heavily upon him. It gave him a timely reminder of just how vast the Soviet empire was - stretching from the Pacific coast in the East and engulfing Ukraine, Belarus, Georgia in the West, the Baltics of Latvia, Lithuania and Estonia in the north, and from Tajikistan to Azerbaijan on the Black Sea in the south, and everything in between. And that was before counting the entire so-called 'Eastern or Soviet Bloc' - the group of communist states that were controlled by the USSR and spanned everything from Poland and East Germany down to Yugoslavia and Albania, which formed what had become known as the Iron Curtain - a Soviet Union line that you could not cross. The size and scale was mind-boggling. To Nikita, sat in the heat of Tajikistan, it was hard to imagine that he was still in the same country as the likes of cold northern states like Estonia.

The helicopter flew low over the city centre before turning to the east of the city, where the look and feel became a little more familiar. The edge of the centre became a grey wall of concrete, more befitting of a city once called Stalinabad. Concrete high rises and narrow streets became a uniform shade of granite that could have been anywhere in the USSR. The helicopter landed on the roof of a wide, squat building with a helipad on the roof, and Nikita hastily climbed out and descended into the KGB's Tajik communication centre.

A young KGB officer was there to welcome him and salute him. 'Major Allochka, an honour to meet you, sir,' he said brightly. 'I am Agent Sharipova. To what do we owe the pleasure?'

How times have changed, Nikita thought to himself. Word of his defeat of the traitorous KGB agent Taras Brishnov and his ally, Dmitry Vasilevsky, the leader of a Neo-Nazi group, Pamyat, who had sought to overthrow the government and reignite the Cold War, had spread quickly through the KGB, and he found that he now enjoyed a certain celebrity status with some. With others, things would never change.

'I need your most secure line and an empty room, Sharipova. It is a matter of extreme urgency.'

The young agent nodded eagerly and led him from the roof into a dark, concrete staircase that took them down several floors. He opened the door to the first floor, which revealed a brightly lit room full of communications equipment and a lot of noise from the dozens of operatives working the machines. Most were too engrossed with their work to notice the pair as they walked through the room, although more than one operative ogled him, with looks ranging from curiosity to open disdain. Nikita ignored all of them and followed Agent Sharipova through to a small room adjoining the larger one. It was a simple room with a desk, empty apart from a chocolate brown telephone.

'This is the phone the station chief uses for urgent, secure communications, mainly with Moscow. It was little used, but the independence movement is growing at pace here in Tajikistan, so now he spends much time in here.'

'You are sure it is secure? The matter I must discuss is highly delicate.'

The young agent looked desperate to ask what it was but just about bit his lip. 'It is fully encrypted, sir.'

'Good. That will be all, Agent,' Nikita added with an air of finality, and Sharipov nodded, failing to hide his disappointment, and left the room.

Nikita wasted no time sitting behind the desk and lifting the receiver to dial the Lubyanka Building in downtown Moscow, where the KGB director was based, and asked to be put through immediately. There was a short delay before the thin, reedy voice Nikita recognised as Maxim Denisov, the man who had risen so rapidly to become the KGB director only months before, answered.

'Da?'

'It is Agent Allochka.'

There was a pause as Denisov hesitated. 'Is the line secure?'

'Yes, sir, I am calling from the secure line of the Dushanbe station chief. I've been assured it is safe.'

'Dushanbe?! What are you doing in Tajikistan when you are meant to be hundreds of miles south of there, overseeing the most important mission currently being undertaken by the KGB and Soviet forces?'

'I have not abandoned post. I will be returning there immediately following this call, but the information that I came upon last night is, dare I say, even more important.'

Denisov snorted disbelievingly. 'If it isn't, there's a gulag I know of still in operation in Siberia that you will soon become familiar with.'

Nikita ignored the clumsy threat, knowing that he was too valuable an asset to send to a gulag, especially since the last of the gulags had been wound down at least twenty years ago.

'There is a plot, a plot to strike East Berlin,' Nikita almost spat out. 'Thousands, perhaps millions, will die. We must stop it.'

Again, there was silence at the other end of the line. This time, it lasted so long that Nikita would have thought Denisov had hung up were it not for the ongoing sound of his wheezy breathing. Eventually, he broke it.

'Tell me everything, Allochka.'

'Last night, we finally captured one of the Mujahideen fighters who have been collapsing our caves and threatening the viability of the grand plan—' Nikita paused for a moment, leaving no doubt as to his personal feelings about the plan. 'The man had much to say that has caused me great concern. As I had suspected, they now have a leader who has brought them together as a more organised and cohesive force.'

He paused to take a breath, and when Denisov said nothing, he forced himself onwards. 'His name is Bedar Al-Zalmay, and they are calling themselves Kula Alqasas. The man I interrogated was not a senior member of the organisation, so he did not know many details, but what he told me was that Kulu Alqasas are planning a retaliatory strike on East Berlin—'

'East Berlin?' snapped Denisov. 'You are sure this is what he said?'

'Of course, sir. It was not a piece of information I took lightly. Nowhere could hurt us more.'

'Indeed,' said Denisov, again falling silent.

After an excruciating minute of hearing nothing but Denisov's wheezy breathing, Nikita could bear it no longer. 'What will we do?'

'Berlin is a tinder box at the moment,' Denisov mused, almost talking to himself. 'It's the symbolic Soviet capital in Europe. This could undermine communism across the entire Eastern Bloc.'

This time, Nikita fell silent, unsure what to say.

After another minute of silence, Denisov cleared his throat, as if snapping out of a trance. 'It is clear we must act. I will make the arrangements.'

'Arrangements, sir?' Nikita asked, confused.

'For you to journey to Berlin, Allochka. Do not pretend to be anything other than delighted to leave those god-forsaken caves. I would lose my trust in you if you did. I need you on the ground in East Germany. You will leave as soon as a plane can be readied.'

'Almost two years has felt like a lifetime,' Nikita admitted, trying to stop his burgeoning grin from creeping into his voice. 'But what will become of the Tora Bora mission?'

'That is no longer any of your concern, agent.'

'Very well, sir.'

'And where are we at with the Americans?' Denisov asked, chuckling. 'I still enjoy that we sent you there as a secret agent, and they sent you back to spy on us, unaware that you were a Soviet agent. It is too perfect for words!'

At this, Nikita did not smile. He had spent a year embedded in the CIA in Langley, Virginia, as an analyst before getting caught in a very public pursuit of the traitorous KGB agent - and Nikita's nemesis - Taras Brishnov and losing a woman he cared for in the process. The CIA had responded to his televised high-speed pursuit by 'turning' him into a full field agent and posting him to the USSR in the hope the Soviets would try to recruit him, allowing him to become one of the only operational US spies on Russian soil.

'I have been unable to communicate with them for some time, sir. They most likely believe me dead.'

'That is unacceptable. It is too powerful a hand we have been dealt to throw it away so carelessly. I expected better of you, Allochka. You must make contact with them immediately and inform them that you are being posted to Berlin.'

Nikita physically had to bite his tongue to prevent his retort about Afghan caves not having a lot of mailboxes. The opportunity to get away from the ludicrous mission and into Europe was too good an opportunity to turn away from.

'I will send instructions for your mission to the East Berlin HQ. Do not fail me, this is critical.'

'Have I ever?' Nikita asked daringly.

He was greeted by the sound of the dial tone.

CHAPTER 2

Nikita was met at Berlin Schönefeld Airport in the German Democratic Republic, or GDR, by the station chief Ivan Rosin, a tall, thin man with a pencil moustache, small spectacles and Bryl-creamed pale brown hair. He looked like something from the French Resistance, complete with hangdog eyes and a pale brown suit, which almost matched his carefully slicked hair. It was just after 9 a.m., and the cobalt sky swirled overhead, but the bitter cold made Nikita almost feel like he was back in Moscow.

'Komm,' said Rosin, speaking in German, looking nervously around him. *Come.*

The airport was strangely quiet, at least by the standards of a capital city, which struck Nikita as distinctly odd, and he felt the sixth sense that he had learned to trust tingling, the hairs on the back of his neck standing slightly on end. Rosin led him to a small, boxy car, a Zaporozhets ZAZ G-200, which would compete hard against a number of other Eastern Bloc rivals for the title of the least attractive vehicle around. Painting it beige had definitely not helped its chances.

'Where is everyone?' Nikita asked in Russian as soon as the doors were closed. Rosin said nothing but pulled off carefully and began to drive through empty streets in the direction of the city centre.

'Well?' Nikita snapped, pushing for a response.

'They attend a rally,' the station chief replied curtly.

'What rally? What aren't you telling me?' Nikita asked with more urgency.

Rosin sighed, and his face sagged slightly. 'An illegal demonstration has been organised this morning in Alexanderplatz. They are protesting against the GDR.'

'How many will protest?' Nikita asked, gazing around the unusually quiet East Berlin, looking even gloomier for the absence of life. 'Surely no more than 50,000?'

Rosin swallowed. 'Our early indications suggest there may be rather more.' He pulled a packet of Cabinet cigarettes from behind the wheel and lit one up, a cloud of cloying smoke from the high tar, high nicotine cigarettes instantly filling the car. He offered one to Nikita, who declined with a shake of his head.

Rosin took another deep inhalation. 'Rumours are there may be a million or more.'

Nikita spluttered, both from the thick smoke of the notoriously low-quality East German cigarettes and the station chief's pronouncement.

'A million?! Surely not, Rosin. That would be unprecedented. It would totally eclipse the Hungarian Revolution and the Polish Poznan Protests combined.'

Rosin just took another drag on his cigarette, his elbow propped on the door frame and a bitter look on his face. It was happening on his watch.

'I am surprised the station chief has been spared for a simple airport pick up when such a rally is going on.'

'You misunderstand, Agent. We are going directly to Alexanderplatz—you are going straight into the field.'

Nikita sat back in his chair, his face impassive.

'I hope you slept on your flight, Allochka. It could be a long day,' added Rosin as he turned the car into Lichtenberger Strasse. Nikita rolled down his window slightly to let out the thick cigarette smoke. Over the whistle of the cold wind, he could just begin to make out a sound of a different kind. At first, it was barely perceptible, but as the car made its way along the wide street, what had started as little more than a whisper was building in a steep crescendo into a roar akin to a fighter jet flying overhead. More and more people were now visible, all moving in the same direction. By the time the car reached the end of the street and turned into the broad Karl-Marx-Allee Boulevard, the sound could be heard more clearly - the sound of hundreds of thousands of angry East Germans crying out for change.

Rosin attempted to make his way along the street through the crowds, beeping his horn frenetically. Eventually, it became clear that it was fruitless, and the car came to a stop. Rosin only just managed to nudge it to the side of the road.

'Perhaps now you can give me some idea of what you're intending me to do here,' Nikita said blandly. 'I do, after all, already have a mission in Berlin.'

Rosin lit another cigarette, drawing on it nervously.

'I think you need a drink,' Nikita said drily.

'I hear that since your time in America, you drink enough whisky for us all, Allochka,' Rosin snapped back acidly.

'I try, but it's hard to keep on top of it.' Nikita shrugged nonchalantly, but the comment had stung. And what's more, now he wanted a drink.

If Rosin was amused, he did not show it. Instead, he just took another long drag on his already half-finished cigarette. Nikita noticed he had a slight facial tick, likely a recent development, he surmised. 'Your mission, then, Allochka. We need someone who can operate in the shadows, someone who can blend in, which in East Berlin might be a little difficult for someone who looks... ah, someone with your... ah...'

'Yes?' Nikita said with a gently raised eyebrow.

Rosin coughed. 'Yes... well, you know. I'm sure you'll get the job done.'

'That remains to be seen, Rosin, on whether you ever manage to tell me what the job is.' Rosin made a sour expression.

'You think you know everything, Allochka. I know a little of your story, and you have lived a little. But nothing you have done, no horrors you have seen, can prepare you for the festering shit soup that is Berlin.'

'East or west?'

Rosin shrugged. 'Two halves of an atomic bomb desperate to go off.'

The car was being jostled gently by the heavy crowds, which showed no signs of dwindling. 'Whatever your intentions for me today, Rosin, they might be redundant if we're unable to get out of the car, which will soon become the case.'

'Yes, of course, we must make haste. As you're now aware, the rally is centred in Alexanderplatz, up ahead. The rooftops and buildings surrounding the square are being patrolled by armed police, all waiting for the order to open fire from either the Stasi chief Ernst Schleicher or his puppet Julian Rausch, the head of the East Berlin Volkspolizei.'

'A police presence is standard procedure for any rally anywhere in the world,' said Nikita.

'Yes, but the decision to gun down the entire rally was taken some time ago. The authority came all the way from General Secretary Petrenko himself.'

Nikita's face rarely registered surprise; his training did not allow for it. But now he struggled to hide his incredulity. 'They have ordered the murder of up to a million East Germans who are peacefully protesting?'

'It may not be violent, but there is nothing peaceful about this protest, Allochka,' snapped Rosin. 'They seek to tear at the very fabric of the Soviet Union and everything we have worked for since Lenin himself. The protest must be crushed.'

'This is insanity. It will ignite and unite the entire Eastern Bloc against us.'

'I was told that you were the best, Allochka. The rumours that you are the finest weapon in the KGB's arsenal were clearly greatly exaggerated, as no KGB agent would question the decisions of his superiors so brazenly,' said Rosin.

'Just tell me what the plan is here, Rosin. The day grows old,' Nikita said wearily.

'Whether you approve or not, the protest will be crushed. There is reason to believe the purpose of your visit and the more immediate mission may overlap.'

Nikita looked up sharply.

'I see I finally have your attention, Allochka.'

'Which is incredible considering how long you're taking to tell me what's going on,' retorted Nikita, struggling to hide his exasperation.

'Your mission is to prevent an Afghan bomb from being detonated in East Berlin. If that were to happen, the trickle of people finding their way west via Hungary would become a flood, and the wall would surely fall. No time would serve their purposes more than when so many of the people are gathered in one place—the loss of life would be appalling. The demonstration must be stopped, and the people dispersed as swiftly as possible.'

'Do you have any intel to suggest they are planning to strike today?'

Rosin shrugged.

'You mean to say you're planning to open fire on innocent citizens just based on a hunch?' Nikita asked in amazement.

'Any plans for violence are not mine. I, unlike you, do not question my orders, Allochka,' the station chief quipped. 'Leave the crowds to Schleicher and Rausch. Your job is to find and eliminate any terrorists at the scene.'

'Well, that shouldn't be a problem, in a crowd of hundreds of thousands squashed into a square,' Nikita muttered. 'The Stasi and the police, they are happy to work with the KGB?'

'They know the rules of the game, particularly the Stasi. And as for the police, I do not care if they are happy about it, but they will do it. Equipment has been left for you at a useful vantage point, where you will also be able to see when Schleicher gives the order to disperse the crowds. Much depends on you.'

'Not least my own life, as if a bomb goes off, I'll be right in the middle of it.'

'Better that than the bomb going off and you living to tell the tale. Here's the address and a map of where to go. I suggest you make haste,' Rosin said, handing Nikita a scrap of paper.

'Nikita glanced at the address and immediately ripped it up, instantly committing it to memory. Without saying anything more to Rosin, he pocketed the map and opened the door to climb out of the car. Rosin grabbed his arm and pulled him back slightly.

'Allochka. Berlin has not known real freedom since before the Great Depression. The people here think they want it, but it would only bring chaos. Capitalism would see a rise of the right once more. We cannot have another Hitler,' he said earnestly, his eyes shining with communist fervour.

Nikita's face remained impassive, and he pulled his arm away, turned and began forcing his way through the crowd, leaving a disgruntled Rosin slumped in the seat of his car.

'One man's Hitler is another man's Stalin,' Nikita muttered to himself, shaking his head slightly, glad

Denisov wasn't around to hear him say such treasonous things.

It took him over half an hour to make it to the concrete block lining the south side of Alexanderplatz using Rosin's map. The crowd was packed shoulder to shoulder inside the square itself, and the going was slow. The security guard, nervously barring the front door, immediately stood to one side upon seeing Nikita and pointed him in the direction of the stairwell to find what he was seeking. *So much for a covert mission*, Nikita thought to himself, making his way as quickly as he could.

He had been directed to a small, boxy room on the third floor, which gave an adequate view of the square, flanked on the left by the Galeria Kaufhof and on the right by the Hotel Stadt Berlin. In the centre of the crowd, a makeshift stage had been erected, and a middle-aged woman with high cheekbones and short hair was speaking, almost in tears, of peace and freedom of speech to the roars of approval from the crowd.

An old army-issue green canvas holdall bag was underneath the window, and Nikita pulled it open to reveal a sniper rifle, a Walther PP handgun, the pistol of choice for the Stasi, which he checked before pushing it into the belt at his lower back, and a walkie-talkie, which he picked up and turned on. It was on a frequency that immediately picked up the crackle of Stasi chatter. He listened to it while swiftly putting together the rifle, a brand new Dragunov, a weapon with which he was exceedingly familiar. He lifted the window slightly and poked the barrel of the gun out of the window, adjusting the reticle in the scope to bring the square fully into focus.

He cursed silently to himself as it became clear that his placement gave him little in the way of a vantage point over the surrounding buildings or a clear view of the crowd itself. A typical decision made by the likes of Rosin, or the police, who had no experience of sniping.

A voice with authority announced itself as none other than Julian Rausch, the police chief, and asked for various teams to confirm their position before ordering them to ready themselves to open fire.

'Südmannschaft?' he barked. *South team?*

Various voices confirmed they were in position, from the rooftops to various other

windows and vantage points from around the building.

'Und unser besonderer Gast?' he added impatiently. *And our special guest?*

'Requesting a change of position,' Nikita replied in German.

'Request denied, hold your position,' came the unerring response.

Nikita swiftly took apart his Dragunov and tossed the pieces back into the bag, which he slung over one shoulder.

He lifted the receiver to his mouth. 'Need a better vantage point. Will report new location once in position.' He threw the walkie-talkie into the bag and smiled as he heard Rausch's fury explode through the device.

Either of the buildings he had faced would be much better for finding a target, and in the interest of speed, he began to make his way towards the closer one, the Galeria Kaufhof. But the going had become even slower, and even trying to skirt the edge of the square had become near impossible. His bag did nothing to help his progress. He was forced to dig his elbows into people to create space for himself and was greeted with a lot of shoves and the occasional punch in the back as he passed. But for the sake of the crowd as much of his own, he kept his eyes on his destination and ignored the disgruntled protestors he left in his wake. The crowd was beginning to build itself up into a frenzy of chanting, and Nikita feared that Rausch and Schleicher would give their order any moment. He threw frequent glances up at the windows and rooftops of the surrounding buildings and saw the occasional curtain twitch from a clumsy police officer but little else from where he was standing.

After what felt like an age, he reached the door of the Galeria Kaufhof but found it heavily barred, and with no heads up as to his coming, the security guards eyed him with deep suspicion, laughing openly when he asked to get inside.

Getting increasingly anxious, Nikita cast his eyes around, looking for another way in. Huge banners and flags were fluttering above the crowd, which must now be at its likely capacity. He pushed and shoved his way around the side of the building to a cul-du-sac, which was much quieter and gave no view of the square. Out of a side door came a shop assistant wrapped up against the cold, her curly hair barely visible above the collar of her coat. Nikita waited out of sight and then darted to catch the door before it closed and walked inside, pulling the door closed behind him before the shop assistant even registered that the door had not clicked shut after them.

He found himself in a brightly lit corridor, but, with access to the department store currently barred, all staff were at the front of the building, and he was relieved to meet no one. Now that he was inside the silence of the building, the walkie-talkie sounded like a foghorn, and he retrieved it from his bag and turned down the volume, pressing it to his ear to listen in. And it was well he did, for there was a cacophony of commotion crackling through the tiny speaker.

'Chef runter! Feindliches feuer!' *Chief down! Enemy fire!*

'Das ist Agent Allochka. Woher kam der Schuss?' Nikita asked, demanding to know where the shot had been taken from. He quickened his steps, finding the stairwell and leaping up them two steps at a time. His message was greeted only with confusion as the police and Stasi officers struggled to process what had happened.

As Nikita neared the top of the stairs, he saw what looked like fresh spots of blood on the floor and, when he looked closer, on the handrail.

'There is blood close to the top of the stairwell in the Galeria Kaufhof. Approaching the rooftop now,' he reported to the speaker in German, turned off the device before it could give away his location, and approached the emergency exit door for the roof. He noticed the wire to the alarm dangling down and knew he was in the right place for the shooter. He withdrew the Walther from his lower back and turned off the safety, easing the rooftop door open as quietly as possible and moving through it at pace, covering all angles with the weapon and ducking down to avoid any snap shots.

But he could immediately see that he was too late. Two crumpled bodies lay in growing pools of blood, contorted like demons under the granite November sky. Nikita kept his weapon raised as he crossed to them, his eyes everywhere and his knees soft and ready to leap at the first sign of danger. His senses told him the danger had passed, and a quick reconnaissance of the rooftop confirmed his suspicions. He turned his walkie-talkie back on and called in the situation.

He looked closely at the bodies, without touching them, and saw that they had not died well. There was little of the face remaining of one of them, with clear signs of a knife wound in his knee also, and the other had something akin to a small crater in his chest. He'd seen worse from close quarter shotgun wounds, but it nonetheless wasn't pretty and he didn't need an autopsy to know that both had died from point-blank sniper shots, and he didn't need to be a detective to see that they were not the targets of the shooter.

He moved to the edge of the building and looked across the square to the hotel opposite. He could see little with his naked eye, but the location of the shooting was clear. The windows were thrown open wide, and heads kept looking nervously outside before ducking swiftly back in. The rooftop was the perfect location for the shot.

The door behind him burst open as a swarm of police and Stasi officers raced onto the rooftop, automatic weapons pointing frenetically in every direction as if they expected the shooter to appear out of the clouds. Then, as one, they all trained their weapons on Nikita, who rolled his eyes and raised his arms. A short, bespectacled man in plain clothes but with an air of authority moved to the front and waved down everyone's weapons.

'He is with us,' he stated and walked over to Nikita. One by one, the guns were lowered, although the expressions of suspicion remained deeply engraved on the faces of many of them.

'You are the Russian?' he asked Nikita loudly so as to be heard above the crowd, his mouth tight with stress.

'Da, Nikita Allochka,' Nikita replied. 'And you?'

'Polizeidirektor Kielhorn,' he replied and, to Nikita's surprise, extended his hand. Nikita shook it, maintaining eye contact with the serious man, whose brown hair was combed in a side parting and his earnest face clean-shaven.

'You know that Rausch is dead?' he asked Nikita.

'I surmised as much from the comms. The shot was undoubtedly taken from this rooftop, but I would guess he had not reckoned on being interrupted,' he added with a nod to the bodies, who were now being given a wide berth by the officers. If you keep the site clean, I'm certain you will find sniper bullet shells.'

Kielhorn nodded and shouted at some of his men to cordon off an area.

'And Schleicher?' Nikita asked.

'What of him?' the police director asked sharply, his eyes snapping back to Nikita.

'He is unharmed?'

'Yes, he has been escorted away from the protest to safety. Why do you ask?'

'I would imagine that he was the ultimate target. With respect, Polizeidirektor, the head of the Stasi would represent a rather larger coup than the chief of the East Berlin Police.'

'With respect, of course,' Kielhorn said, arching an eyebrow and looking coldly at Nikita.

'You disagree?'

When Kielhorn said nothing, Nikita looked back at the crowd, now being entranced by a new speaker.

'Will the crowd still be dispersed?' Nikita asked, fearing the answer.

'That is beyond my authority,' the director replied. 'But now, I think not. Whatever that may mean for Berlin.'

'It will mean less blood on your hands,' Nikita asked. 'And from one who knows a little of such things, believe me when I say that is a blessing.'

Kielhorn looked closely at Nikita now and dropped his voice so it was barely perceptible over the crowd. 'This is not Moscow, agent. Here, a whisper kills you just as well as a gun.'

Nikita gave a small nod, holding intense eye contact with the inspector.

'And what are the whispers telling you about the shooter?'

'That whether Rausch or Schleicher was the target, they succeeded in the goal, which was to stop the order being given to open fire on the crowd,'

Kielhorn said, unable to hide a hint of relief showing in his body language. 'And you?'

'I have been in Berlin for a total of two hours, Director. I do not pretend to know the ins and outs of the situation. But I do have my own whispers to follow, whispers that may yet change the landscape of the day and of Berlin.'

The director started at this. 'Something other than the shooting?'

'That remains to be seen. I suspect the ship has sailed, but you can never be too careful. Can you secure me a vantage point on top of the hotel?'

'The focus will, I think, remain on Rausch's room so I can arrange for the rooftop to be yours.'

'Danke,' Nikita replied and turned to leave.

'Allochka?'

'Ja?' Nikita replied, turning back to look at the director.

'Take this,' he said, handing him his card, embossed with Polizeidirektor Walter Kielhorn and his contact details. 'Sometimes it can be all about who you know in this city,' he added.

Nikita took it and nodded, trying to judge the man and his intentions. Random acts of kindness made him very nervous. As he made his way back through the throng to reach the hotel, he scrunched up the card, but just as he went to toss it away, something stopped him. He buried it in his pocket and carried on his way.

***

By mid-afternoon, the square was beginning to clear as the demonstration ended and protestors made their way back across their half of the city.

Nikita's hands were frozen in place around his Dragunov as he continued to cast back and forth across the crowd, looking for any indication of someone from Kulu Alqasas, but with no leads and no idea if it was someone from Afghanistan or someone acting on their behalf, he was trying to find a needle in a haystack.

Even when the early November darkness fell, and all that was left of the demonstration were the tattered remains of banners littering the square, Nikita waited. He was certain now that no bomb would be going off in the area, but he found it was often after dark that the most interesting things could happen. Watching the people come and go throughout the day, he was struck by the innate nervousness by which all the East Berliners seemed to be afflicted. They rarely made eye contact; their collars were pulled up and their heads down, and they moved as quickly as anyone could without looking suspicious. *What a way to live*, he thought to himself before remembering how similar Moscow often felt.

A clock somewhere had just chimed midnight, and the wind was reaching gale-force proportions when he eventually made the decision to pack up. His stomach was rumbling angrily, and hypothermia didn't feel too far off. He could easily have endured it longer, but wasn't sure what was the point, the sniper and the bomber, wherever they were, seemed to have opposing goals. He packed his things away in the canvas bag and stood to leave. But one last glance around the square made him stop and crouch back down.

Back on the rooftop of the Galeria, which had long since been cleared by Kielhorn's men, a lean figure was moving in the shadows. Nikita quickly pulled the scope of his sniper back out of the canvas bag and lay it back down on the cold concrete rooftop. He focused on the figure who had stopped close to the edge of the rooftop and seemed to be scrabbling with something next to the drainpipe, but it was impossible to see what was going on.

Nikita's mind whirred as he tried to decide on his next move. Stay, shoot, or try and engage. He knew what Denisov would say if he was here - be decisive and shoot. But the wind was so strong that making the shot would be highly difficult, and the worst thing he could do was miss and alert the shadow to his presence. He made a snap decision, throwing the scope back in the bag and running full speed to the door from the roof and towards the elevator, which took a painfully long time to reach him.

He ran from the hotel, keeping to the edge of Alexanderplatz and as out of sight of the Galeria rooftop as possible. He weighed up his options and went back to the side entrance he had used earlier that day, this time finding it locked. He quickly picked it and made his way inside, treading silently in the pitch-black windowless corridors, his ears alert for the slightest sound and his Walther pistol held firmly in both hands. As he came to the turn-off for the stairwell, he paused. He had thought he had heard the slightest hint of a breath. He froze, his back pressed against the wall, completely focused and ready.

After several minutes, there had been no further sound, and he swung around into the stairwell - and was hit by an almighty force.

CHAPTER 3

The figure from the rooftop had been waiting like a coiled spring on the stairwell and, when Nikita moved into it, had propelled themself with enormous force straight at his midriff, beneath his outstretched gun.

The wind was driven from Nikita's lungs as he crashed back into the wall of the hallway, which forced his head to snap back and crack into the wall. He fell to the floor, gasping for breath and struggling to get his eyes to focus. The darkness of the corridor was the only thing that saved him from a killer blow, as he heard his attacker roll away and a bullet thud into the wall above where he landed. Blinking to clear his head, he rolled onto his front as quietly as possible and drew a rattling breath. Another gunshot echoed around the hall, again missing him. He aimed off a shot in the direction that the shot had come from and heard a cry that, to his surprise, was the unmistakable sound of a woman. He moved down the corridor towards it, zigzagging, staying low and treading silently, ears pricked. He heard a ragged breath that he judged to have come from just a couple of metres ahead and kicked out as hard as he could. He caught both body and wall, which sent an enormous jarring through his knee. Still, he pushed the pain away and leaned forward to throw a punch but was stunned by a fist cracking into his temple. Despite the blinding pain adding to the concussion he had already suffered, he held onto the arm of the fist that had struck him and pulled it closer to him.

The woman had a scent that wanted to transport his senses to a place far from the frigid Berlin corridor, but the knee thrust that narrowly missed his groin brought him swiftly back to the present. She chopped with one hand at Nikita's neck, and he lost his grip on her arm as she spun away and reversed with a kick of her own into his stomach. This time, he reacted quicker, and despite the kick catching him in the side, it didn't drive the wind out of him. Instead, he moved with great agility to one side so the momentum of the kick carried his attacker past him. She lurched forward, unable to stop her momentum, and he took the opportunity to land an massive blow to her side. She fell to the floor, retching. He drew his weapon and was about to fire the killer shot when the lights crackled and buzzed on, momentarily blinding him.

When his eyes adjusted, looking up at him from the floor, one leg bleeding heavily from where his bullet had pierced, it was a face that caused the breath to leave Nikita's lungs harder than when he had been attacked. He choked, and the gun fell from his hand and clattered across the floor.

'No, no, no, no, no,' he moaned, pain digging into every part of his body.

Looking up at him was the face of the woman he loved. The face of Elysia.

***

'Jake?' she gasped, referring to him by the alias he had used when based in the US at CIA headquarters. Her usually golden-brown Greek complexion was drained of colour, and her mass of curly brown hair was stuck to her face, which was sweaty from the fight.

Nikita could not summon any words and just continued to stare down at her dumbly, faintly aware of a growing ache in his heart. An ache that felt like a betrayal.

The silence between them was interrupted by the sound of footsteps appearing from the front of the building, and sirens could be heard in the distance, getting louder by the second.

'We must go,' Nikita said, picking up his gun, torn between a desire to embrace her and to run from her as his mind churned to make any sense of what was happening.

She nodded, and he pulled her up. He put her arm around his neck to support her walking on her injured leg. The only indication of any pain was the faintest of gasps as she put weight on the freely bleeding leg, but she then gritted her teeth, and they began limping as quickly as they could.

'Du da drüben! Halt!' shouted the voice of a security guard who had appeared a long way down the corridor. Nikita threw a glance at him and took a shot at the light above the guard's head, which shattered into pieces and caused the guard to run back and take cover.

Nikita booted open the door to the side street, and they moved out into the frigid night air. The street was deserted, but the sound of sirens was very close.

'We don't stand a chance of escaping them on foot,' Nikita said as they shuffled down the street towards the main highway, noticing that he was having to take increasing amounts of Elysia's weight. 'Do you have a vehicle?'

She shook her head, focusing only on staying upright.

There was only a single car parked on the side street, already with a parking ticket shoved underneath the windscreen wipers. Nikita pulled Elysia with him towards the car, which was an ancient Trabant 601. The Trabant was meant to be the people's car of East Germany, but this one looked like it had been *a lot* of people's car along the way. But that suited Nikita's needs just perfectly, as the rusting lime green passenger door wasn't even locked.

He pulled it open and eased Elysia in with a tenderness he simply could not help. He walked round to the driver's side, only to find it locked. He rolled his eyes at the half-hearted efforts at security and walked back around, having to lean across Elysia to open the driver's door, which forced their faces closer than they had for many months. He worked hard to focus only on the door handle and not look into her eyes.

Once in the driver's seat, he swiftly hotwired the car, and the old two-stroke engine sputtered into life. And not a moment too soon, as police cars could be seen flying along Karl-Liebknecht-Strasse but aiming for the front, not the rear of the building. Trying not to draw attention to themselves, Nikita turned the correct way onto the highway and followed reluctantly in the direction of the police cars. He cursed as the lights turned red, and he had no option but to pull up alongside one of the green and white polizei vehicles, which did not have its sirens sounding. He shoved Elysia's head down below the window frame and gave his face a quick wipe, aware that any sort of close inspection would show signs of his fight.

He glanced at the police in the car and was relieved to see that they were talking amongst themselves, laughing and smoking, clearly only backup for the callout to the Galeria. Nikita pushed the seat back so his face was hidden by the doorframe, but then he saw Elysia pushing herself up groggily and placing her gun on the dashboard. The policeman in the passenger seat glanced nonchalantly towards Nikita's car before going to carry on his conversation. Then he froze, and his head snapped back around as he spotted the gun and Elysia's blood-covered hand, and he began shouting. Whether he was shouting to his partner or to Nikita, Nikita did not wait to find out. Despite the stream of traffic flowing across them, he hit the accelerator and flew through the red light. The world turned into a blur of cars whipping either side of them and car horns blaring. He swerved to avoid a dumper truck which was trundling towards them and was forced to chicane back the other way immediately afterwards as a motorbike was due to clip them. They avoided the motorbike, but its rider toppled off, sliding across the street and into the wall of the Galeria on their right.

The siren call leapt into life behind them as the police officers tried to make their way across the flood of vehicles, but to Nikita's relief, many had skidded to a stop and blocked the way of the police.

He floored the accelerator, which took some time to make any difference at all, and charged on ahead, heading east.

The flashing blue lights of the far superior police cars began to appear in the rear-view mirror as word spread that the suspect was headed away from Alexanderplatz. Nikita threw the car into a sharp left turn down a side street, but the police cars had followed and were gaining on them. He began taking every turn he could, right, left, left, right, as frequently as possible to try and lose the tail, and he thought it had worked until two police cars swung into the residential street they were hurtling down. They were about 500 yards away, and with no other option, Nikita hit the handbrake and spun the car around back the way they had come. To his right, there was an old flight of stone stairs leading to a street below, and he flung the car into it, bouncing down it and hearing the crack of suspension breaking. At the bottom of the stairs, he hit the brakes, skidding the car to one side, and wound down the window. As the first police car appeared, he shot once at the front tyre, which exploded, and the police car swerved, skidding sideways, and the following car, unable to stop in time, smashed into the side of it, crunching them both into the wall of the house next to the path.

Nikita glanced at Elysia and saw that her eyes were drooping, her face sickly pale in the glow of the streetlamps, and, with a screech of the tyres, he pushed the old car forward once more. The police who had crashed would have called in their location, and he could hear sirens getting closer. The car was also starting to make a high-pitched whining noise. The street they were on was heavily lined with cars, and he swung the Trabant into a shadowy residential car park, parking it as out of sight as possible. He leapt out and began trying the handles of other cars until he got lucky with what he saw, with a sigh, was another Trabant, albeit a much newer model. He dashed back, grabbed Elysia and transferred her to the new, pale turquoise alternative. He snatched a quick look at her bleeding leg - it looked like the bullet had passed straight through, but the wound needed to be treated immediately, or she would bleed out.

'Elysia, stay with me,' he said, gently slapping her cheek to rouse her. Her eyes flickered with some recognition, and she gave a weak smile.

'Hasn't our problem always been that I can't stay with you?' she said.

'Time for that discussion later,' he said curtly. He ripped a piece of cloth from his undershirt and tied it tightly around her leg as a tourniquet to try to stem the bleeding a little. He stood up and heard sirens again and dashed around to the driver's seat.

The newer car was no less easy to hotwire, for which he said a silent prayer of thanks, and the engine thrummed into life, sounding like liquid gold after the previous car. He eased the car out slowly and turned down the street. He could hear the sirens getting closer, but as of yet, he couldn't see any on the street. At the end of the road, he found himself on a dual carriageway and turned into it just as he saw flashing blue lights appear in the rear-view, screaming down the street behind him. More police cars were flying down the other side of the highway but were not giving the new car a second look as Nikita kept his head down as much as possible and eased into the trickle of late-night traffic heading out of the city.

Elysia let out a low moan next to him.

'Come on, Elysia,' he said, shoving her slightly and trying to rouse her, but consciousness was slipping away fast. He sped up, risking drawing attention to them, but he was running out of time, looking searchingly for any shops, doctors or pharmacies that might give him what he needed.

Up ahead on the right, he could see a dark blue sign for *Tierarztpraxis,* a veterinary practice. It would have to do.

He turned the car off and drove under the concrete archway to the car park at the rear of the practice. All the lights were off, and the practice was empty, which was perfect for his purposes. He leapt out and picked up Elysia, cradling her in his arms. The back door of the practice looked heavy and solid, so instead, he threw his elbow into a large rear window, kicked out a hole large enough for the two of them, and stepped inside.

There was a dim green glow of security lighting, which made it possible for Nikita to find his way past the reception desk and into a small operating room. He laid Elysia down on the stainless-steel table, which was too small for her, and her legs hung down over the edges. He turned her onto her side and hefted her legs up, bending them in the process to make her fit, and tore the black leggings away to get a closer look at the damage to her calf. To his relief, it did not appear to have hit a major artery, and the tourniquet had slowed the bleeding, but she had still lost an enormous amount of blood. He turned on the lights, blindingly bright after making his way in the dark, and scanned the room for any equipment that he could use. A large white cabinet filled the wall on one side of the room, and inside, he found everything he would need to treat the injury. *If it wasn't already too late*, he thought to himself.

He squeezed liquid antiseptic into the wound, which caused Elysia to scream before passing out fully, and then continued to wipe it clean with alcohol at both the entry and exit points. He heavily padded the side facing down with swabs to help it clot before pushing down firmly. While leaning on the leg, he threaded a needle and hoped that whatever thread vets used for stitches wasn't harmful to humans, and roughly sewed it up.

Elysia coughed a few times, and her leg kicked, but whether she was conscious or not, she no longer had the energy to fight what was happening to her. Once Nikita had tied off the thread, he cleaned the wound again and hoped the stitches would hold. He turned Elysia over to look at the other side. Peeling the swabs off, it appeared they had done their job in helping it to start clotting. He repeated the process from the other side and looked down at his work. A medic he was not; two coarse, uneven lines of thread pulled the skin tightly around both sides of Elysia's previously unblemished calf, but so far, it seemed to be holding. He found a bottle of water and some food in a small kitchen on the second floor of the surgery, which restored a little strength and began to turn his attention to what must happen next.

He didn't fear for himself - the Stasi and Police would bow to the KGB no matter how big their objections were, but he knew nothing of Elysia's role and could not contact Rosin or even the CIA until he knew more. Again, his heart burnt with pain at the thought of her treachery.

He sat on the floor, leaning against the wall and looking up at her, lying unconscious on the surgery table.

'What have you done, Elysia,' he whispered.

In a city he didn't know, in which the Stasi had eyes everywhere, where could he hide?

CHAPTER 4

A pale autumnal sun bathed the room but did little to brighten the brown and beige décor of the seedy room Nikita found himself in.

He had found the run-down hotel in a forlorn-looking area on the edge of the city and chosen it for the fire exit stairwell he could see at the rear. He had checked in with the spotty young night attendant, who gave him a wink and a thumbs-up at the woman who was clinging to the dark stranger so hard she wouldn't even turn to look at him.

Nikita grinned back and made a show of picking Elysia up in his arms and holding her like a baby. 'Let's get you to bed, baby,' he crooned in German and carried her up to the room.

That had been over twelve hours ago, and still she slept.

Once he'd done a reconnaissance and scoped out the building's location more fully, Nikita had dozed fitfully on the dirty hotel room floor, unable to bring himself to share a bed with Elysia and unable to sleep, wondering if the walls had ears. He knew the stats, that at least one in a hundred East Germans were Stasi informants, and the paranoia that came with that made him wish he had a stiff drink to hand.

He looked down, saw the blood still on his hands, and took a shower. When he came out, Elysia was sitting up on the bed.

'Water,' she croaked feebly. He handed her a bottle he had brought with him from the vet, and she emptied it before asking for more. He filled it at the bathroom sink and handed it back to her.

'It's up to you if you want to risk that water,' he said, but her red-rimmed eyes just focused on the bottle, which she drank half of.

'Not sure it was worth the risk,' she said, pulling a face and wiping her mouth. He handed her a soggy-looking corned beef sandwich wrapped in clingfilm. She tore off the wrapping and began to eat hungrily, some colour beginning to return to her cheeks.

Nikita stood watching her, saying nothing. He had a million questions, but as he so often found to be the case, he had no idea how to ask them. Instead, he held his hands behind his back, clasping them tightly, while Elysia worked hard to look anywhere but at him while the silence and the tension in the room grew.

It was only when Nikita turned his back and gazed out of the window that she found that she was able to speak.

'I'm sorry,' she said in a hushed voice full of emotion.

Nikita closed his eyes and stayed silent, afraid to ask what it was she was sorry for, as his mind worked to convince him of every worst-case scenario.

'I'm not what you think,' she said.

'That much is clear,' he said, eyes staring fixedly at a concrete wall across the street.

'Are you not going to look at me?' she asked.

'I don't know what or who I'd be looking at other than a liar.'

'That's pretty rich, Jacob—or wait, is it Nathan? Or are you someone else today?' she snapped caustically.

He snapped round at that, his eyes ablaze.

'I told you everything I could. In fact, far more than I could or should have. Can you say you did the same... Elysia, or are *you* called something else today?' Then, unable to help himself, he added, 'Was anything you said true?' He immediately felt more vulnerable than he ever had in his life and wished he could swallow the words back up.

'How can you even ask that?' she said furiously as she tried to lift herself but was still so weak her arms gave way, and she fell back down.

'Just answer the question,' he said, coldly ignoring her feeble state.

She stopped trying to get up and sat back, looking him in the eyes.

'Yes, I love you, if that is what you're asking,' she said, her deep brown eyes full of emotion.

'Then why didn't you tell me what you are? Tell me everything, now.'

'I want to, but I'm so tired,' she groaned. 'I need to rest.'

Nikita resisted the urge to shake her. 'If I am to keep you safe, I need to know from what... and who.'

Elysia glared at him coldly.

'What are you?'

'I am still the same woman you knew before. The only reason you are hurting is because you thought it was only you who was allowed to have the secrets.'

'Bullshit. I told you there were things I couldn't reveal. You did not return that favour.'

'You would have told me nothing if I had not figured it out for myself,' she retorted hotly.

'Well, now I know how you were so able to unpick that puzzle,' he threw back. She was the only person he'd met since his training that was able to make him lose his cool so much, and the fear of vulnerability spiked in him again. 'Just answer my question,' he added.

'You already know enough to know that there is much I cannot tell you,' she said with a sigh.

'If you were CIA, I would probably know, so I would have to go with Mossad—' She shook her head imperceptibly. 'Or MI6,' he finished. She looked up at him, neither confirming nor denying it but holding his gaze with a smile.

'An American would, of course, only consider these to be worthwhile agencies.' She smirked. 'Trust me when I say who I do or do not work for is of no moment to you.'

'When did you join... whoever it is you work for?' he asked. She arched her eyebrow, and he rephrased. 'How long have you been a spy?' He felt his heartbeat quicken at the question.

'Long enough,' she answered cryptically. 'You know these are questions I can't answer.'

'Okay—but were you spying on me when we met back in Skyros?' He could not help but let his memory drift back to their meeting on the Greek island. He was there for his first mission to take out a Soviet double agent in hiding, and she was working in a shop he had entered, and they had hit it off right away. It had all felt so natural, but it was beginning to seem so dirty to Nikita.

'No...' she started and hesitated, 'and yes,' she finished as her shoulders slumped slightly. Nikita's eyes blazed, but she held up her hand to stop him before he exploded at her. 'Let me explain. I was only a *very* low-level asset, asked to keep my eye out and report anything suspicious if I came across it due to the amount of time I spent in the Greek Islands, as well as going back and forth to Athens. Nothing ever happens on Skyros, but because of its location close to Turkey and the East, my employers felt it worth having someone there with their eyes open. It was perfect. I got paid for doing nothing, which helped prop up the shop, which barely ever sold a thing. Other than little wooden carvings of Black Russian terriers,' she added with a wink, referring to the item that had drawn Nikita into the shop in the first place.

Nikita cringed inwardly. Buying something that had become his calling card from a secret agent of another country would have been enough for his KGB recruiter, the late Colonel Klitchkov, to have him shot.

'Then what changed?'

'You,' she answered simply.

'Me?'

'When you came to the island, everything changed. At first, I honestly had no suspicions about you. I didn't even phone it in. Then I lost my uncle, and still, I was ignorant at first, so I came to you in grief... and we...' She looked at Nikita, her mouth drawn thin with anger. Nikita's chest tightened - his part in the death of her uncle Giorgos was a secret he had kept from her that had, at times, engulfed him with guilt.

'But it was no innocent car crash that took him... was it, Agent?' she added coldly. Nikita involuntarily sat on the edge of the bed, wanting to hold her but unsure how to.

'Elysia... I so badly wanted to tell you the truth.' He sighed.

'You don't know how to tell the truth,' she bit off.

'Truth isn't a word that comes up much in our line of work,' he said, 'the stories we tell are what keeps us alive.' She nodded, both of them understanding what that meant.

'Giorgos was a good man, and I was very sorry that he died. I did not kill him, though, if that is what you fear.'

'Your mere arrival on the island killed him,' she said.

'Perhaps, and perhaps not,' Nikita said, shrugging. 'He had a role to play in all of this, and he played it of his own volition. But like I say, I was very sad that he died, and I have wrestled every day with the fact I could not tell you anything.' Then, seeing her incredulous look, added, 'Believe me or don't, that is your choice. Now, continue with your story. What about my arrival changed the sort of agent you were?'

'Only that when you left, I felt lost. I barely knew you at all, but meeting you, I had felt something...' She softened for a moment before collecting herself. 'The island didn't feel the same anymore. I had a reason to get back out into the world.'

'And they posted you to follow me to the States?'

'Actually, no, finding you in Baltimore really was just an unbelievable coincidence. They had posted me back there, as I was already from there, and it was a strong Greek community that I could hide in while close enough to Langley to keep an ear to the ground.'

'They?' Nikita asked.

'Nice try,' she said with a small laugh.

Nikita stood up, frustrated, and went to gaze out the window once more. 'You're going to need to tell me, Elysia.'

'Why?'

'Because it seems our friend on the reception desk was sharper than he looked. The police are here. Now, talk fast. We have only minutes. You are unable to run anywhere, and I need to know who to hide you from and where I need to get you to.'

'What makes you think you can protect me?'

He looked at her, his eyes telling the story that he was unable to voice. She tried to hold his gaze but broke under the emotion within it.

'I am Greek Secret Service,' she said, looking at the floor. 'And we are working a little with the British.'

'Then we must get you out of East Berlin. You are not safe here, particularly after what I'm guessing was your assassination of the head of the East Berlin Police, of which I would like to know more.'

Elysia shrugged. 'You know as well as I do that the order to open fire on the crowd had to be stopped. It would have been a blood bath. I'm only sorry I didn't get both of them. They are evil men.'

Nikita thought of protesting but knew it would only be out of stubbornness. 'We need to get you out of East Berlin,' he instead repeated.

'You have a way of crossing the wall?' she asked, ignoring his other point.

'I do not, but I'm sure I can think of something,' he replied, shrugging.

'Then you have not spent much time at the wall. Crossing is no small thing, but I have a way through if you can get us there.'

He nodded and scooped her up, not waiting any longer. He climbed out of the window onto the fire escape, careful not to make a sound. The police cars were visible parked on the main road at the front of the building, and one officer had been posted at the bottom of the fire exit, where he stood languidly smoking a cigarette.

Instead of going down the escape, Nikita threw Elysia over one shoulder in a fireman's lift and climbed carefully up the steps until he reached the flat roof of the hotel, which was squeezed between two other tall buildings. He climbed over the wire separating the rooftops with ease and made his way across the neighbouring building. It came to a narrow alleyway separating it from the next building, but he approached it at a run and leapt over. It was only a gap of around five feet, but with the added weight of Elysia, he only just made it and landed with a grunt. To her credit, Elysia said nothing.

He continued across the next building, angling and jumping across another building that backed onto it. He walked with confidence as it was an escape route he had already mapped out following his reconnaissance of the area while Elysia slept.

At the rear of that building, he stopped and peered over. Beneath was a balcony jutting out from the distinctly drab-looking apartment block fifteen feet below.

'I will lower you down as far as I can, but you will have to land as best you can without harming your leg,' he said brusquely to Elysia, who bit her lip and nodded once more as he put her down. She shimmied backwards over the ledge and held on tightly to his arm. Nikita lay flat on the roof and pushed himself over as far as he dared. He lowered her down until the distance had been almost halved and then released her.

Wounded she may be, but a trained secret agent she was also, and she landed with barely any pressure on her damaged leg, dropping and rolling silently onto the balcony. Nikita landed noiselessly beside her. They could see into the apartment block behind the windows. Although closed, the heavy sash window was easily lifted from the outside, and they climbed inside, clambering down onto a heavy wooden chest placed beneath the window for climbing in and out. Nikita quickly searched the apartment and confirmed that it was empty. In the kitchen, he found more food, as well as a small bottle of schnapps, which he quietly took a swig of before pocketing, relishing the burn of alcohol as it rolled down his throat.

'We can afford to wait here for a few minutes,' he said, throwing her an apple, which she bit into hungrily. 'Let me check your wound.'

Understanding the importance of her mobility for the mission, she complied, peeling back the bandages and wincing only slightly.

The wound had not seeped too badly but would still need proper medical attention. 'It will do for now,' he said and bandaged it back up once more.

'This way you have to West Berlin—you know how to find it?'

'I do. We need to get to the north of the city. Where are we now?'

'I am not sure precisely, but I judge us to be northeast,' he replied, chewing on something similar to a stroopwafel, but without the flavour. 'This point of crossing—does it need to be done under cover of darkness?'

'No. In fact, I would judge daytime to be better.'

'Then let us go at once. Can you walk?'

Elysia stood up and tested her leg. 'I can, but only slowly.'

'It is better that you walk. It will attract less attention. Try not to limp,' he added.

'Helpful,' she said, rolling her eyes.

CHAPTER 5

It was thirty minutes later that Nikita pulled to a stop in another stolen car on Eberswalder Straße, and up ahead could see the wall running across, blocking Bernauer Straße and the French sector of West Berlin from sight. The pair had remained undetected by the police who had been called to the hotel, but still both looked around anxiously.

Nikita looked up at the grey wall, which stood firm and unmoving, cutting not only the city in two but also families and friends, and had done ever since its sudden overnight erection in August 1961, and all at once understood much more the damage it had caused. The damage his country had caused to the people of a place hundreds of miles away, a place they had no business being in.

'How do we cross?' he asked.

'There is a tunnel, but the way is not easy,' she said, looking nervous.

'If it is not easy, are you able to make it with your leg?' he asked.

'Whether I'm able to or not is irrelevant, I have to make it,' she said.

'Then lead the way, and let's get it over with as quickly as possible.'

She led them to a street running parallel to the wall where there was a low-rise building that had once been a warehouse but now stood padlocked and with boarded-up windows empty. She knocked on the huge metal garage door and waited for an answer.

After a long, nervous wait, a door that had been carefully cut out of the garage door opened, revealing a small, furtive-looking man in a black beanie hat. He had bushy ginger sideburns running from under the hat, which brightened upon seeing Elysia before darkening when he saw Nikita standing behind her.

'What is this?' he demanded in German with a curious accent.

'Let us in, Remo, and I'll explain,' she replied. The sound of German from her mouth sounded alien to Nikita, for so long used to her Greek-American-generic European fusion of an accent.

Remo looked uncomfortable and then, seeming to make up his mind, opened the door further.

'Okay. Quick, quick, come in.'

Nikita followed Elysia inside, into exactly what it looked like from the outside; a dark, cold, empty garage. He began to talk, but Elysia turned and put a finger to her lips as they were led through to the back of the warehouse and through a thick, rusty iron door.

Behind it was another empty room, darker than the first and much smaller. All Nikita could make out as his eyes adjusted to it was an old table with a couple of chairs in the middle of the room, caked in so much dust that it didn't look like they had been touched for generations. Remo closed the door tightly behind them and then turned to Elysia and Nikita.

'What are you doing, bringing a stranger here? You will get us all killed!' he barked at Elysia in choked whispers.

'We spoke to no one, and we were not followed. I can vouch for him,' she replied calmly, also keeping her voice low.

'But who can vouch for you? We agreed to only one return trip for you. You never mentioned anyone else. The success of this place depends on trust and absolute secrecy. You have betrayed that.' He looked utterly furious, his eyes unblinking in the gloom.

'I have betrayed nothing,' Elysia retorted. 'This man is not only an old friend, but he has also saved my life on more than one occasion since I saw you last. He is on our side; you have my word.'

Remo breathed deeply, releasing some of his anger, and turned to Nikita.

'Who are you?'

'I would think that you prefer to not know too much about the identities of those who come to you,' Nikita said calmly.

'That is a Stasi answer if ever I heard one,' Remo grunted.

'I assure you I have no love for the Stasi. But I do have a love for anyone who can aid me in a passage to the West. I am on your side; of that, you can be certain.'

Remo chewed on the inside of his cheek, wrestling with it and staring intently at Nikita. Eventually he shrugged. 'There is no guarantee you or anyone else can give. You have money?'

Elysia handed him a wad of marks der GDR, which he flicked through and grunted again.

'Betray us, and you will die,' he said to them both coldly. He then turned and walked to the far wall, an old, chipped concrete wall, and knocked in a long pattern. After a moment, a short burst of knocks returned, to which Remo replied with another different pattern of taps.

There was a moment of silence, and then, to Nikita's surprise, the entire wall swung outwards, running smoothly and making no sound at all. Behind the wall appeared a hole the size of a large portrait painting, which had been cut directly into the concrete, where Nikita could just make out the dark shape of a woman silhouetted against a dim glow deeper into the hole.

Without a word, she moved to one side to allow the other three inside. Nikita clambered into the cramped hole with some difficulty and moved past the woman who smelled of stale cigarettes. She eyed him suspiciously but said nothing as he passed, instead turning back to swing the false wall closed behind them.

In front of them was a short tunnel that opened into roughly hewn steps that cut through the foundations and into the earth below, going sharply downwards. They followed, stooped over and, working not to topple over, down into increasingly oppressive heat. The narrow stairwell then opened out into a large room lit by more oil lanterns and candles, making for a smoky cavern. In the room were two others, sat at a table not unlike the one in the room above them, playing cards.

At that moment, the room began to shake and shudder, dust falling from the packed earth ceiling as a distant roar seemed to grow closer. Nikita grabbed Elysia to him but noticed that Remo and the other two men were laughing at him, seemingly unconcerned by the apparent earthquake. As quickly as it had arrived, the shaking and roaring faded away, and the room was again still.

'What was that?' Nikita demanded.

'That is the sound of the West Berlin U-Bahn,' croaked one of the men at the table, an unshaven man with thick, dark eyebrows, moustache and a beer belly.

'On this side of the wall?' Nikita asked, surprised.

'It bends briefly under the wall and east at this point of the line to run through Bernauer Straße U-Bahn station, which was closed as it sits right on the split with the French sector,' Elysia explained. 'It is a ready-made tunnel.'

'It is a ready-made tunnel for underground trains, Elysia, not people. Surely it's policed?'

'Of course,' said Remo. 'But you don't need to worry about that.'

Nikita strongly begged to differ but saw that he didn't have any choice.

'Come, the next train is in ten minutes,' Remo continued, leading the way out of another narrow tunnel which had been cut through earth and rock, angling downwards.

Nikita pulled Elysia back as she went to follow. 'You trust him?' he whispered.

'Of course, why?'

'His accent... he is not German.'

'Well, that depends on who you ask in this part of the world. He's from Strasbourg in Alsace—it's in France, but it was part of Germany until about seventy years ago.'

'Then why would he come to Berlin?'

'His father was part of the French Resistance against the Nazis. I think he feels resisting German oppression is in his blood.'

'You do not need to worry about Remo,' said the other man sitting at the table. He was stocky, with white-blond hair and noticeably large hands, and was looking at Nikita coldly with crystal blue eyes. 'He is small, but he is fierce, and his heart is true.'

'And what of yours?' Nikita retorted.

'His heart is blacker than you,' chortled the man with the moustache. He stopped when he saw Nikita's cold look. 'Calm down, man. I mean no offence.'

'You'd be amazed at how often people have to clarify that,' Nikita said.

'I suggest you go with Remo,' said the blond man calmly, removing a revolver from his coat pocket and aiming it at Nikita. 'You are making me nervous, and I would hate to get twitchy. We are all on the same side, after all, jah?'

Nikita raised his arms placatingly and followed Elysia down the tunnel to where Remo was waiting impatiently.

'Come, come. We do not have long.'

'Long for what?' Nikita asked but received no reply.

The tunnel continued to angle downwards, the heat getting oppressive, but eventually, Nikita began to feel a breeze rising upwards towards them. The tunnel flattened out, and Remo stopped at a long wooden board, which he slid to the side to reveal an equally long hole, around five metres across, cut into the floor of the tunnel, which was supported and reinforced by a wooden frame and brickwork. Below, Nikita could see the train tracks of the Berlin metro system snaking away in the darkness, and he began to have an uncomfortable suspicion about the plan.

'The northbound train is due to pass in'—Remo checked his watch—'two minutes. This one knows how it works,' he said with a nod to Elysia, 'so I suggest you follow her lead. Aim for the rooftop closest to the end of the final carriage. The roof is stronger there, and the thud of your landing is dampened so people do not hear over the roar of the train.'

'Aim for the rooftop?' Nikita said as the reality dawned on him. 'You mean us to land on the roof of a moving underground train?' He turned to Elysia. 'This is crazy, Elysia!'

'If it was easy, everyone would do it,' she said with a shrug. She looked clammy and was clearly in great pain, but her face was determined.

'You have to be desperate and quite crazy to cross the wall,' Remo said.

'As crazy as a Frenchman who chooses to spend his days in the Berlin underground?'

Remo grinned. 'Oui, monsieur. I am craziest of all,' he said with a wink.

'I think you dropped something,' interrupted Elysia from behind him. He turned to find her holding the bottle of schnapps he had lifted from the apartment, her brow furrowed in displeasure. 'Some things never change, do they, Jake?' she said. He went to grab it, but she pulled it away.

Nikita tried to look nonchalant. 'I needed something to warm me up. You have it if you want.'

She unscrewed the cap and took a sip. 'The difference is, I can take just a sip.'

Nikita felt the familiar anger roiling up in his stomach, the anger only she ever managed to elicit in him, but at that moment, the floor began to shudder, only a little at first but then growing in intensity.

'Here we go. The train slows right down at this point while it curves east, but it's still moving. Keep your head low, monsieur. The ceiling on this stretch of the line to Voltastraße is higher than at other points, but I still would not recommend standing up. Many have died this way,' he added much too casually for Nikita's liking.

Seeing Nikita open his mouth to protest, Elysia put a finger to his lips. 'Do shut up, Jake. Just do what I do, and you'll be okay.'

Nikita frowned but did as she said as the roar grew with a mighty crescendo that was almost deafening. The hole filled with light from the headlamps of the train as it rolled along the tracks. It was noticeably slower than you would normally expect, but it was still an awful lot faster than Nikita was comfortable with.

The train appeared below them, about two metres down, a mass of cream-coloured, corrugated, reinforced PVC that looked anything but a comfortable place to land.

'Drei,' Remo began.

'Zwei.' Elysia was crouched low, ready to drop into the hole, and Nikita did the same, every fibre of his body protesting the danger he was willingly entering it into.

'Eins... GEHEN GEHEN GEHEN!' shouted Remo over the cacophony of clacking wheels and rushing air.

Elysia looked at Nikita, her doe-brown eyes alive with excitement, and they both jumped.

One of Nikita's feet hit the rooftop, but the other missed and slipped off the back of the carriage, and he flailed helplessly, his arms windmilling as he sought something to cling to as he began to fall backwards.

But then Elysia's hand closed on his and pulled him back upright.

'Duck!' she then shouted before he'd fully had a chance to gain his balance, and she pulled him down flat to the roof of the train, as a sign hanging down from the ceiling informing the driver they were approaching a station threatened to take Nikita's head off.

He missed it by a fraction and lay face down on top of Elysia, her arms wrapped around him. For a moment, he closed his eyes and could almost imagine them back in Skyros, back in a different time. A time he found himself longing for.

The train rattled through the empty Bernauer Straße station, and Nikita rolled off Elysia and lay to one side, peering through the gloom at one of several stations that had become known as geisterbahnhofs. Ghost stations. The platform was barely visible in the pitch-black, a single flicking security light casting eerie shadows towards the vacant stairways that had once led thousands of people up to the street beyond every day. Another time in another world. Torchlight suddenly flashed across the train, and he saw two GDR Security Guards monitoring the train. Elysia pulled him back down flat against the roof.

'You didn't think the platform would be unmonitored, did you?' Elysia chastised in a loud whisper. 'We're directly under the wall now,' she added as the train moved past the platform, 'hold on tight, we're going to pick up pace.'

Nikita looked around for something to hold on tight to, but there was precious little, and he was forced to cling to either side of the train as best he could. As Elysia had predicted, the train gathered pace as it re-entered West Berlin, and the wind pushing against them was huge. Nikita could feel his fingers starting to lose their grip as the train wound its way under the city and could see that Elysia was also struggling.

They stared into each other's eyes, unable to see anything else, as the train carried them further north, silently willing one another to hang on. As they swung around a particularly large bend, Nikita's tentative grip on the edge of the train was lost as his left hand slipped free. He tried to regain a purchase, but the force of the wind was proving too strong to reach. Instead, he had no choice but to hold on to Elysia, and he could see tears of pain flooding her eyes. He realised that she had hooked herself on with her wounded leg stuck through a large iron handle at the edge of the gap between the two carriages. He tried to let go, to ease the weight on her, but she held him tightly to her.

'If you let go, I'll kill you,' she shouted into his ear, and he stopped trying to pull free.

After what felt like an eternity, the train began to slow, and another low-hanging sign overhead instructed the driver to begin slowing for the entry to Voltastraße station, and relief flooded through Nikita.

'Now comes the difficult part,' Elysia said to him, speaking directly into his ear. He pulled away and saw she was grinning as light from the station up ahead began to creep into the tunnel. He laughed in spite of himself and let go of her as the pace of the train slowed to such a degree that he no longer felt a danger of sliding off.

'Follow my lead,' said Elysia, who eased herself down the side of the train using the iron hoop she had been holding on to. Before her head disappeared over the side, she added, 'Keep to the corner of the train so you cannot be seen by the passengers, and do not touch the train tracks. They are electrified, and to touch them is instant death.'

'A lovely end to the perfect trip,' Nikita muttered. He followed Elysia as swiftly as he could and noticed that the iron hoop was slick with blood. There was no chance to stop and check if Elysia was okay, however, as he squeezed next to her on a tiny ledge at the rear of the train. Both had their arms above them, holding onto the iron hoop awkwardly to hold themselves flat to the side of the train.

'When I say jump, do it immediately,' Elysia said as loudly as she dared with such close proximity to the passengers. 'You must jump sideways, away from the tracks.'

'Into the wall?!' Nikita protested.

'Just do as I say,' she snapped. 'Time it wrong and you die horribly. You must jump immediately when I say.'

Then, the sound from up ahead changed as the front of the train rolled into the bright lights of the subway station. He could hear the sound of a Tannoy announcing the arrival of the train and the voices of hundreds of people milling around the station. The wheels began to screech as the train driver hit the brakes hard, and Nikita felt like his back was going to snap from the angle at which he was holding his body.

'Ready?' Elysia said swiftly.

'No,' Nikita replied drily.

'GO!' she shouted and launched herself directly at the wall just moments before the rear of the train entered the station.

CHAPTER 6

Without hesitating, Nikita flung himself directly after Elysia, fighting every instinct of self-preservation, and shot towards the solid brick wall as the train ground to a halt just metres in front of them, blocking the platform from view. He braced himself, flinging his arms up to protect his head and closed his eyes tight.

But then he landed, higher and more comfortably than he had expected, albeit with the wind driven from his lungs as he crashed clumsily on top of Elysia.

He briefly registered a metal doorway embedded deeply in the brick wall before it slammed shut behind them, plunging them once more into darkness. He pushed himself to his feet blindly, pulling Elysia with him, and held himself in a fighting stance as he heard the heavy breathing of a man nearby. But then there was a click, and an electric light buzzed into action above them, stinging their eyes after the relentless darkness of the past few minutes that had felt like an eternity.

They were stood in a small room built from the same bricks as the tunnel. It was filthy and with little in there other than old tools and equipment long since discarded by the rail engineers who inhabited these tunnels day and night to keep them running. The man standing in front of them was clearly one such worker; he had a hunched posture, and his face was blackened with grime, save for the strip where a headtorch was strapped around it.

'Willkommen im Westen,' he announced with a grin. *Welcome to the West.* His grin suddenly faded as Elysia collapsed to the floor, her face deathly pale.

'Where is the nearest hospital?' Nikita barked in German, thankful that his rigorous years of KGB training had ensured he was fluent in several languages and at least passable in others.

'About ten minutes by car, thirty by foot,' answered the man with a shrug. 'What has happened to her?'

'That story would take longer than she may have,' Nikita said. 'How do I get up to the ground?'

The man looked shaken, particularly when Nikita lifted Elysia into his arms, and they both saw that her trouser leg was soaked with blood. His raggedy stitches might have done the job for someone committed to bed rest but less for a hair-brained escape on top of an underground train. She was barely conscious and was muttering a stream of insensibilities under her breath. 'Which way, man?' repeated Nikita.

The man said nothing but pointed to a door at the rear of the room. Nikita marched towards it, pulled it open and found himself in an empty, tiled corridor that looped around to connect with the main stairwell, where the last stragglers were filtering up the stairs from the platform. No longer caring whether they were seen or what people thought of them, he took the stairs two at a time, ignored the long queue for the elevator, and instead took the emergency stairs. He ignored his knees screaming at him and instead just focused on taking each step and pumping upwards around the spiral staircase to the increasingly cold air.

He burst out onto the street and was immediately stunned by the total change in look, feel and demeanour. Where there had been few people on the street in the East, with little activity and a general sense of nervousness, the West was a complete contrast despite being only a few hundred yards away from the wall. Brightly coloured billboards adorned the sides of walls, and there was a thrum of activity around the station. To his shock, he even saw some non-white faces amidst the crowds leaving the station.

He didn't allow himself long to acclimatise; however, a soft groan from Elysia brought him back to his senses. He ran towards a taxi rank in front of the station, ignoring the looks he was receiving from passers-by at the unconscious woman in his arms. As he approached the first taxi, the driver gave him a sour look and gunned the engine to shoot away into the traffic. *The West wasn't so different after all*, Nikita thought bitterly.

The next taxi driver wagged his finger at him as he approached, but the third was happy to take the fare, provided that Elysia put her leg in a plastic bag, which he handed them.

'Sorry, but I have to keep the car blood-free for business!' he announced cheerfully as he pulled away.

'Thank you for taking the fare,' Nikitia said earnestly.

'Why should your money be any worse than anyone else's?' the driver replied with an endearing shrug.

'Not everyone sees it that way. If you run some red lights to get us to the hospital, I'll double the money,' Nikita said, turning his attention to Nikita as the taxi driver nodded and accelerated and began winding through the cars ahead.

Elysia's eyes cracked open slightly, and when she saw Nikita above her, she smiled beneficently.

'Are you trying to save me again?' she murmured.

'Always and forever,' he whispered back and blinked back any wetness in his eyes. When he looked back at her, she had slipped once more into unconsciousness. Nikita took the chance on the journey to peel back her trouser leg and lift the sodden bandages. The stitches had torn, and blood was again seeping heavily out of the wound, which already was showing the signs of possible infection.

Only five minutes later, he screeched to a halt outside the front of the sprawling granite hospital and turned, smiling, as if eager for praise for making the journey so swiftly. Nikita thanked him, pulled a wad of cash from Elysia's pocket, and handed him more than treble the fare, which made the taxi driver's eyes bulge with gratitude.

'Danke mein Herr,' he blubbed. Nikita nodded at him and lifted Elysia gently out of the taxi. 'If you need a taxi again, you can call me any time, I am Helmutt. Everybody knows me,' the taxi driver added, handing him a card. Nikita took the card, nodded again, and turned to hear Helmutt shouting through the car window, 'Good luck to your friend, mein Herr!' as Nikita marched towards the entrance to the accident and emergency department.

He walked straight past the queue to the front desk to the protests of the others waiting, all in varying degrees of pain and distress. The harried-looking nurse, however, took one look at Elysia and yelled for an orderly and a doctor.

'What has she done?' the nurse asked matter-of-factly, pointing to Elysia's leg as an orderly raced towards them pushing a gurney.

'Bullet wound,' Nikita replied as quietly as possible.

To her credit, the nurse showed no surprise or alarm and instead wrote a note on a piece of paper and handed it to the orderly, who in turn passed it to an equally harried-looking doctor who was running towards them. He took one look at Elysia's leg and instructed the orderly to take her straight to surgery.

'Surgery?' Nikita asked the doctor dumbly, and he hurriedly followed the gurney. 'Surely she just needs stitches?'

'A wound bleeding that much needs a lot more than stitches. The artery must have some damage—if we do not repair it right away, she could lose the leg.'

Nikita had seen enough bloodshed to know what a damaged femoral artery could mean, and like a sledgehammer, the full reality of the fact it was his shot, his bullet, that had done this damage to the woman he loved hit him. Or the woman he thought he loved. He didn't know if the woman he loved was the same person as the one lying on the gurney before him.

He noticed the doctor was still talking.

'... Any details you can give us may help.'

'It happened late last night, around midnight, and the shot was fired from a Walther PP handgun, and it appeared to be a simple in and out wound, which was treated, albeit roughly, with stitches,' Nikita said as matter-of-factly as the nurse on reception. Both had seen enough to know when practicality was more important than anything else. 'There was nothing to suggest the artery had been damaged, so I suspect that has happened since.'

The doctor looked up at Nikita sharply, looking at him properly for the first time. 'Happened since the gunshot wound?' he asked suspiciously.

'Her journey to the hospital was more than a little perilous,' Nikita said, giving the doctor a knowing look.

The doctor's mouth tightened, and Nikita wondered if he had misjudged him. 'You seem to know much of this,' he said, looking down at his notes.

'I was there.' Nikita shrugged. 'I would see her leg saved.'

'She is not the first to arrive here following a difficult journey. Let us see if we can make sure it was worthwhile,' he said, without looking at Nikita as they arrived outside of surgery. 'We must inform the police as it is a bullet wound, so I'll need you to stay until they arrive.'

He looked up, but Nikita was no longer there.

***

It was hours later that Nikita slipped discreetly back into the hospital and into the room where Elysia lay asleep and heavily medicated. He checked her notes and knew enough to understand that she was weak but was unlikely to suffer any loss of limbs or permanent damage. It was dark outside, and the lighting in the corridors had been dimmed to give the hospital that strangely muted feel unique to hospitals after dark the world over, where noise and night-time met somewhere in the middle.

He sat next to her for a time, drinking in the features that he still could not believe were really here, in a hospital in West Berlin. From a shopkeeper on a distant Greek island to a secret agent working for both the Greek Secret Service AND MI6, she had been one of his only links to a world outside of espionage, an anchor he had clung to during the long months in the Afghan caves. Now he felt rudderless, in love but betrayed, vulnerable but closed off. But his overriding feeling was one of guilt for all the things she still did not know about him, about the lies he must perpetuate. It was a feeling that sat deep in the pit of his stomach and made him want to be violently sick.

'You love a lie, and I love a shadow,' he murmured to her as he stroked her tumbling golden brown hair back from her face.

He heard the sound of voices in the room next door as the doctor made his evening rounds. When the doctor entered the room, he found Elysia sound asleep, and the perfect carving of a Black Russian Terrier stood on the table beside her.

***

Nikita walked aimlessly for a while, soaking up the energy of West Berlin, an energy he hadn't felt since being in Cuba, a place he longed to return to for the company of his father and sister. After losing his mother to Soviet Neo-Nazis, he had never been afforded the chance to grieve with his family, to repair the wounds that were left open and festering. Before he knew it, his feet had led him, with a certain inevitability, to a bar. It was a dingy place, with rock music playing from a jukebox and enough people in it for him not to be conspicuous, which suited him just perfectly.

Ignoring the usual raised eyebrows that greeted him the world over, he took a seat at the bar and called for whisky.

The first drink was in his stomach before he'd even noticed, and he ordered another. This one he drank slower, noticing it was Jameson's Irish whisky, a rare luxury to a man from behind the Iron Curtain, and he thought through what his next move should be. He had to return to the East to track down the bomber, but with little in the way of leads, he had no idea where to start.

He ordered another drink and, while the barman poured out the whisky, asked him if they had a phone he could use. The barman nodded his head towards the far side of the bar, and Nikita took his whisky over to the phone. Handily, no one was sat at that end of the bar, and Nikita lifted the phone, whirring in a number that he had long since committed to memory.

The phone rang twice before a cool voice answered in a generic American accent.

'Welcome to Johnson's Shipping Supplies. May I take your reference number?'

'Twenty-eight,' Nikita said, reciting the field agent number he had been given and covering his mouth to block out the blaring music as best he could and preventing any interested observer from lip reading. He may be in the West now, but who knew how far the Stasi's eyes could reach.

'And can you confirm if your delivery is secure?' asked the woman calmly.

'Negative,' responded Nikita.

'Please state your present location.'

'French sector, West Berlin. Exact location unknown,' Nikita added, eyeing a woman suspiciously as she passed him on the way to the toilet.

'One moment, please,' said the woman, and he was met by some smooth jazz holding music, which he had to endure for almost five minutes.

'Please proceed to Leopoldplatz. There is a laundromat named Waschhaus at the corner of Müllerstraße and Luxemburger Straße, where you will find a payphone. You have a great day now,' she said pleasantly, and the line went dead.

Nikita swallowed the rest of his drink, threw some Deutschmark notes down on the bar and left without a backward glance. After several empty taxis had driven straight past him, he found his way to the nearest U-Bahn and studied a map from which he learned, with relief, that Leopoldplatz had a station. Sitting on the rattling train was infinitely more comfortable than riding on top of it, but with three double whiskies sitting in his empty stomach, it afforded him too much time to dwell on Elysia, and his mood darkened.

He found the laundromat with ease and saw that the phone was in a small, grubby booth at the back of the room. He was grateful that, while the machines were whirring, there was no one inside at that moment. The second he had closed the door of the booth behind him, the phone rang.

Nikita froze, and his eyes searched the room. He saw the tell-tale glint of a camera lens hidden within a clock hung above the entrance, aimed directly at the booth.

Giving it a sarcastic wave, he picked up the receiver.

'Agent 28, you're a long way from home,' said a deep voice Nikita was unfamiliar with.

'Who's that?' Nikita said, sliding back into the Floridian accent he had used for his American alias.

'You are speaking with CIA Deputy Director Barker,' said the voice with a tone that gave Nikita the distinct impression he had a permanent smirk on his face. He knew those guys. He didn't like those guys.

'Where's Sykes?' Nikita asked, referring to Gordon Sykes, Department Chief for the Soviet Counterintelligence Branch in Langley and Nikita's former boss when he had been stationed undercover as an analyst at CIA HQ.

'Sykes does not handle field agents, agent.'

'Nor does the deputy director,' Nikita commented pointedly.

'Every now and then, we have to debase ourselves and mix with the rabble when we have agents who go off the grid for the better part of two years. That's an awfully long time,' he finished, leaving his meaning uncomfortably clear.

'I have been undercover, as ordered,' Nikita said.

'Interesting, I thought your job was in Moscow. Yet now we find you in West Berlin.'

'You missed Afghanistan. I had a blast there for most of that time. Not a lot of phone reception in the desert, though, which is a bit of a drawback.'

'The thing is, Agent, sometimes when agents disappear off the grid when they're undercover, sometimes, it's because they've forgotten which side they're on.'

'Sometimes bosses forget that too. And sometimes agents are just getting on with their jobs,' Nikita responded coldly.

There was a silence that sounded a little too much like a sceptical sneer to Nikita, which Barker eventually broke.

'What brings you back to us, 28?'

'I have been sent to East Berlin to uncover a bomb threat. There is a new Afghan organisation named Kulu Alqasas that is planning to strike at East Berlin in retaliation for the Soviet invasion of their country.'

'Funny. I thought the invasion was over,' said Barker in a vaguely mocking voice.

'If only you'd had an undercover agent who could inform you otherwise,' Nikita said.

'Continue with your story,' ordered the deputy director.

'I have been sent here by the KGB to head off a bomb threat from Kulu Alqasas, who are led by a man named Bedar Al-Zalmay. If it succeeds, East Berlin could erupt.'

'East Berlin is forever on the cusp of erupting,' Barker commented.

'Perhaps, but the chaos would undoubtedly spill over into the West.'

'You forget there's a wall stopping anything from spilling into the West.'

'Be that as it may, the bomb threat remains.'

'And you came by this information, how?' Barker asked.

'Does it matter? It's a serious enough claim that Denisov himself sent me to Berlin to investigate.'

'You must have really earned his trust,' Barker said, the mocking tone returning.

'Which was the job you guys sent me to do!' Nikita responded angrily. His temper remained quite cool, but Jacob Marshall was known for being rather more emotional than his Soviet counterpart.

'And how well you appear to have done it.'

'You sent me, an untrained field agent, into Moscow where you have no other agents, provided me with no handler or means of contacting you, and now question my motives after everything I have given for our country?'

'We do expect a degree of creative thinking from our field agents, but perhaps we have expected too much in this case,' Barker said acerbically. 'Don't think you're irreplaceable. There are thousands of guys around the country just like you we could pick up who have been bred to do what they're told and would be only too glad to do something a little different to selling drugs.'

'What will you do about the bomb threat?' Nikita asked, trying to avoid being drawn into whatever game Barker was trying to play. If he thought casual racism would get under his skin, it just went to show he didn't have the first clue where Nikita had come from.

'That is none of your concern.'

'As I'm an active undercover agent in East Berlin charged with containing the threat, I would say it's 100 per cent my concern.'

'Suffice it to say, we have no jurisdiction in East Berlin. The Soviets made absolutely sure of that long ago.'

'Oh, come on, cut the bullshit. I'm sure the place is teeming with our people.'

Ignoring him, Barker continued, 'By all accounts, the place is falling apart. Not just East Berlin but the whole Soviet empire. A bomb would only hasten the fall of the whole communist experiment.'

Nikita paused, hoping he had misunderstood the meaning of Barker's words.

'You mean... you want it to happen?' he asked hesitantly.

'The United States government would not condone any bombing in East Berlin,' he replied.

'But you would also not do anything to stop it?'

'How could we stop a bomb that we never knew about?' Barker said meaningfully.

'But all those innocent lives...' Nikita began.

'—that could be saved with the fall of the Iron Curtain,' interrupted Barker.

'Then what do you want me to do? If I don't hunt for the bomber, my cover will be blown.'

'You *try* to do what they have asked of you, and this time, keep the channels of communication a little more open. Do you understand me, Agent 28?'

'Understood,' Nikita said curtly and hung up.

He walked back out into the cold November night and exhaled heavily, his breath steaming in front of his face, and tried to decide on his next move. His hands were almost shaking, not from the cold but from the weight of pressure upon him. Yet again, he found that his feet led him to a bar. This time, it was a dimly lit blues bar, full of blue and red lighting and thick with smoke. Much like the place he had been to earlier in the evening, it was not very full, and Nikita realised that it was a Monday night.

He slid into a booth with another whisky and stared at the amber liquid. *The difference is I can take just a sip.* Elysia's words played through his mind, tightening his stomach uncomfortably. He took a sip and put it back down. Who knew if anything she had said was true. She knew nothing. She had not been forced into the KGB to protect her family, she had not had to kill countless people, had not lost her mother to Neo-Nazis, to be a spy in the CIA, and then be a double agent, acting out the whims of powerful Russians and Americans who cared nothing for him. She had not been ordered to ignore a bomb that would kill thousands of innocent people.

Seconds later, he was at the bar ordering another, this time ordering two to save the trip.

By the time he had lost track of how much he had drunk, the churning in his stomach had eased, but his mood had darkened further. *Bred to do what they're told* were the words now in his mind. Maybe Barker's words had stung more than he'd thought. As if hearing his thoughts, Sam Cooke's civil rights song A Change Is Gonna Come came on to the jukebox.

He suddenly found himself paying more attention to the lyrics than ever before, as the soul singer talked of being born in poverty, and how he had been running from it ever since. Out of nowhere, Nikita was overcome with memories of his mother, Sophie Allochka, being shot dead when the Russian Neo-Nazis led by Lev Veselovsky came en masse to kill his entire family, at a place deep in Siberia they had been shoved away to, just because they were Black. He remembered the shack made of scrap metal he had been raised in. *I've spent my life running from it too.*

The words continued to resonate with Nikita's soul, as now Sam Cooke spoke of life being too hard, but the thought of death being even harder. Taxis passing him by, constant taunts, reluctant handshakes, disdain from those he was trying to help; anger began to roil inside him that he hadn't felt before. A TV screen up behind the bar was showing images of the

Alexanderplatz protest of yesterday but suggesting that even tougher restrictions on travel could be brought in tomorrow, especially in light of the assassination of the chief of the East Berlin Police.

The song finished with the Cooke's claim that it's been a long time coming, but he was sure that change would come. Nikita emptied his glass and slammed it down on the table so hard that it shattered, cutting his hand.

'It's true, you guys cannot handle your drink, jah!' said a blond man at the bar whose bleary eyes told Nikita he couldn't handle his drink either. Nikita leapt up, ignoring the blood tricking from his hand.

'What do you mean, friend?' Nikita asked, grinning intensely at the man, feeling a recklessness he had never experienced before. What more could anyone do to him?

The man laughed at Nikita and winked at the barman. 'Another nigger getting a little too big for his boots.'

He didn't get any further, as Nikita crashed a fist into the side of his face and sent him flying to the floor, immediately unconscious. There was a moment of silence, in which Nikita began to feel remorse hit him, but then a baseball bat swung by the barman thudded into his side, forcing him to his knees. Two other men descended on him from across the bar, too, and Nikita felt a sharp kick to his side in the same place the bat had struck. He let out a hoarse laugh. *Let's give these white folk a taste of what it's like to be beaten down*, he thought to himself. He punched the side of the knee of the leg, swinging back to kick him again, and felt the twang of a cruciate ligament snapping as the man screamed and fell to the ground. Nikita jumped up and took a punch straight to the face from a bulky bald guy who looked enraged.

Nikita's head snapped back, but he moved aside to dodge the next blow, instead ducking inside the punch and aiming a blow to the centre of the ribcage of the man, who immediately gasped as the wind completely left his lungs and fell to one knee. Nikita finished him off with a kick to the face, and the man rolled over, clutching his nose and still trying to draw breath. The barman now had come out from behind the bar and was approaching cautiously with the baseball bat.

'I thought this is meant to be the liberal West?' Nikita said blearily.

'I suggest you walk away now,' said the barman.

'But I'm having so much fun,' Nikita said, grinning recklessly, and then was thrown forward by a heavy impact to the back of his head.

CHAPTER 7

Nikita opened his eyes and felt like his head was stuck in a bell tower, such was the ringing between his ears. It must have only been minutes since he had been unconscious as he saw the barman disappearing around the corner of the alleyway he'd been deposited in. He tenderly touched the back of his head, and it was wet and sticky with blood from when he'd been hit by some kind of heavy, blunt object with an enormous amount of force. He groaned loudly. The imprudent adrenaline that had coursed through him just minutes before was long gone, and now he was left with a sick feeling in his stomach and the taste of blood in his mouth. He pushed himself up and staggered sideways, crashing into the dumpster they had so unceremoniously left him beside, and he realised how drunk and concussed he was and wished there was an instant way to sober up. The pain he could deal with, he had been trained to ignore it, but the shame was something else altogether.

He zigzagged his way back up the alleyway and followed the roads towards the centre of West Berlin. He found a public toilet, which was much like public toilets the world over; dirty, cold, and with a lot of suspicious puddles across the floor. He doused his face in cold water, slapping his cheeks. Then, filling the sink, leant backwards and washed the back of his head, ignoring the stinging that knifed through his cranium. As he massaged his scalp, he could feel that nothing was broken, but the blow had split the skin enough to know he would be feeling it for some time and that he wouldn't be sleeping on his back for a few days.

He turned and looked at himself in the cracked mirror and slapped his cheeks again.

'Well, you got what you were looking for, and how did it make you feel?' he asked himself. His usually clean-shaven face was lined with stubble, and he was pretty sure he had fractured a rib or two from the baseball bat. Hard to believe he was still only twenty-three, and he wondered if he would live to see twenty-four.

He cracked his neck from side to side, splashed some more water on his face and strode out of the washroom, feeling more stable on his feet. Somewhere, a clock was chiming for 10 p.m., but it felt like it should be the small hours of the night. He found a café still open and inhaled a strong black coffee and a large, salty pretzel and, his head feeling much less fuzzy, worked through his next steps.

It was time to get back to the reason he was in Germany in the first place: the bomb. It was one of the few occasions he was glad to be from behind the Iron Curtain; it was a lot easier to fulfil his Soviet orders of stopping the bomb than his CIA ones to allow people to die. But there was a small temptation within him to do as Barker had said, let it all play out, and then maybe, just maybe, with no USSR, there would be no KGB, and he could taste what real freedom felt like. *No*, he said to himself, *no freedom is worth that much blood on my hands.* But to stop the bomb he needed to get back over the wall. It was important that Rosin and the Stasi did not know he had crossed to the West, as it would mean unmasking Elysia and her assassination of Julian Rausch. Nikita did not know yet how or what he felt about the new Elysia he had discovered, but he was not yet ready to throw her to the Stasi wolves or, worse, his KGB cronies. Getting back without them knowing, though, meant going back the way he had come, which was not an experience Nikita had any desire to relive.

He had heard of the other creative methods people had conjured up in a bid to get across, from jumping out of buildings next to the wall to homemade hot air balloons - all were notable by the bloody end the participants invariably came to.

Perhaps the high-speed underground train roof-ride wasn't such a bad option after all. As he journeyed back to Voltastraße U-Bahn Station, he passed the hospital where he had left Elysia, who would almost certainly be conscious again now, and debated going in to see her but decided against it. He needed to forget about her for now. If she was a spy, she would be tough enough to get over a bullet wound. God knows Nikita had recovered from his own share of them.

Not for the first time, he wondered if he would ever see her again.

***

THE KREMLIN, MOSCOW, USSR

General Secretary Misho Petrenko strode irritably along a corridor of the Kremlin, away from the meeting chamber of his Politburo and muttered furiously to himself. The group of eighteen men were essentially his cabinet, but right now, Petrenko felt like they were as much his enemy as the US.

He heard footsteps running to catch him up but carried on striding ahead as best he could with his considerable girth.

'General Secretary,' wheezed the familiar voice of Maxim Denisov, his faithful KGB dog, drawing level with him.

'What is it, Maxim?' Petrenko asked curtly, not lessening his pace and instead forcing Denisov to fall into stride beside him.

'Do not pay heed to the short-sightedness of the Politburo,' he said breathlessly.

'Ha! Short-sighted is certainly what it is. Why must they fight me on every decision?'

'They lack your vision, General Secretary.'

'My position would be stronger if our covert Afghan operation had succeeded,' he responded pointedly.

'All is not lost yet, sir,' Maxim said.

'Oh?'

'I do not deny that the situation is bleak. But the fact remains that we have an entire nuclear arsenal that the US believe to have been destroyed, lying hidden. Albeit in an admittedly unsuitable location.'

'This is true. But other than the success of deceiving the US, I don't see how it benefits us. The entire Eastern Bloc is on the cusp of dissolution. We've had revolutions in Hungary, Berlin, Bulgaria, Czechoslovakia, and Romania. Poland has even elected itself a new government! Our grasp grows tenuous.'

'The world sees you as a hero. Your Glasnost and Perestroika policies are viewed very favourably.'

'Not by the Politburo, you heard them. They think I am the man allowing the empire to crumble. Is it my fault that Schleicher didn't open fire and disperse the Alexanderplatz demonstration in Berlin? My fault that his police crony was shot? Whether I tighten my grip or loosen it, my list of enemies only grows.' He grabbed Denisov by the arm. 'It is you who must help me unite the nation once more, Maxim,' he said pleadingly, stopping to look at the man he had made head of the KGB, 'you're the only one of those vultures that I can trust.'

Denisov's long, flat mouth curled slightly at the corner into the hint of a smirk.

'I do have one idea up my sleeve, sir. It involves our old friend, the Black Russian...' he began and started walking. This time, it was Petrenko who followed him, and this time, Denisov allowed the smirk to spread right across his face.

***

Nikita once more sat in a car beside Ivan Rosin, whose hair was ruffled and the usually carefully shaped pencil moustache unkempt.

'You don't look well, Rosin,' said Nikita, who did not feel well himself after another hair-raising journey back under the wall. It had, at least, sobered him up.

'Where have you been?' responded Rosin with suppressed anger, staring determinately at the wall in front of where they had parked.

'Doing my job,' Nikita replied with a shrug.

'Your job was to stop any terrorist activity, and yet I have a dead chief of police on my hands and a KGB agent gone AWOL for two days afterwards, who then returns stinking of alcohol.'

'Firstly, my job was to stop a bomber, not to prevent anybody from shooting a policeman I'd never heard of. I didn't notice any bombs go off unless there's something I've missed?' he asked with a raised eyebrow. 'Secondly, I do not answer to you. I answer to the Kremlin.'

'Well, the Kremlin has wasted no time harassing me for answers,' Rosin retorted and lit up a cigarette from a crumpled packet in the driver's door. 'Where have you been?' he repeated.

'After I saw the shooter—'

'You found the shooter?' Rosin asked with a gasp, which caused him to choke on his cigarette and explode into a coughing fit.

'No, I saw the shooter from a distance.'

'Tell me,' said Rosin, recovering.

'After finding the terrible location you had originally posted me to, I proceeded to a better location on top of the Galeria, where I discovered the aftermath of the shooter's location. As the roof was then teeming with Stasi and police officials, I moved on to the rooftop of the Hotel Stadt Berlin, which gave me a prime view of the demonstration. I stayed there long after the protest had abated, and just after midnight, I saw movement on the Galeria rooftop. I saw them retrieve the weapon from somewhere the clearly inept police force had overlooked, and then they quickly made their escape.'

'You did not pursue them?'

'I tried, of course. But by the time I had reached the Galeria, they were gone, and police cars were converging on them. Again, I made the mistake of assuming that what sounded like the entire East Berlin Police force might be able to catch one getaway shooter. Since then, I have been focusing my attention on trying to find any leads that might reveal the mysterious bomber rather than searching for the shooter.'

'In bars by the smell of it,' Rosin said with a scowl.

'In my experience, bombers don't usually hang around in art galleries.'

'And where have you got to?'

'That is where I need your assistance.'

'Do tell,' said Rosin, lifting an eyebrow.

'Firstly, what can you tell me about Schleicher?'

'The head of state security?' Rosin said, looking surprised. 'He runs probably the greatest intelligence agency the world has ever seen. He is everything you expect from such a man.'

'And what should I expect from such a man?' Nikita asked.

Rosin shrugged. 'He is ruthlessly efficient, unerringly loyal to the socialist cause and does not suffer fools.'

'And you're sure of that, are you? That his loyalty to the cause cannot be questioned?'

Rosin chuckled. 'Not only has he been the head of the Stasi for thirty-two years, but his roots in the party go much, much deeper. He is said to have murdered two Berlin police captains in 1931 on the orders of Stalin himself and then spent years in Moscow, even taking part in the Great Purge, where hundreds of thousands were murdered, if you believe such far-fetched anti-Soviet propaganda. After that, he returned to East Germany after World War II to ensure it became a socialist satellite state. Then came the Stasi, the reach of which cannot be underestimated.'

'The ultimate communist CV. Murder, betrayal, power lust, oppression of the people and a total absence of the equality communism is meant to stand for,' Nikita summarised.

'If Schleicher heard you say such things, you would be dead before you even knew you'd been arrested.'

'Then I pray you aren't a Stasi informer,' Nikita said, looking Rosin directly in the eyes.

To his credit, Rosin held his gaze. 'I am here representing the same organisation as you, Allochka. I am no traitor.'

'Good,' said Nikita abruptly, and he rubbed his hands together to get some warmth through them. It had started to rain again.

'You think he is involved in the bomb plot?' Rosin asked, his voice dripping with scepticism.

'Not at all, but I think if I was a bomber looking to destroy the fabric of East Berlin, then taking out the head of the secret police, which controls every aspect of its society, would be one of the first things I would consider. I need two things from you, Rosin.'

'Da?'

'Firstly, I need somewhere to stay, somewhere without ears—'

'Such a place does not exist this side of the wall,' interrupted Rosin. 'Every door has ears.'

'Then have your people sweep the room first,' Nikita retorted. 'And secondly, I need to be able to pass with ease over the wall as and when needed.'

'That is the sort of thing a defector might ask for,' Rosin said, spitting the burnt-up stub of his cigarette out of the window and immediately lighting another.

'I find our conversations incredibly tedious, Rosin.'

'You sound like my wife,' Rosin snorted.

'What a lucky woman she is.'

'You've no idea, she's back in Leningrad,' Rosin said grimly and started the car.

'Where are we going?'

'You'll need a passport and papers to be able to cross through the checkpoints,' he said.

***

Not long after, Nikita sat in the apartment Rosin had provided him with and leafed through the papers that would enable him to cross to the West when needed. He also had a map of the city, with a big circle drawn in permanent marker around where the Stasi HQ was. There was also a circle around the Volkspolizei's East Berlin HQ, and it was there that Nikita decided to go first.

The wide, low concrete building was not difficult to spot, with the Volkspolizei flag flapping despondently from a high pole in the November drizzle. Nikita walked in and was surprised to find no security checks and only the usual suspicious or frightened looks that followed him everywhere. Clearly, in East Berlin, they rarely had to deal with people entering police HQ of their own volition.

The reception desk was also unmanned, so he proceeded to the elevator, which was to the right of it. With no indication of where he should go, he opted for the top floor.

The cramped, wood-panelled lift opened onto a long corridor with little natural light, lined with offices on either side. Nikita walked along it, reading the names on the doors as he went. Towards the end of the corridor, he spotted what he was looking for:

Walter Kielhorn
POLIZEIDIREKTOR

He knocked on the door.

'Jah?' came a tired response, and Nikita entered. If the director was surprised to see Nikita, he didn't show it and instead walked around his desk to shake his hand.

'Agent Allochka, please sit,' he said, gesturing towards a chair. 'It's not often we enjoy a visit from our friends in the East.'

'You could venture into politics when you tire of the police if you continue to be that diplomatic, Director,' Nikita said with a smile.

'What can I do for you?' Kielhorn said, sitting in his own chair. He gave a meaningful look at the phone on his desk, and Nikita immediately understood.

'I was wondering if you made any progress with the shooter?' Nikita asked.

'I am afraid not. Whoever did it knew what they were doing and left no indication of who they were, but it looks like it was a professional hit rather than an angry protestor.' Again, the director gave Nikita a meaningful look. 'And did the whispers you were chasing get any louder?'

'I find myself in a similar position to you, Director, with no progress and no leads.'

'I am sorry to hear it. We will, of course, offer you every assistance you require. Even if it could be helpful to know where is good to go for good food,' he said with the slightest hint of a wink.

'Of course. Being new to the city, I have eaten little other than sandwiches since my arrival. A good German meal would be most welcome.'

'Here, let me write down some good places for you,' Kielhorn said and handed Nikita a scrap of paper.

Nikita glanced at it. There were no restaurants, only an address he did not recognise and a time.

He looked up at Kielhorn. 'I thank you. I will be certain to visit your suggestions. I won't take up any more of your time, Director, but if you do make any progress with your case, please do let me know. Perhaps we can be of assistance to one another.'

'My pleasure, comrade,' Kielhorn replied, rising to again shake Nikita's hand.

***

LENINGRAD, USSR. 1983

'You cannot prepare too much for a mission, and if you are not early, then you are late,' raged Dima Balabanov, the KGB instructor famed throughout the agency for his skills in espionage. 'A failure to prepare will lead, without question, sooner or later, to your death. When you operate in the shadows, you must know the shadows inside and out. You must master them, and only then can you become them. PREPARATION!' he barked once more.

Nikita sat with another trainee, squashed behind wooden school desks made for people much smaller than the strapping young men, both of whom looked deeply uncomfortable.

Balabanov turned on an overhead projector, which shone an image of a map up on the screen at the front of the room.

'This is your first real-world exercise in espionage and subversion, and if you fail, you will get an early start to your torture resistance training, but the focus of it will not be education. I know the political correctness brigade likes to call it Resistance to Interrogation instruction, but let's call it what it is: torture training.'

The young man sat next to Nikita, Igor Malafeyev, chuckled, thinking it a joke, but stopped abruptly when he saw the deadly serious look on the teacher's face.

Balabanov brandished a telescopic pointer, swinging it like a sword, and pointed to the map.

'What you can see is a map of the central business district of Tallinn, the capital of our satellite state, Estonia, which is just across the border from us here. The job of you two is to get into the government offices here'—he stabbed with the pointer at the centre of the map - 'and plant subversive evidence in a key location.'

'What is the subversive evidence, and what is it for?' Nikita asked.

Balabanov's eyes flashed, and he smacked the telescopic pole down onto Nikita's fingers, causing him to roar with pain.

'Two years in the KGB, and still you question orders! Your job is to follow, not to lead Allochka!' he spat.

Malafeyev again sniggered but went unpunished by Balabanov.

The teacher regained his composure and continued. 'You must remember, both of you, that more than anything else, espionage requires patience. You cannot rush it; you cannot force it. You have to expertly coax others to your will. Now, where was I? After World War II, following the Soviet occupation of the Baltic states, a resistance movement was formed called the Baltic Forest Brothers. We infiltrated and broke them by the mid-fifties, but the evidence shows that they have again risen. Planting this evidence that we will arrange for our people in their government to find will justify an invasion by our great country. Estonia does not know it, but it needs more than just a Soviet umbrella. It needs to be part of the Soviet Union itself.'

Massaging his stinging knuckles, Nikita said nothing, and Malafeyev had also learned his lesson.

Tonight, you will be taken to Tallinn. There, you each have individual pieces of evidence, and each of you has a duty to ensure you are not identified. While the task should be easy, which is why we are happy for it to fall to trainees, there is a great deal riding on it, and if you should fail, well, I already have warned you of the consequences.'

Later that night, Nikita and Malafeyev sat in silence in the back of an army truck as it bumped along an indirect route across the border into Estonia. Malafeyev was six feet tall and strapping, with muscled arms and a square jaw, and was staring at Nikita with a look of complete disdain. Nikita ignored him, being used to such hostility from his fellow trainees, and rested his head in his hands, gazing at the floor.

'Why did I have to get paired with you?' Malafeyev grunted.

'My thoughts exactly,' Nikita said, looking up at his comrade with a smile.

'Are you being funny? Just because you're the golden boy doesn't mean I don't see you for what you are,' he said, glaring at Nikita with malice in his eyes.

Nikita's two years in the academy had taught him enough about the other boys' feelings towards him to bother asking Malafeyev exactly what he meant, and instead, he went back to looking silently at the floor.

'You're just a chernozhopiy who will betray us all at the first chance you get.'

Nikita's head snapped up at the use of the highly offensive term, and he looked at his compatriot coldly.

'What?' said Malafeyev, smirking, his eyes challenging Nikita to respond.

Nikita had learned the value of silence and said nothing other than eyeballing him. The grin fell from Malafeyev's face as he realised Nikita was not playing ball.

'You people are too used to submission,' he added, further trying to provoke a reaction from Nikita, who just looked up and smiled virtuously at him while imagining being able to put a bullet straight into his face.

'You're either stupid or crazy,' Malafeyev continued. 'Either way, I would rather do this mission alone than depend on you,' he said and, quick as a flash, drew his gun, into which he had already screwed a silencer.

Quick as he was, there was a reason Nikita was hailed as the best recruit the KGB had seen for a decade. Without his facial expression changing, he swiped sideways to aim the gun away from his head, moved inside the arm and bent Malafeyev's hand backwards until he heard the trigger finger snap. He then pulled the gun off the limp finger, spun round and delivered a blow to the temple that caused

Malafeyev to immediately crumple to the floor of the truck, where he lay unconscious.

The entire episode lasted no more than four seconds. Nikita sat down again and used his unconscious colleague as a footrest for the remainder of the journey.

When they arrived at the drop point on the edge of Tallinn, Nikita found that a sluggish Malafeyev was a lot more placid towards him, albeit with eyes that were not fully in focus. Nikita nodded to him, and they went in different directions, both with their own task to complete in the government offices on the west side of the city. Both would take their own route there and their own method to get inside.

The sky was beginning to faintly lighten behind him with false dawn as he made his way through a residential area in the south of the city. The envelope of doctored information felt awkward sewn into the lining of his jacket. He had studiously pored over maps of the city all day in preparation for the mission so as to be able to look as much as possible like he lived there. He walked confidently to the commuter railway station in the Nõmme District and arrived, as he had planned, just in time for the first train of the day to roll into the station. Balabanov's words echoed around his head, '*You cannot prepare too much for a mission,*' and that was what Nikita had done. He must stay alive for his family, and failure was not an option. He had no doubt Malafeyev was also doing everything he could to get to the drop site and scope it out as far in advance as possible.

The train was almost deserted at such an early hour, with only the occasional bleary-eyed passenger leaning against the window, doing their best to pretend they were still in bed, and Nikita did much the same thing. But while his eyes were closed, his mind was racing, and he replayed the steps he had worked through to ensure his mission was a success.

He arrived hours before most of the workers would be arriving and, after doing a detailed reconnaissance of the building, stationed himself in a coffee shop opposite the main entrance, glad for the hot liquid and caffeine. He had identified three possible entry points, two of which were manned by security. The final, potentially unmanned, entry would have been the ideal candidate, but after watching it for some time, he became convinced it would be a poor choice. A close inspection of the door revealed a barely visible wire that showed it was alarmed, and he dismissed that as an entry point, adding it only to a list of emergency exit points. He had watched the gradual stream of people entering both of the other two entrances, and the main entrance seemed to be where the suits entered, while the other was used mainly by service staff. He leafed through the ID papers he had lifted from both front entrance and side entrance workers, evaluating his options while replacing the photographs on both with ones he had of himself.

The trickle of people had turned into a stream, and Nikita swallowed his coffee, making his decision not to enter through the front but to join the service staff. He unzipped his jacket to reveal the baggy overalls underneath that he had donned in preparation for such an approach and walked at a leisurely pace to the side of the huge brick building to join the small crowd of people, which he was grateful to see, was not exclusively white men. This would help his anonymity no end as he headed to the service entrance. He looked relaxed and ready for work and joined the back of the long queue of tradesmen waiting to enter the building. As he joined the line of workers, a large garage door next to the entrance began to be raised with a loud rattling as a garbage truck crawled noisily towards it. Nikita made a snap decision to change his plan, and acting quickly on instinct, he waved at the driver with a look of great familiarity. The driver waved back but looked completely confused.

'Tere hommikust Mihkel!' Nikita greeted him, grinning, in one of the very small handful of Estonian phrases he had memorised in preparation and gained a few vaguely interested glances from other bleary-eyed workers. He ran around to the other side of the truck, blocking him from view of the entrance where workers were moving towards the door and metal detector beyond. At a jog, he jumped up and grabbed a metal rung of the truck, staying out of sight from both the door and the wing mirror of the truck driver, and held on as the garage doors trundled down behind them.

As soon as they had clanged shut, he hopped nimbly to the ground and, staying to the rear of the truck and out of sight, jumped and crouched behind a dumpster until he was fully out of sight of the truck. He took the opportunity to remove the papers from the lining of his jacket, which he bundled up and deposited in the dumpster, then he stood and, walking like he belonged, opened a door at the rear of the underground carpark and entered the maze of corridors beyond.

He knew exactly where he needed to go and, entering a stairwell, climbed swiftly to the fourth floor. It opened onto a vast office floor that was filled with desks, people, and noise, including men in similar overalls, allowing him to move hurriedly through without drawing any attention. At the far end of the large room was a series of closed-off offices, and it was towards them that Nikita headed. As he made his way through the corridors of desks, he spotted, to his delight, a mail cart that was unattended as the chubby post-room clerk chatted animatedly to an equally chubby blonde woman who was twirling her hair bashfully, keeping them both nicely distracted.

He leant on the cart and began steering it along the various pathways between desks and cubicles, moving as quickly as he dared until he reached the office he was looking for. It was a much wider one than those on either side and also glass-fronted, although, fortunately, obscured by venetian blinds. On a large wooden plaque, read:

BOARDROOM, MINISTRY OF THE INTERIOR

The door was ajar, and the room was empty, although place names and binders had already been laid out on the long table of polished birch for the conference that would be happening that morning. At the head of the table was a place marked for Mart Leppik, Estonian Minister for the Interior, while at the opposite end of the table was a card for Konstantin Sollogub, USSR - Estonia Foreign Affairs Liaison, a title which Nikita doubted was fooling anyone. Withdrawing papers from his envelope, he filtered through them and slid them into the binders in each place around the table. Without hesitating, he turned and pushed the mail cart back out, leaving it a few desks away from the clerk, who was still engrossed in conversation and oblivious to the loss of his cart for a few minutes. But as Nikita began to make his way back through the office, the alarm sounded overhead, causing everyone to stop mid-sentence and look around.

With an enormous amount of grumbling, everyone began making their way towards the exit. Nikita followed, but his mind was racing. He did not believe in coincidences, especially ones that made his escape so much easier. He hurried into the men's toilets as the crowd passed and, dashing into a cubicle, removed the overalls to reveal a suit underneath. He hastily pulled on a tie and slid back in amongst the back end of the crowd, putting on a trilby hat from a hatstand as he passed and pulling it as low onto his head as he could without looking suspicious. With eyes everywhere, he continued down the stairwell and followed the crowd towards the main exit that he had been sitting watching from the coffee shop earlier. As he left the main entrance, he saw police running down the side of the building, and he casually followed and saw them milling around the unmanned entrance he had considered and then dismissed earlier. It proved him right that it was alarmed, but only one thing was going through his mind. Malafeyev.

Nikita was caught in two minds. His mission had been a success, and if he left now, he may be untainted by any failure on the part of Malafeyev. On the other hand, leaving his comrade behind or his mission incomplete would not endear him to his tutors or his fellow trainees. Nikita approached the crowd of police and interested observers, ambling by as slowly as he could without attracting attention, and saw that the door he had inspected early that morning and judged to be alarmed was hanging off its hinges. Malafeyev using brute force did not surprise Nikita, but the lack of subtlety for such a high-profile mission very much did. Continuing to walk past the crowd, it was then that he saw, on the floor further along the pedestrianised street, Malafeyev's envelope of documents. The heavy A4 manila envelope was identical to Nikita's own and addressed to the Estonian Prime Minister himself. Whether he had dropped them or tried to dump them, Nikita was unsure, but he did know that Malafeyev had come far enough through his training to never discard such important and potent information accidentally. It did mean that he had failed in his mission. He picked up the manila envelope, which was wet and muddy from being walked over, and folded it into the inside pocket of his suit jacket. Getting back into the building was out of the question, but at least now he had ensured the information did not fall into the wrong hands. It at least appeared that Malafeyev had managed to make his getaway.

Balabanov's face, however, had gone beyond strained and into an explosive puce as he struggled to get the words out when facing them back at HQ in Leningrad that evening. Malafeyev sat bruised and forlorn under the glare of their famed teacher while

Nikita sat in his usual rigid position, braced for what was to come.

'Malafeyev, you are a disgrace to the agency and to our glorious nation! You failed on every front! What is it I always say? PREPARATION!' he roared before either of his students had the opportunity to reply. 'You did not prepare, you did not arrive early, you did not operate in the shadows, and you certainly did not master them. Why did you choose to bludgeon your way through an alarmed door?'

'I did not know that it was alarmed. It seemed the most obvious way in without being seen,' grunted Malafeyev, a crumpled shadow of the giggling young man of the day before.

'That is because you did not PREPARE!' spat Balabanov, his eyes popping out of his head.

'Allochka arrived in ample time, scoped out every entry and exit point, devised a clear plan, and spent hours memorising the entire layout of the building. As a result, he made a successful drop.'

Nikita was going to ask how his instructor knew that, and then it dawned on him that he had been observed the entire time.

'Yes, Allochka, you did not think we would abandon two green recruits to such a vital mission,' Balabanov said as if reading Nikita's mind. He turned back to Malafeyev, whose finger, Nikita noticed, was heavily strapped up.

'But you, Igor, you did not prepare. You did not come to know the shadows. You arrived late and made a rash decision which cost the mission. You returned beaten and with a broken trigger finger, and you had to rely on Allochka to happen upon your muddied documents, which had been left in the street! This is not espionage; this is amateur foolishness, and you have shamed the KGB.'

Malafeyev's face was tormented but prepared for what was coming. 'I am ready for my torture training,' he said, hanging his head.

'Torture training?' Balabanov said, lifting his eyebrows. 'No, no, no, Igor, that is for KGB recruits —'

'No!' Malafeyev exclaimed as realisation dawned on him. 'But Allochka broke my finger, sir, and knocked me out! This is why I was late!' he screamed desperately as two burly KGB agents appeared, stony-faced and in long grey coats, from behind the door and walked towards Malafeyev.

'Goodbye, Igor,' Balabanov said coldly as the young man was dragged screaming from the room. The door closed behind him, and the sounds faded away.

Balabanov turned his attention to Nikita.

'You showed the promise I have heard about, Allochka,' Balabanov said as if nothing had happened. 'But your mission still failed. Your former comrade's negligence meant that our backup agents were unable to remedy the situation. Without both pieces of subversive evidence being dropped in the correct places, there is doubt over the Estonia plan being successful. One-half of a successful mission does not make for a success. Wounding your comrade was unwise' - Nikita went to interrupt, but Balabanov held up a hand to quiet him - 'do not take me for a fool, Allochka. Your emotions still make you weak. There is no room for weakness in the KGB.'

The lights in the windowless room suddenly went out, casting them into pitch darkness, and a bag was thrown over Nikita's head. He fought to remove it, but another pair of hands forced his arms behind his back and tied them up.

He vaguely heard the muffled sound of Balabanov's voice as he left the room. 'Torture training begins. I hope you survive.'

***

The memory of Leningrad and Balabanov would forever be etched into Nikita's memory, and it was with that in mind that he made his way to the address Kielhorn had given him. *You cannot prepare too much for a mission, and if you are not early, you are late.* The mantra had been beaten and tortured into every recruit that survived their KGB training, and Nikita no longer knew any other way. Preparation is what had kept him alive this long.

The address Kielhorn had given him at first looked wrong; it was a corner building with boarded-up windows that looked like it had long been empty. It was an area that looked to be mainly residential but that had once been a small high street of sorts. There were still a couple of neglected-looking shops further along the road; a clothes shop, a greengrocer with a meagre selection of vegetables on display, and a bakery that was just closing for the day. Nikita walked in just as the baker was turning the sign to say closed and picked up the last remaining baton of bread, now hardened and going stale. It wasn't much, but 'eat when you can' was another message that had been drilled into him. He stationed himself in a shadowy alleyway, gnawing his bread in the cold November drizzle and watching the corner building. As he had found with all parts of East Berlin, few people moved about openly in the streets, and those that did were stooped as if seeking to be invisible. *This place is making Moscow look cheery*, Nikita thought to himself, almost missing the place that had become his home city of a sort. At least there was some life and energy there, but East Berlin was a place that seemed to have had the life sucked out of it.

After about an hour of waiting, he saw a young couple approach the corner building, looking around them as they closed on the front door. They banged on it three times, and to Nikita's surprise, the door opened, momentarily revealing a warm glow from inside, before banging shut behind them. As the minutes went by, the same thing happened with a middle-aged man and later a trio of women in their late twenties. All had been dressed smartly, and Nikita began to have a hunch about the building, which was reinforced when he went for a stroll past it. Turning the corner, he pressed his ear to the concrete wall and heard, very faintly, the sound of music creeping up from what he suspected was the cellar.

There were no rear entrances, and it infuriated him to not be able to get inside for a full reconnoitre, but if his suspicions were correct, there would be a hidden route out of such a building. With nothing else to do but wait, he returned to his secluded spot and counted down the minutes until Kielhorn's arrival. The director himself was early, wrapped up in a heavy coat with a woolly hat pulled down over his head, giving no indication of his occupation, and Nikita could guess why. Nikita slid out of his hiding place and moved towards Kielhorn, who was walking slowly down the street and looking around for a sign of Nikita. He nodded in recognition when he spotted Nikita and quickened his pace. They met outside the decrepit-looking building. Kielhorn said nothing but banged three times on the door as Nikita had seen everyone else do, and after a few seconds, the chipped, black door creaked open.

It revealed an overweight man with spiky blond hair and a stretched t-shirt not quite covering his ample belly. He had a nose ring and several rings on his fingers, and his dilated pupils suggested he had been enjoying himself in a way that an on-duty Kielhorn would definitely not approve. Behind him was a grimy room, lit by several standing lamps around a couple of old sofas, a sunken armchair and a TV set blaring in the background. Food wrappers littered the floor.

'Jah?' he mumbled, eyeing the pair in the way that the doorman the world over does, a gaze that makes you instantly feel guilty.

'Wir sind für einen Tee,' said Kielhorn, suggesting they were here for the tea. It must have been the password that the doorman wanted to hear as he grunted and stepped aside so they could enter and swiftly closed the door behind them.

He then stepped past them and shoved the armchair to one side with his black hobnail boot. Underneath was a rug, which he then pulled aside to reveal a trapdoor. He lifted it, allowing the sound of loud punk music to roar into the room. It revealed a staircase, which he gestured to them to go down. Kielhorn, looking unperturbed, walked briskly down the steps, and Nikita, more hesitantly, followed. The trapdoor slammed shut above him, but the way was dimly lit by glowing lamps placed haphazardly along the corridor at the bottom of the stairs. Nikita was on high alert; entering a meeting point without proper reconnaissance and with no visible exits other than a trapdoor was the worst possible scenario. They followed it around a corner and through a door, which then opened into what had once been a very large cellar but was now very clearly an East Berlin punk speakeasy.

The Sex Pistols were being pumped out of a PA system at one end, and the room was hazy with the smoke of cigarettes and marijuana, which explained the doorman's pupils. It was busy with people, some dancing, but not full to brimming, which was probably due to the fact the day was still relatively early. Kielhorn led them to a small table at the side of the room, where they both, from habit, turned their chairs outwards so they could view the whole room but did not look at each other.

'Why are we here, Kielhorn?' Nikita said, surveying the room. He spoke loudly to be heard over the volume of the thrashing guitars.

'Please, call me Walter. Do you know what would happen to me if I were found to be here?' the German replied.

'I can take a guess. I don't think places like this even exist in Moscow,' Nikita replied.

'Oh, they find a way to exist everywhere, my friend,' Walter said with a chuckle. 'Everyone needs a place to be free.'

'An interesting choice of words,' Nikita said, looking sideways at the director.

'In East Berlin, the places where the walls don't listen are few and far between. As you saw in my office, even a director in the East German Police Force is not exempt from the ears of our friends, the Stasi.'

'This is something you object to?' Nikita asked, trying to size him up.

'It is something I suspect we both object to,' Kielhorn said, looking Nikita in the eye.

'Perhaps you are right, perhaps you are not,' Nikita said evasively. 'What gives you reason to think you can trust me?'

'My friend, I lived most of my life in East Berlin, I have never even left East Germany. I have learned to never trust anyone!' He laughed.

'That I can drink to,' Nikita said as a waitress with a bubble-gum pink Mohican, leather jacket, trousers, and black lipstick slammed what looked like two cups of tea down in front of them. When Nikita lifted it and took a tentative sip from the chipped teacup, he realised it was schnapps and some brown colouring.

'You two should lighten up. You look like cops,' she said with a leering smile.

Nikita swallowed his schnapps in one gulp. 'Bring me another of these, and maybe I will,' he said with a wink. She grinned at him and walked away.

'You're good,' Kielhorn said with a chuckle, sipping his schnapps far more conservatively and making a face. 'I'm afraid I never was much of a drinker.'

'It keeps us warm in the East,' Nikita said with a shrug. 'Now come on, Walter, what's this all about?' he asked again.

'I think we can be of mutual benefit to one another,' Kielhorn said, taking another sip and looking out across the room.

'How so?'

'I know you know something about the shooter on the roof, and I also think I know why you are in Berlin. It is something I can help you with,' he said, looking briefly at Nikita, who held up his hands.

'Don't let me stop you when you're on such a roll,' he said, half smiling.

'I know you are searching for someone. I don't know who or for what exactly, but I have a feeling who might be involved.'

'That clears that up,' Nikita grunted.

Kielhorn turned his chair and leant forward to Nikita, beckoning him to do the same, which Nikita did with a sigh.

'Let us stop talking in riddles, my friend.'

'Let's,' Nikita agreed witheringly.

'Your country is failing, and the empire is crumbling. And here? You saw the demonstration; you know of the revolutions rolling across Eastern Europe. It is only a matter of time before the wall comes down and Berlin is united. The communist government in East Germany is floundering; they are an embarrassment to any decent German, and we are tired, so very tired, of the lies, the whispers, and the treachery. I am a policeman, but I feel like a prisoner.'

'So you want my help in escaping to the West?' Nikita said bluntly.

'No, my friend! I told you, I have never left this country. This is my home, but I may be able to help you to hasten the winds of change.'

'You credit me with a great deal of power.'

'Even a KGB foot soldier has the power to effect great change. But I think you are rather more than a foot soldier,' he said knowingly.

'Let's assume I want to hasten these winds of change. How would you suggest I do it?'

'You are here looking for someone, am I right?' Nikita nodded. 'You have been tasked with stopping this person from doing or saying something undesirable, correct?' Again, Nikita gave a tiny incline of his head. 'Then I believe that not only is Schleicher the problem, but he also may be your solution. For some time, I have believed him to not be everything he says he is.'

'Of all the people to be above suspicion, the head of the Stasi is surely top of that list,' Nikita said with a snort, recalling Rosin's defence of the man.

'Do you still not understand? This is East Berlin! Nobody is above suspicion. Here I am, Polizeidirektor, and I have to meet you in an illegal speakeasy to be able to talk freely.'

'What makes you suspect Schleicher?'

'Call it a hunch.'

'That's reassuring,' Nikita said with another snort.

'You are speaking to me because you have no other leads, am I correct?' Kielhorn said with a knowing look, and Nikita could see how he had risen to such a level in the police force.

'You seem to know a lot, Walter. Anyone would think perhaps *you* were Stasi yourself.'

'The secret police and the police force do, of course, work closely together. It does not mean we like them.'

'From what I can see, nobody likes them,' Nikita commented.

'Now that *I* can drink to,' Kielhorn said, taking another sip of his schnapps and scrunching up his face. The barmaid brought another over to Nikita, this time with more of a smile.

'Danke,' Nikita said, raising the cup to her and watching her walk away as she threw a glance over her shoulder. 'Now, Walter, what can you give me of substance.'

'I can give you Schleicher's itinerary. It is something I have procured at great personal risk, but I am certain that with the right equipment - which I'm sure is readily available to you - you will come across information useful to your hunt. Schleicher's movements, once as routine and predictable as the rising of the sun, have become erratic, and he spends more and more time outside of Berlin. And the shooter - do not tell me that Rausch was a more desirable target than Schleicher.'

'Perhaps the shooter made a mistake?' Nikita said.

'A sniper from that distance, making such an accurate shot? I do not think it was a mistake to shoot Rausch, but why him instead of Schleicher? Rausch was not a bad man. He was corrupt, of this I am certain, but he was no friend of Schleicher. Perhaps Schleicher knew something of the shooting in advance? But perhaps you know more of this than me?'

'Very little, I'm afraid, Walter,' Nikita said, and the policeman could not hide his disappointment.

'I do not believe you,' Kielhorn said. 'You are well-trained, but I did not get to where I am without being able to smell a lie a mile off.'

'Yes, I can believe that. But I do not know much more about the motives of the shooter other than it seems clear to me the intention was to prevent any attempts to stop the demonstration. But... I did see the shooter,' he said tentatively.

Kielhorn's eyes snapped up to meet Nikita's, and he smiled. 'I knew it! I knew you had information.'

'Not a lot, I'm afraid, but I can share what I have. I will also tell you a little more about my mission because I will need any intel you can give me.'

'Now it is *you* asking a great deal. You are asking me to become a traitor,' Kielhorn said, shaking his head.

'A traitor to a nation you believe is crumbling?' Nikita said, spreading his hands, to which his companion grimaced. 'I only ask you to share information that may help us both. If I can find the person I am looking for, and Schleicher is involved, it may bring down both the Stasi and, if your theory is correct, the shooter, too. And who knows? Maybe the wall will follow!'

'That cursed wall,' Kielhorn said bitterly. 'I have family on the other side, you know? I have not seen my sister or father for twenty-eight years. I was only a boy, and they had gone to stay with our cousins, and when we woke up the next morning, the wall was there, like a great snake slithering through the heart of my home town.'

'And you tell me you don't want to cross the wall?' Nikita said sceptically.

'Are you kidding? Every day, I dream of seeing my father and sister again. But a man of my position cannot be seen crossing the wall. My only hope is to see the wall fall.'

'There is the honesty I was looking for,' Nikita said, waving for another schnapps. 'And I know a little something about being separated from family. I agree, maybe we can be of help to each other. Let me explain. I am looking for a bomber, probably but not definitely from Afghanistan —'

'Afghanistan?' interrupted Kielhorn, looking surprised.

'If you can pass me any intel that crosses your desk that may help me find him, I can ensure there is great credit in the bank for you all the way to the General Secretary himself. Extracting your father and sister may then start to become a possibility. I care little about whether the wall stands or falls or what happens to Germany; it is not my concern. I have other concerns that are far more pressing to me, but I think our ambitions may align.'

Kielhorn nodded and drained his schnapps tea, a bitter look on his face.

'You are a KGB man to the core.'

'Now you are just trying to hurt me,' Nikita retorted with a grin, which caused Kielhorn to laugh heartily.

'I like you, Allochka. God only knows if I can trust you, but I like you.'

Nikita raised his teacup to him.

'Tell me about the shooter,' Kielhorn pressed.

'I saw only from a distance as I kept my position atop the hotel long after Alexanderplatz had cleared.

But a figure in black returned to the rooftop to collect what looked like their weapon.'

'My team did a sweep of the entire rooftop,' Kielhorn protested.

'Then your team is not good at their job,' Nikita said plainly. 'The figure clearly claimed a sniper rifle from somewhere near the edge of the roof. At this point, I raced to the Galeria, but they had gone,' Nikita said, reciting the story he had told Rosin. 'There were police cars descending from every direction, so I assumed that the shooter would be caught,' Nikita added, rolling his eyes.

'That was... regrettable,' admitted Kielhorn. 'In a city so closely controlled by the Stasi, it is rare for my men to find themselves in a high-speed car chase. I am feeling the heat for it at the office. You saw no features of the shooter?'

'Not really. They were slim, quite short for a man, but even through my scope, I could see little more detail than that in the dark. They had cloaked themselves well - it was most certainly a professional, I could tell by the way they moved.'

'That isn't much,' Kielhorn said, looking seriously over his glasses at Nikita.

'It isn't,' Nikita admitted. 'But I can also pass any intel your way if I come across it. Do we have a deal?' he asked.

Kielhorn's gaze bored into him, and Nikita felt that he was looking right into his very soul before he cleared his throat. 'Jah, we have a deal,' Kielhorn said, extending his hand.

Nikita shook it before pulling the director towards him. 'But if you cross me, I will kill you,' Nikita breathed, and Kielhorn, looking nervous, nodded.

CHAPTER 8

Nikita lay back on his bed, sipping at a bottle of vodka he had been able to procure from a convenience store on his way home. He let his mind sift through everything he had experienced since landing in Berlin. His senses were dimmed, but no matter how much he drank, it no longer seemed to free his mind from the thoughts that bounced around inside. From the memories he longed to forget. Sometimes, their vividness made his skin crawl and his hands feel dirty, the recollections of the things he had done to stay alive, to keep his family alive. But at what cost?

He had followed Kielhorn all the way back to the police HQ, but nothing in the director's movements had given Nikita any cause for suspicion. It seemed he had found a green leaf in a wintery storm.

He jumped up and forced himself into his usual routine of 500 press-ups and sit-ups to try and force the pain out of his pores. As he was doing his sit-ups at the end of the bed, he saw, from the angle he was lying, a small piece of wire under the table that sat in front of the mirror. He propped himself up on one elbow and sidled under the table to take a closer look, his fingers tracing the wire. It led to a small round button-like object stuck to the back of the face of the table, which he peeled off.

Inspecting it, he could see that it was a highly modern listening bug, and he gently placed it back in position. He then scoured the room for more and found a similar bug wired into the handset of the phone next to his bed and another in the lampshade. He then eased the curtain back slightly at one side and looked out at the street. A car was parked about fifty yards down the street where two men in fur hats sat smoking.

Kielhorn was right. No one was safe from Stasi ears. *The question is*, thought Nikita, *are Rosin and the KGB listening too?* He was no stranger to being followed, but it didn't mean that he liked it.

***

KYIV, SOVIET UKRAINE. 1984

Nikita walked swiftly and silently along the street on the east side of Kyiv, which was split into two halves by the Dnieper River. It was a foggy night, and the street was lit by streetlights, but many were broken, throwing long, misty shadows across the city streets. The cracked tarmac road was lined by ill-looking trees and bushes, and tall concrete tower apartment blocks rose up on either side, the tops lost in the swirling mist.

He could hear the footsteps of his pursuer behind but remained confident he could lose them, especially in such murky conditions. He quickened his pace, turning left down a narrow alleyway between two buildings, and almost walked straight into the black waters of the river as it appeared out of nowhere beneath him. A path led off to his right, and he took it, following it along the grassy banks of the river, which wound its way south through the Ukrainian region of the Soviet Union and down to the Black Sea. From his vantage point on the banks of the river, he could see the fog rolling along the water and spilling over the edges, and he walked straight into the thickest part of it, intent on losing himself.

The fog led him away from the river, and he followed it back into an empty street which curved through brown scrubland before leading to a bridge crossing to the western side of the city. He darted off the street and slunk back towards the river. There was no longer a path, but that suited him just fine. The city was quiet, such was the hour, but that was why this was all happening now. It had all been planned in this city he had spent so much of his time in since leaving home. An unhappy city, a place where many wanted freedom. Feelings Nikita had every right to empathise with, but instead chose to bury.

A tree appeared out of nowhere, and the branch cut the side of his face. He felt a bead of blood trickling down one cheek like a tear and wiped it away. Tonight, he wanted to celebrate, not cry over a defeat.

The fog began to glow as the lights of the Paton Bridge reached like fingers into the mist, and the sound of cars pierced the muffled silence. He broke out of the smoggy clouds and clawed his way up the bank to the bridge, confident he had lost his pursuer. All he had to do was reach the other side.

'Bang bang, you are dead,' said a flat, reedy voice from behind him, and there was a sharp sting on Nikita's spine.

Nikita's head sank. He was so sure he had been safe. He turned to see his commanding officer, the man in charge of the KGB military training school in Kyiv, Maxim Denisov, sauntering towards him, holding an air pistol. He squeezed the trigger, and another ball bearing struck Nikita, this time on the wrist, causing a sharp stab of pain, but Nikita gave no outward sign that it had hurt him and instead stood to attention.

'That was sloppy, Agent. Already I consider you little better than shit on my shoe, but you still manage to disappoint me.'

'It will not happen again, sir,' Nikita said.

'If it does, it will not be an air rifle I am holding, and you will find yourself floating face down towards the Black Sea. Do I make myself clear?' Denisov crooned, getting uncomfortably close to Nikita's face. His breath smelled of cabbage and smoke, and Nikita worked hard not to let his distaste show.

'Always, Allochka. Always, always, always, be three steps ahead of your pursuer,' he whispered into Nikita's ear and then pressed the air rifle into Nikita's side and pulled the trigger.

***

Nikita absently rubbed his side, where a small scar would always remain. He decided to leave the bugs where they were, to do everything he could to stay three steps ahead of his pursuers. To do so, he would need to leave without being followed by his new friends. He folded the piece of paper Kielhorn had given him with Schleicher's movements for the days ahead and pushed it into a tear in the lining of the new jacket Rosin had given him and then sewed it up. He'd memorised it anyway.

He left the building through the front door, allowing the Stasi to see him, and ambled along the street in no particular hurry. He heard the engine of their car fire up in the distance and smiled to himself. They were clearly amateurs. To try a covert pursuit by car on such a quiet street was a very basic error, and sure enough, they soon had to drive past him as another car came behind them, forcing them to speed up. They pulled over and tried their best to look innocuous as Nikita walked by. Both were still wearing fur hats and looked so thoroughly Stasi that Nikita nearly laughed out loud. One was balding and wearing wire-rimmed glasses and a beige coat buttoned up to the top. The other had a thin, pale brown moustache, pot belly, and one of the sternest faces Nikita had ever seen, with pinched cheeks, thin lips and a square, jowly jawline. On the upside, they couldn't be taking their surveillance of him too seriously if they were sending these two to watch him.

He heard a car door slam shut behind him once he was fifty yards beyond the car and didn't bother to look around. He knew that they had finally come to the conclusion that at least one of them should follow on foot. Nikita quickened his pace, striding out, and smiled again, quite enjoying the game as he heard his pursuer forced into a jog, his shoes slapping onto the pavement. Shoes! Nikita couldn't help but chuckle to himself. He assumed *everyone* knew to wear soft-soled shoes when pursuing a target.

He came to the end of the road to a large crossroads and saw the tramlines crisscrossing the tarmac. From the right, he could see one of the trams trundling towards him, and he slowed his pace and, at the same time, saw another tram approaching from the opposite direction. The footsteps stopped behind him, and he chanced a glance around, seeing the man with the wire-rimmed glasses skipping sideways into a doorway. Nikita took his opportunity and walked quickly towards the two trams, walking past the one from the right just as it passed and then turning to jump onto its rear platform as it trundled on by, just as the tram from the opposite direction rushed past. He moved quickly inside and sunk low into a chair, leaving his two Stasi friends floundering, unsure where he had gone.

Now that he had lost them, he needed to make his way to the location he had memorised on the Schleicher itinerary. He had a feeling Schleicher was not a man to abandon an itinerary or arrive late. The tram was taking him in roughly the right direction, meandering out to Northeast Berlin. He took the opportunity to close his eyes and dropped into a fitful doze, enjoying the rocking motion of the ancient tram and caring little what the other stern passengers thought. It was an hour later that the tram ground to a halt at its final destination of Ahrensfelde, a green town right at the city limits of East Berlin.

It was colder here, with fewer buildings to block the chill of the early November wind. Still, for a man who had grown up in the Soviet Union, the late German autumn did not phase Nikita at all. He thought back to where his parents and sister had been forced to live in Siberia for the past few years, a place with an average winter temperature of -20°C. Just the thought of Siberia brought back the harrowing image of his mother, Sophie Allochka, being shot dead by the Russian Neo-Nazis, and Nikita closed his eyes, shaking his head fiercely to rid himself of the memory.

He stopped to inspect a colourful map of the town on a sign outside the tram station and saw where he needed to get to. It was a long walk, following the roads leading further out of the city towards the eastern edge of the Berlin Control Zone. After more than an hour of fast walking, Nikita closed in on the place where he should find Schleicher, and it soon became clear. A sprawling mansion rose from behind a dip in a rolling field that had been recently ploughed, making the landscape look brown and barren. Beyond the house, the land continued rolling down to a long plateau, and he could see in the distance the edge of the Berlin Control Zone, which was merely perfunctory as East Berliners could move quite freely into the rest of East

Germany. Alongside it was Werneuchan Airfield, a military airport famous for launching fighter jet night flights in World War Two, and was now a Soviet Airbase. *Like a little slice of home*, Nikita thought grimly. Even from this distance, he could see several Yak-28P Jet Bombers and a long line of Mig-23 Fighter Jets, all ready to take off at a moment's notice. But it wasn't what was visible above ground that had made Werneuchan notorious in the past twenty years. It was what was underneath it. In the early seventies, Leonid Brezhnev, the previous General Secretary of the Soviet Union, had ordered a nuclear storage facility to be built at the airport. It was a gutsy move, being as it was still technically in the airspace of Berlin, meaning France, Britain and the United States could fly right over it and see exactly what they were doing. Nikita made a mental note of its location in case he needed to reach Soviet soil or make a quick getaway at any point while fervently hoping he wouldn't have to go anywhere near the place.

Looking across the terrain, there was only one option for getting close to the property unseen, which was a long tree line running down the hill parallel to the property and sweeping in behind it. Nikita made his way to it. The spruce woodland was quiet and very dark, and his ears were sensitive to every noise. It was a long way around, with the Sitka spruce forest killing most plant life and creating little in the way of an animal haven, meaning there was no path or trail to follow. Nikita could feel his shirt sticking to his back despite the cold. Eventually, he had looped through the trees and around to the back of the country house, where the windows were flickering from the flames of a fireplace Nikita could just make out through the back window. He stood behind a bushy young spruce, peering across the grassy lawn that banked sharply downwards and rolled down to the trees, which formed a natural boundary to the garden.

The rear of the house had floor-to-ceiling windows, granting the occupants a fantastic view out over the trees and across East Germany, but Nikita did not think about the view. Getting closer to the property would be difficult. It was perched above him, and there was no cover from the room, although it appeared empty from Nikita's poor vantage point. He had just decided to make a break for it when he saw the top of a door open at one side of the room, and moments later, the unmistakable figure of Ernst Schleicher stepped into focus, gazing out of the windows. His pudgy, short stature and flat, pouty mouth reminded Nikita strongly of Denisov, and the likeness did not end there. He stood in a stiff grey suit with the look of a man who was comfortable with enormous power and unaffected by the suffering he caused to so many. But unlike Denisov, this was a man who looked incapable of smiling or joy. He looked cold and merciless.

Nikita swayed back on his heels and remained motionless. Kielhorn's intel looked to have been correct so far, but it begged the question, why was the head of the Stasi hanging out in the countryside in the middle of the day? According to Kielhorn's itinerary, it was only a brief stop, and it was a long trip to take just to look out of the window.

Schleicher started talking but did not turn to look behind him to whoever he was conversing with, instead keeping his eyes fixed on somewhere off in the distance. His mouth tightened a little, and to Nikita's trained eye, he could see that whatever he was being told, he did not like it. Then, another man moved beside him but was looking at the head of the Stasi rather than out at the view and began talking animatedly. The man had heavily greying hair, with darker streaks on either side and a flabby neck, which was wobbly, as he demonstrated with Schleicher. Then, unseen by the man with grey hair, Schleicher made a gesture with his hand and a small man with a whiskery face and long pointed nose, making him look like a ferret, instantly appeared stealthily from behind. He looped a cord around the greying man's neck, who was too slow to react to get his thumbs underneath it. He flailed around, writhing wildly, trying to push off the person accosting him, but the small, ferrety man was clearly much stronger than he looked and out-matched the older man for strength. He pushed a knee into his back and pulled tighter on the cord. Gradually, after what felt like an age, his movements began to slow as his face turned to puce, his eyes bulging out of his head, eventually slumping to the floor, lifeless.

At no point had Schleicher even looked at him, continuing to stare off into the distance. As the man fell to the floor, his arm flopped against Schleicher's leg, and without looking down, the head of the Stasi just took a step to one side, with a slight wrinkling of his nose. The assassin said something to Schleicher, who gave a tiny nod of the head, and then he grabbed the body by the legs and dragged it off awkwardly. Once the door closed, Schleicher sighed and turned away from the window. Nikita, who had been waiting patiently for a window of opportunity, took the opening without a second's hesitation.

He ran out from behind the treeline, crouched as low as possible to stay out of sight from the windows, and ran up the sloping lawn, his feet slipping on the wet grass. He leapt off the grass and into a flowerbed that was lining one side of the lawn to avoid his footprints being left tellingly in the damp grass and hurtled upwards as fast as he could.

He ran to the side of the house, where the windows ended and had been replaced by old cut grey stone and mortar, and held his back to it. He looked up and could see it was a squat building connected to the house, like an old storage room, a little higher than a shed. With a quick look around, he turned, jumped and hoisted himself onto the roof, crouching low on top of it. He moved across the roof to the main body of the house, where there was a sash window leading to the first floor. It was too high to reach, but an old lead drainpipe ran up alongside it. Without pausing, he went arm over arm up the drainpipe, which creaked a little under his weight but did not give way until he was level with the window. He gave a quick glance inside and saw that the room was empty and, palm flat against the glass, pushed it gently upwards. To his relief, it wasn't locked, and why would it be - no one would be crazy enough to break into the country retreat of the head of the Stasi. He scrambled catlike inside, landing softly on the floor and standing stock still while he listened for any sounds or movements nearby.

He was in a dark guest bedroom that looked like it was not currently in use. Nikita didn't get the feeling that Schleicher was the hospitable type. He eased the window down behind him, and to avoid creaking any floorboards, he propelled himself onto the king-size bed and rolled across it to land softly on his feet on the other side next to the bedroom door. He teased the handle millimetre by millimetre, afraid of a squeak; these old houses were a nightmare for spies, but the handle did not cause problems. The door hinges were another matter, however. As he pulled the door open, it let out what felt like an almighty creak. He heard the sound of voices downstairs and then the tell-tale sound of footsteps climbing the stairs. Nikita quickly rolled under the bed and gave the duvet cover several tugs to remove any suggestion that it had been disturbed by an intruder and lay still. The bedroom was gloomy, but there were lights on in the hallway outside, and he could see a shadow approaching as someone came to investigate the cause of the creaking.

The door opened fully, this time not creaking, to which Nikita clenched his teeth in frustration, and the person walked into the room. From the way they moved and the thickness of the feet and legs, Nikita was immediately confident that it was the ferrety man, a man whom he was sure was a professional. Nikita held his breath and silently moved his hand down to his boot, where he kept a dagger, his fingers closing firmly around the handle.

However, after a few moments, the footsteps went back out of the room, and the shadow faded, while Nikita heard him similarly checking other rooms before then descending the stairs. He let out a long, slow breath and rolled out from under the bed, grateful that the ferrety man had left the door wide open. He moved softly along the landing, keeping to the edges to minimise the chance of any loose floorboards, but was not overly concerned - he had not heard the ferrety man hit any creaks, and the floor was covered with a plush, deep, cream carpet. The hallway had rooms along his right-hand side and bannisters to his left, which looked out on a now deserted entrance hall. One by one, he tried the other rooms, all of which were empty, although he soon found Schleicher's bedroom, a lavish room with an enormous bed, ornate furniture and a level of luxury that the head of the secret police worked hard to deny the people of East Germany. *It's the same from here all the way east to the Pacific*, Nikita thought to himself, *communist governments talking of equality for all while denying themselves nothing*. In Nikita's experience, the West was no better, just a different method of the rich getting richer and the poor getting poorer. Either way, the results were always the same.

He looked around the room, searching for anything that might be of interest. The room was immaculate in its tidiness. Schleicher clearly kept his bedroom like he kept the Stasi - in total order and control. There was a desk next to the window, which afforded a view out to the Werneuchan Airfield, and papers were neatly piled to one side of it. Nikita rifled through them quickly, searching for anything that may give further reason to suspect Schleicher of alternative motives. Nothing stood out as untoward, many of them personal household bills and notices, which made sense with this being his retreat and not his office.

Nikita was reordering the pile when one page caught his eye. It was a deed for another property, an absurdly cheap one, somewhere near Rostock, a port city on the north coast of East Germany. Nikita grabbed a pen and a scrap of paper and jotted down the details from the sheet, which named the property Meeresfarm, before placing it carefully back into the pile and leaving everything as he had found it. He then moved gently back out of the room and onto the landing, where he could hear voices from downstairs. He moved swiftly back towards the room he had first entered from and lay flat on the corridor carpet, unseen from downstairs but able to hear most of what was being said.

It had clearly been a short meeting with whoever had arrived in the car as they were returning to the front door.

'When will it be there?' he heard Schleicher's monotone voice say in clipped German.

'Tomorrow, unless there are any unforeseen delays,' replied an unfamiliar voice. Nikita lifted his head a fraction and saw that it was the ferrety man.

'Make sure that there are not,' retorted Schleicher, who then turned and disappeared from view. Nikita made a mental note of the conversation and then, not wanting to push his luck any further, made his way silently back to the guest bedroom and back down the way he had come. As his feet touched the ground, he heard a car engine start up. He peeked around the corner and saw Schleicher sitting in the back of a black government vehicle, the gravel crunching under the tyres as it wheeled away along the private road, cutting across the fields and back to the main road.

Nikita exhaled and debated his next move, leaning against the building with one shoulder and gazing after the car. Out of nowhere, however, he was struck from behind with a heavy snapping force, that dropped him straight to the ground.

CHAPTER 9

Nikita rolled quickly forward as he hit the ground and dodged a crushing blow which shuddered into the ground, missing him by a fraction.

He leapt back to his feet and saw that it was Schleicher's ferrety assassin who hurtled at him again, expertly stopping Nikita from gaining a footing, throwing a darting punch with one hand and sweeping his foot with the other. Nikita stumbled backwards, warding off the torrent of blows falling on him from the smaller man who moved like an acrobat, forcing him back into the wide driveway at the front of the sprawling house that looked much bigger from this side.

Nikita pulled the Walther pistol he kept at his back out, but he had barely withdrawn it from his belt when it was kicked from his grasp, clattering away from reach.

'Tut tut, that is cheating,' said the man in a surprisingly deep and gravelly voice and, to Nikita's surprise, a British accent. Nikita did not have time to dwell on that, however, as the raining blows continued to the point where he fell to one knee. Then, he took a powerful boot to the face, forcing him onto his back. The man stood over him, his long nose twitching with glee, and withdrew from his own waistbelt a long, thin, lethal-looking weapon akin to a rapier.

'It is just not sporting to spy on spies,' said the man, grinning widely and showing some missing teeth, lifting the rapier.

Nikita threw a handful of gravel as hard as he could into the man's face, which caused him to roar in pain and rub his face with his arm. Nikita took the second of distraction to pull the dagger from his boot and drive it into the back of the British man's ankle, severing his Achilles tendon and causing him to roar in pain once more, unable to stop himself from falling to the ground. Nikita leapt up and picked up the rapier that the man had dropped to the ground. He stood above him and held the long, thin blade to his throat, applying just enough pressure to draw a little blood.

'You fight dirty.' The man smiled, whose nose had stopped twitching and now was just dripping from the drizzling rain, which had started up again.

'You are not as impressive as I had imagined. I caught you so easily.'

'Yet here I stand above you,' Nikita said coldly.

'I know who you are,' said the man, with a calm look on his face, the look of one who has accepted his fate.

'Who are you? Why is a Brit working for Schleicher?' Nikita demanded, pushing harder on the rapier and causing the man to retch.

'You are a candle trying to stay ablaze in a gale, Black Russian,' he whispered enigmatically. 'There are forces at work that cannot be stopped.'

Nikita nicked the man's throat with the dirk, causing a trickle of blood to bead down his throat.

'Talk plain, man. What is Schleicher up to? Tell me everything, and I can keep you safe.'

'Safe?' The man coughed. 'Nowhere is safe,' he said. He then bit down his teeth hard, and there was a cracking sound. His mouth started to foam, and his body began to twitch. Spotting the cyanide symptoms from a hidden cyanide tooth common to spies, Nikita quickly turned the man over and tried to splash water from a puddle into the man's mouth to wash it out. The man choked and spluttered and then fell still. Nikita turned him back over and saw that he was dead, his eyes glassy and foam continuing to bubble from his lips, which were quickly turning blue.

Nikita looked around him, a final check to confirm that no one remained at the property, and pushed the needle-like dagger and his Walther into his belt. He made sure there was no evidence of what had happened remaining. He checked the man's pockets for any evidence of who he was - there was an ID card with a picture of the man, with the name Karl Von Nixdorf alongside it. After hearing his accent, Nikita highly doubted it was his real name, but he pocketed it nonetheless, along with the wallet, which contained some loose change. Then, he hoisted the man over his shoulder and carried him into the woods, where the sounds of the wind and drizzle quickly died away as his feet fell silently on the spruce needle-strewn ground. He walked deep into the woods, looking for somewhere to dispose of the body discreetly, with no shovel to bury him. Eventually, he found a small hollow beneath a fallen tree, which he rolled the body into and covered with branches. Without a backwards glance, he sighed and angled back up the hill, through the forest to the road. As he walked, he debated his next move. To head directly to Rostock or to return to Berlin? He opted for the latter; he needed more information.

When he finally arrived back at his apartment a couple of hours later, he saw that his Stasi friends were back in place in the car. Looking out of the corner of his eye, he saw the relief on their faces at his return, but again, he pretended not to see them. He had barely taken his coat off, however, when there was a knock on the door behind him. He opened it and saw before him an unshaven postman in full Deutsche Post regalia.

'Guten abend,' he said in a gruff voice. 'Du hast Post,' he added and thrust a letter into Nikita's hands before spinning on his heels and heading back off down the corridor.

Nikita held the letter suspiciously in a pincer-like grip, letting it dangle and touching it as little as possible. He knew enough of KGB methods to know not to trust random postal deliveries, especially when all mail in the building went into trays in the foyer.

He laid it on the table and inspected it from all angles, gently sniffing it without touching it and looking closely to see if it had been tampered with. He retrieved some cutlery from the kitchen drawer and, after wrapping a scarf around his face, prised it open with a knife and fork, sliding out the letter within. With no more evidence or suggestion of poisoning, he picked up the letter, albeit with gloved hands, and read through the note. It consisted of two pieces of paper - one was a printout, and the other an image. The printout was a border security form that gave details of Ghulum Ubaid, an Afghan national who had arrived in East Germany just over a week ago at the Polish border, and the Berlin address where he was staying. Stamped across it, in large red print, were the words 'Verdächtig'. *Suspect.*

Behind it was an A4 photograph showing the man in question, a handsome man in a sharp black suit with combed-back hair, pale brown skin, long eyelashes and a Shenandoah moustache-less beard. There was no other note or personalised information, aside from a large 'WK' scrawled in pencil on the back of the printout, and Nikita memorised the information before ripping the paper into scraps and putting it through the garbage disposal. He then grabbed his jacket, checked his Walther was loaded, and, after pausing for a moment, slid the assassin's dirk into his coat sleeve and headed out. This time, he definitely did not want to alert the Stasi to his movements at all and instead went out the back door of the apartment block to a small walled-off square where rubbish was piled up. He climbed on top of an old, broken chair and pulled himself up and over the brick wall and into the courtyard behind, which belonged to a different building. He ambled casually across the small garden and through the open doors to the adjacent block of apartments and out into the street beyond. A quick glance told him that the Stasi officers had not thought to cover this street as well, and he moved off.

It was beginning to get dark by the time he arrived at the address, with streetlights flickering on and shadows growing, and he spent some time scoping out the premises. It was a modern building with lots of glass and steel, a world away from the dingy place Rosin had put him up in, and the doors showed signs of much greater security, too. One thing that surprised Nikita was the absence of any obvious surveillance for a man marked as suspicious. Grateful for the gathering darkness, he kept to the shadows and eyed every vantage point, hidey-hole, car or window for any hint of Stasi or police operatives, nervous that it could well be a trap, but identified nothing. Something seemed strange.

After more than an hour of waiting for his opportunity, he saw someone leave through the front entrance, and as soon as their back was turned, he darted across the street, just catching the door with his fingertips before it closed. Sometimes, the easiest ways were the best.

Moving into the foyer of the building, there was an elevator and, next to it, a stairwell. On the wall, there were post boxes for each apartment with handwritten name cards stuck to each one. He was not surprised to find there was no Ghulum Ubaid listed anywhere, but on the top floor was a sticker for gastbewohner, or guest resident. He entered the elevator and punched in the button for the top floor, and caught sight of himself in the mirror. His young, handsome face was unblemished but haggard and exhausted looking, and his hair longer than he would usually allow.

'You need to get more sleep. To drink less and eat better,' he said to himself, and then, hearing his mother's voice in his words, saw his face fall and turned away. The memory of her murder still churned in his stomach like a canker, something he had not faced up to and did not want to face up to. His thoughts were interrupted by the door pinging open to a wallpapered corridor lit with soft lighting. He stepped into it and followed the numbers on the door until he reached the gastbewohner apartment. The door was closed, and he pressed his ear against it, listening for any sounds from within. There was no light shining under the door, and with no other real option, he rang the bell. He stood to one side of the door and slid his pistol out of his waistband, easing the trigger silently off. But still, there was no sound from inside and no indication that anyone was home. From within the folds of his coat, he withdrew some needles and set about picking the lock, which soon clicked softly. He gently pushed the door open, again standing to one side and peering around.

The apartment was dark and silent, but Nikita knew not to take that for granted. He softly closed the door behind him so that his shadow wouldn't enter the room before him and, with his gun held out in front of him, moved slowly inside. There was a small entrance hall, with the apartments' rooms all leading off from it. He could immediately see a kitchen to his left, a mass of glass and brushed aluminium, and he could see the edge of a bath in the room directly in front of him. The doors to the remaining two rooms were closed, one second on the left beyond the kitchen and the other on the right next to the front door. After nudging the door of the bathroom open and quickly confirming that it was empty, he opted for the door on the right, which opened onto a living room.

Large fish-bowl style windows wrapped around the corner room, which, when the venetian blinds were pulled, would give a view across the surrounding city. The room was fairly bare, with black leather furniture and only a single picture of flowers in a vase on the wall. There was a large dining table on one side of the room, which showed little signs of use, and only one chair was pulled slightly back.

Increasingly confident that nobody was home, Nikita retreated to the entrance hall and searched the bedroom. There were some clothes and rumpled bedsheets and a few personal items, but nothing noticeably untoward. That was until he opened the wardrobe and saw a large black holdall pushed towards the back of one of the cubby holes. He pulled it out, opened it, and saw some equipment that was definitely not something an ordinary citizen would have lying around. Inside were the beginnings of the making of a dirty bomb, with fuses, wires, ball bearings and nails, but nothing obvious to make it all explosive that he could see. Underneath it all were also two weapons that Nikita was all too familiar with: Avtomat Kalashnikovas, better known as AK47s.

'Well, I'm in the right place,' he muttered to himself. He tossed the bag back to the ground and began to feel nervous. Nothing here felt as it should be. What kind of a professional bomber kept this kind of gear in a bag or wardrobe?

He began conducting a search of the property for the Stasi bugs, which he assumed must be present for such an unlikely visitor to East Berlin but found nothing. In a city where everyone was bugged, it almost had to be a deliberate omission for someone to not be. He walked back into the living room and peered out from behind the blind, and all was still and quiet. He felt a prickling sensation on the back of his neck. Something felt very wrong. Where was the bomber at this time of day in East Berlin?

Time to get out of here, and fast, he thought to himself, striding back into the entrance hall.

And then the door exploded.

Nikita was thrown backwards by the impact of the detonation and crashed through the kitchen doorway, coming to a halt underneath the sink. He felt dizzy, but he tried to jump to his feet but fell unsteadily against the counter. Black-clad armed police, their faces hidden by armoured helmets, streamed into the apartment through a cloud of smoke, rifles out in front of them.

Nikita fumbled around blindly to grab a weapon of some kind from the kitchen worktop, but before his hand found anything, he was struck with almighty force by a truncheon to the leg, and he fell down. Still trying to clear his head and find some balance, he sprawled awkwardly on the floor. He felt a boot press down on his back and could hear shouting in German but could not make out what they were saying. He rolled sharply and snapped a punch at the kneecap of the leg above him. He felt a satisfying crunch and a cry as the body fell to the ground beside him. But then he felt the steel-capped boots of a dozen feet kicking and pounding him. The last thing he saw was an incoming truncheon. *That one's going to hurt,* he thought to himself. He was right.

CHAPTER 10

He regained consciousness as he was being carried out of the apartment but kept his eyes closed, allowing his eyelids to flutter just a fraction to see where he was. He must have only been unconscious for a minute or two. His head was splitting with pain, but at least he was no longer dizzy, and his mind began to race at high speed, evaluating all of his options. He could see enough to recognise that these weren't Volkspolizei. This was an armed Stasi unit.

They trudged down the stairs, and he found he was sliding on the stretcher they had put him on and were awkwardly trying to carry him at an angle. The stretcher was just canvas stretched between two poles, and as he slipped down it, he decided to allow himself to keep sliding, but at pace.

With a sudden burst, he tipped his weight down and slid along the stretcher and into the face of the

Stasi officer below him. He was no longer wearing a helmet and took both of Nikita's boots straight into the face. Nikita stamped down hard with one of them, which crushed the nose of the officer with a wet, crunching sound. He continued to slide off the stretcher, and as he landed on his feet, he spun and grabbed the stretcher. He jabbed it into the midriff of the policeman following behind, who bent over just in time for Nikita to hit him with an almighty uppercut underneath his nose. It sent the man sprawling backwards onto the stairs, temporarily blinded by the force of his nose being shoved upwards and with a face covered in blood.

Shouts came from further down the stairs, where another two Stasi soldiers were returning back up the stairs, and shots began to fire. Nikita grabbed the assault rifle of the blinded officer and easily took out one of the men. The second darted behind a pillar, and Nikita, without hesitation, ran directly towards where he was hiding, closing the gap in under a second. The soldier darted out to take a shot and was immediately hit by the force of Nikita, hurtling through the air and crunching him into the far wall, where he then thrust an elbow into his temple, rendering him immediately unconscious. There was nobody else on the stairwell, others having opted for the elevator on the way out. Nikita began walking cautiously down the steps but was stopped by the crack of a weapon firing, and he felt the blood before he felt the pain as a bullet sliced through his earlobe. He grunted and turned to see the first man he had taken out with a raised weapon, spluttering through a bloody face. The man loosed off another few shots from his service revolver, looking terrified and hitting nothing but the wall until there was a tell-tale click of an empty chamber.

Nikita closed in on him, and the man started shaking his head in terror. These weren't police or even soldiers; they were a poorly trained division of some Stasi military wing. In itself, that was odd - the Stasi's success was built on subtlety, and these guys were anything but subtle.

'Bitte, bitte!' he pleaded. Nikita turned his gun around to hold it by the barrel and knocked the man unconscious. 'It's more mercy than you deserve,' he grunted at the comatose officer as he tenderly touched his ear and felt a sharp jab of pain, and his hand came away sticky with blood.

This time, he walked back up the stairs, confident that a stream of Stasi officers would be appearing through the bottom of the stairwell at any moment. He entered the first-floor corridor and walked along it, trying every door handle along the way with no success. When he got to the end of the corridor, one of the apartment doors behind him opened, and a curious woman's head poked out. Upon seeing Nikita, her eyes widened in fear, and she darted back inside, but not before Nikita had got a foot in the door.

The woman cried out in terror and repeatedly crashed the door against Nikita's foot, but he shouldered his way in and closed the door behind them. As his face came into the light and she saw his blood and dust-smeared visage, she tried to scream, but Nikita clamped his hand over her mouth.

'I am not here to hurt you. Some bad men are trying to kill me, and I need to escape. Can I trust you not to scream?' Nikita asked, staring intensely into her wide blue eyes. She nodded slowly, and he eased his hand away.

She stood there trembling, and Nikita looked at her properly for the first time. She was perhaps in her early forties, with a softly lined but handsome face, white blonde hair tied back, and was standing awkwardly in flannel pyjamas. In the next room, he could hear the television blaring, and the smell of cooking was coming from the kitchen. Nikita leaned against the wall as the dizziness struck him again, and all the colours around him swirled momentarily. As he regained his focus, the woman's face swam back into his vision, now with something resembling concern mixed with her terror.

'I am sorry for my intrusion,' he said. 'I just need to climb out of one of your windows, and I will leave you in peace. Believe me, I am having a much worse day than you,' he added with an attempt at humour.

'I do not think you are able to climb out of a window,' she said pointedly, her brow furrowed. Something about her ability to collect herself quickly, for some reason, made her seem quite lovely to Nikita and made him aware of how awful he must look.

'It is not a question of ability. It is a question of necessity,' he said. 'If I stay here, I die.'

'What did you do,' she asked meekly.

'Too many things to mention. But to them? I think it is just the fact that I exist that is the problem.'

She bit her lip and nodded.

'Now, just the window, please,' he said pointedly, hearing noises getting closer in the hallway outside the apartment as the inevitable search began.

She nodded again and led him to her bedroom, where there were two large tilt windows that led out to a narrow balcony no wider than the width of a person. He peered out the window. It looked to be a twenty-foot drop. High enough to hurt. A lot.

He looked outside and saw that the apartment faced out onto the side of the building rather than the street or the backyard, which would work in his favour if only a little. He would probably be seen, but it was his only chance. Any moment now, Stasi would be streaming inside the apartment.

'Thank you for your help,' he said to the woman. 'Any moment now, the police will come looking for me - do not be afraid to tell them I was here.'

'This is East Berlin, sir. If I didn't report you, one of my neighbours would surely report me,' she said with a sigh. She handed him a towel and a bottle of water from beside her bed and handed it to him. 'Take this. You should clean your ear; it will get infected.'

Nikita nodded grimly, took the towel, and climbed out onto the balcony. He heard what he thought was a whispered 'Good luck' from behind him and smiled gently. Sometimes, people really could surprise him. He took a swig of the water, and it tasted heaven-sent to his dry, dust-choked throat. He poured the rest over his head, ignoring the incredible stinging it provoked in his ear, and softly rubbed his face with the towel, feeling better just for the absence of blood and grime.

Staying as flat to the wall as he could, Nikita looked in every direction and strained his ears for noise. To his left, he could see the flashing lights of police cars at the front of the building, and although he couldn't see anyone to the right, he could hear them. Beneath him was a narrow strip of grass next to a wall, and over the other side of the wall was a side street. The wall was just two bricks wide but sat only a few feet beneath the balcony. It was too far away to touch but close enough to try dropping onto; it was nonetheless a welcome discovery. He lowered himself over the edge, dangled by his arms and thrust himself outwards as best he could. He landed clumsily on top of the wall, and his right ankle folded under him, sending a stabbing pain up his leg. *Add it to the list of injuries*, he thought to himself.

He slid down on the other side of the wall and into the side street, putting his weight onto the uninjured ankle and staying in the shadows as much as he could, grateful that there were no streetlights on the side street he was on. He could, however, see police at either end of the street, although no one had seen him yet.

Across the street was a line of houses, and it was to them that he hobbled as quickly as he could, praying that none of the armed Stasi looked behind them as he limped across the road. He dropped down behind a car on the driveway of one of the houses and inspected his ankle. It was sprained or had a small break, but either way, it was still functional, although running anywhere was out of the question. The house behind him was semi-detached with a faux-wooden fascia, and lights glowed inside. Down one side of the house was a path that led to a gate and garden beyond. He moved down it and climbed painfully over the gate, remaining as quiet as he could. The backyard was small and well-kept, with a grassy lawn and flowerbeds lining each side. Light from the kitchen at the rear of the house was illuminating the yard, which forced Nikita to climb over into the adjacent garden, his breath rising in front of him as the temperature began to plummet. This garden proved darker and more silent, and he reached the end of it to look over. It backed onto another garden facing the opposite way, and he scrambled into it. Minutes later, he was on a street on the other side of it, jimmied the door of a car parked on the street, and soon left the police well behind him.

But much as he was desperate to clean himself up, rest his ankle and inspect all the other injuries to his body that he was certain he would soon begin to feel from the bomb blast, he did not dare to go back to his apartment. Everything about what had happened was wrong. How did an unwatched, non-bugged apartment provoke a sudden Stasi invasion just when the occupant was out but Nikita was there? He needed answers, a little rest and some clean clothes.

He pulled the car over next to a phone booth and, inside, found a phone book for East Berlin. He flicked through it until he found what he was looking for; Kielhorn, W, and an address in the city centre. Nikita memorised the address and got back into the car, which was another Trabant. He could barely remember seeing a car in the city that wasn't one of the two-stroke vehicles and headed straight to the address.

The building he arrived at was clearly once a lavish and now crumbling affair - much like many of the buildings in East Berlin, but through the rotating glass door, he could see that inside, it had managed to retain some of its faded glory. He was pleased to find a fire escape at the rear of a building a few doors down and, by crossing the rooftops, was able to break into Kielhorn's apartment with no great difficulty. When he got inside, he found an apartment like something out of a colonial era, with wood-panelled walls, deep rugs and ornate armchairs. The polizeidirektor clearly did himself well, which was no mean feat in a communist police state. The lights were all off, and Nikita moved slowly and carefully from room to room, making sure that Kielhorn wasn't home. He was just conducting a scan of the study when a framed photo on a bookcase caught his eye. In it, Kielhorn was standing in full Russian attire, with a long grey coat, high black boots and a furry ushanka hat. But that was the least of Nikita's problems with the image because stood alongside him, in Moscow's Red Square, with the colourful turrets of the Kremlin in the background, were none other than Ernst Schleicher and Maxim Denisov.

Nikita gazed at the picture with a cold fury upon his face, trying to unpick what this meant. There were forces moving here that did not make any sense.

He took the opportunity to use Kielhorn's shower, commandeered a pair of jeans and a black jumper from his closet, and settled in comfortably with a large glass of what he hoped was the most expensive whisky Kielhorn owned. He sat back at the desk with his aching ankle up, a bag of frozen peas on top of it, and a gauze roughly taped to his ear. He knew what he needed more than anything was some sleep, but sleep would have to wait. His life may now depend on it.

Sometime later, he heard the rattle of a key in the lock, and Kielhorn entered, turning lights on as he went. He almost walked straight past the study and then crashed into the doorframe as he saw the shadowy figure sitting at his desk. When he spotted the gun aimed at him, he froze before slowly raising his arms up in surrender.

'Guten abend Walter,' Nikita said softly.

'What... how... what are you doing here?' Kielhorn replied in shock.

'You mean, how am I still alive after you sent your friends to kill me?' Nikita said in a voice laced with venom.

A look of total confusion crossed Kielhorn's face. 'What are you talking about?'

'You play your part exceptionally well,' Nikita responded. 'I actually believed I could trust you.'

Kielhorn placed a finger to his lips, throwing his eyes towards the walls.

'That is a convenient line for you to take, isn't it, Polizeidirektor. But I think we both know that even the Stasi do not bug the homes of people in your position.'

Kielhorn shook his head furiously but stopped when Nikita clicked the safety off on his pistol.

'Enough now, Walter. I have barely eaten or slept for days and am in all sorts of pain. Thanks to you, I'm likely to now have to live with part of my ear missing. I came here for sanctuary, and then I found this,' he said and tossed the Red Square picture onto the floor at Kielhorn's feet. Kielhorn bent to pick it up and glanced at it, his face paling slightly.

'Strange to see a man who claims to have never left the country standing in Moscow.'

Kielhorn took off his spectacles and polished them on his shirt, his shoulders slumping slightly.

'It is not what you think.'

'I find that unlikely,' Nikita retorted.

'That picture... was taken long ago,' he said.

'No, it wasn't. Denisov has only been head of the KGB for two years.'

Kielhorn was beginning to sweat. 'He is not the head of the KGB in that picture. It was before then. Much has changed since.' Again, Kielhorn mouthed to Nikita that the Stasi were listening, but Nikita dismissed it. He doubted they were, but he also didn't particularly care anymore.

'Why did you send me into an ambush at the Afghan's apartment?' Nikita asked out loud, changing the subject and interrupting Kielhorn's silent remonstrations.

Kielhorn's shoulders slumped now as if accepting his fate.

'I did not. It was, I thought, good intel.'

'You are the only person who knew I was going to be there. But an entire armed Stasi unit seems a little excessive.'

'The fact that you are still standing suggests that whoever sent those men did not send enough. Believe me, I had nothing to do with it.'

'Let me ask you this: if you were in my position, would you trust anything you say?' Nikita asked.

'I would think that in your position, you do not trust anything *anybody* says,' Kielhorn retorted, dropping into one of his ornate armchairs. He looked at the whisky that Nikita was working his way through. 'That was gifted to me by Denisov,' he said. 'He promised to take me with him to the top, yet here I am years later as a mere polizeidirektor and with Denisov's finest weapon pointing a gun at me. The thing you should always remember with Denisov is that you are either vital to him or absolutely expendable. There is no middle ground.' He picked up the Red Square picture up off the ground and gazed at it bitterly.

Nikita was not interested in whatever story Kielhorn might spin. 'If you did not tip off the Stasi, how did they know I would be there?'

'I told you, every wall has ears in East Berlin. It could have been anyone; perhaps you were followed, or perhaps you were not the intended target. I find it unlikely that the Stasi would target a KGB agent. The repercussions could be enormous. Did you follow any more of my suggestions?' he asked tentatively.

Nikita nodded, increasingly feeling caught in indecision. He couldn't deny that he liked the man in front of him, but he had learned long ago that liking someone did not mean you would not still have to kill them. He thought momentarily of Elysia again but quickly pushed her from his mind.

'And what became of them?' Kielhorn asked, eyes wide in curiosity, leaning forward in his chair.

'That perhaps your suspicions were not baseless. Or that you seek to lure me into an elaborate trap.'

'Are you going to kill me?' Kielhorn asked as Nikita hefted his foot off the table and tested it on the floor. It was sore, but with a night's sleep, it should be useable.

'Fortunately for you, I still have need of you,' Nikita said. At Kielhorn's quizzical look, Nikita added, 'I need to rest here tonight. And some hot food would go a long way also.'

Kielhorn bit back a reply and nodded while getting to his feet and gesturing for Nikita to follow. He led Nikita into a spare room where there was a bed already made up. 'You can sleep here tonight,' he said before leading him into the kitchen.

Dinner was classic German fare of sauerkraut served up with fried cutlets of what looked like veal. Not Nikita's favourite, but it was still a heartier meal than he had enjoyed for days. The pair ate in silence. Both had their minds on other things.

When they retired for bed, Nikita was struggling to keep his eyes open but stopped Kielhorn before he turned towards his own room.

'Do not think of leaving or attacking me tonight. Neither would end well for you.'

'Comrade, our paths are now so inextricably linked that there would be no merit in me doing so.'

Nikita eyed the man once more, finding him impossible to read. Nikita's job was to be likeable, to appear trustworthy, to gain confidence, but never to return the favour and never to fully trust anyone. He thought fleetingly of Elysia once more, of the rules he had broken for her and for how she had now broken something within him.

He woke early the next morning, having slept deeper than he imagined he could, and was greeted by the feeling of everything hurting. His head was splitting in two, and as he rolled over, he found that he had brought the bottle of whisky to bed with him, which he did not recall having done. It was empty.

Getting dressed, he saw that dark bruises had sprouted across much of his body from the bomb blast, and the stinging in his ear had not lessened. More welcome, however, was the smell of fresh coffee wafting from the direction of the kitchen.

'I had thought KGB agents would be up rather earlier than this,' Kielhorn said cheerfully to Nikita as he entered. He was standing at the stove, wearing a heavy brown dressing gown, with a cigarette hanging out of the corner of his mouth, frying eggs.

Nikita said nothing but moved to sit at the bar next to the kitchen and poured himself a cup of coffee.

'I'd tell you to make yourself at home, but I don't need to be here for that, do I?' Kielhorn said with a chuckle.

'You're in good humour this morning,' Nikita croaked, scalding his throat on the thick black coffee.

'It is the feeling that comes with suspecting it is one's last morning alive,' Kielhorn said, his smile dropping for a fraction of a second before forcing it back into place. 'I might at least smell the roses a little.'

'I told you - I am not going to kill you,' Nikita said.

Kielhorn sighed. 'I know you will not,' he said, smiling sadly at Nikita. Then he clapped his hands. 'How many eggs do you want? I like mine with a kiss, as they say, but I'm afraid you aren't my type,' he said, chuckling. Then his eyes widened. 'I mean, I prefer women!' he said frantically. 'Not... you know...' His face went a deep red.

'Because I'm Black?' Nikita again finished for him, putting the man out of his misery and watching him deflate slightly. 'It's okay, short, ageing white men aren't my type either,' he added with a crooked smirk.

While Kielhorn continued preparing breakfast, Nikita fetched some paper and a pen from the study and returned to the breakfast bar, where he sketched images of the two men he had seen with Schleicher the day before, both the strangled man and his British murderer. He pushed them in front of the policeman.

'Do you recognise either of these people?' he asked as Kielhorn slid a plateful of greasy eggs and a loaf of stale dark brown bread in front of him.

'You are a terrible artist,' Kielhorn replied, looking at the two images. 'I have seen little children produce better drawings.'

'I was busy learning to survive racist Russians when other children were learning to draw,' Nikita said curtly, which wiped the smile from Kielhorn's face.

'Let's see,' he said, removing his glasses and holding the first sketch up and squinting. It was the picture of the man who had been strangled or a rough likeness. He shook his head and put down the paper. 'This one is not familiar.' Then, he picked up the second drawing.

'Now this one, this one I recognise,' he said, his eyes wide and looking from the drawing of the ferrety British man and then to Nikita. 'Even from your dreadful scrawling, I can see that I know this one,' he said, still picking his words carefully.

'Who is it?' Nikita asked eagerly, leaning forward.

Kielhorn licked his lips nervously and looked around him again. He shrugged, but on the paper, he started writing.

Gregory Muller - Schleicher's assassin and a British spy.

'You know that?' Nikita spoke jarringly out loud.

Kielhorn put a finger to his lips, causing Nikita to roll his eyes again. Kielhorn again wrote on the paper.

MI6 trying to turn Schleicher. Gave him Muller to do his bidding.

Nikita pointed again at the other drawing and wrote. *This man fell foul of Schleicher's bidding.*

At this, Kielhorn looked sad, and he wrote simply: *Many have.*

With a sigh, Kielhorn stood, tore up the pages into fine shreds, and threw them in the bin.

'Eat your breakfast. You must eat when you can,' he said, which caused Nikita to freeze mid-mouthful. Those words, the words of his training. A slip of the tongue, a coincidence or something far more sinister? The fog surrounding Kielhorn was growing ever murkier.

Nonetheless, Nikita took his advice, eating as much as he could stomach and washing it down with more of the strong coffee. He began to feel more human than he had in days, as long as he didn't try to move too much, but he'd endured far worse than bruises and a torn earlobe.

Kielhorn reappeared in his uniform as Nikita was getting ready to go.

'What will you do now?'

'Follow the trail wherever it leads,' Nikita replied.

'You would make an excellent police detective,' chuckled Kielhorn.

'There would be far less blood on my hands,' Nikita muttered and abruptly found himself craving a drink of something much stronger than coffee. He noticed that his hands had a slight tremor in them, and it made him want a drink all the more.

'See what you can find out on the first drawing I showed you,' Nikita said, pulling on his coat. Then he paused and looked at the policeman. 'It would be unwise of you to tell people of my visit here,' he added.

'You still think they do not already know?' the policeman replied with the same unsettlingly forlorn smile on his face.

CHAPTER 11

Nikita stood once more looking upon the Afghan's apartment. There was little sign of the military raid that had taken place the night before, with a full clean-up operation clearly having taken place. The Stasi were good at covering their steps.

But this time, Nikita did not have to wait long to find what he was looking for. Out of the doors, wrapped in a thick jacket, came Ghulum Ubaid, the Afghan who had been conspicuously absent at the time of Nikita's visit and the Stasi's raid the night before.

He looked noticeably less handsome than in the photo Nikita had previously seen of him. His eyes were bloodshot and dark, baggy circles hung beneath them. His hair was unkempt, and his beard untrimmed. He looked as bad as Nikita felt.

The Afghan pulled his coat tight around him and walked quickly down the street, and Nikita followed on from a distance, slinking along the opposite side of the road. Ubaid had a backpack slung over his back, and the way he allowed it to bounce around left Nikita with no doubt that it did not contain any explosives. He walked towards the city, which made it easier for Nikita to follow as the roads grew more congested and the walkways became increasingly crowded. It was a bright, sunny day with the fallen leaves crunchy underfoot and East Berlin looking transformed. The crumbling buildings that had looked so drab in the November drizzle looked majestic in places, and even the mood of those he walked among seemed lifted, albeit with the usual umbrella of fear ever present above them all.

Ubaid didn't seem to be in any particular hurry other than clearly wanting to get out of the cold. After spending almost two years in the brutal heat of Afghanistan himself, Nikita could understand why Ubaid would struggle to adapt to an East German November. Nikita wasn't sure where he expected to be led, perhaps an underground lab or a pharmacy, but he certainly hadn't expected a library. The Afghan man climbed the steps into the East Berlin State Library, a wide, squat concrete building that had partially been given a modernist makeover with some wooden cladding.

Nikita hung back for as long as he could afford to before casually following on. The building was broad and well-lit inside, and the hush that descended on libraries the world over was immediately present here. Nikita's eyes searched the large entrance hall for some trace of his quarry, and at first, thought he had now lost him, but then he picked him out, walking along a first-floor landing above. It was still early, and the library was still quite empty, so Nikita waited as long as he could afford to.

He followed on, climbing the stairs and making his way onto the landing. It was a broad balcony running along one side of the entrance hall, looking down on those below. He followed the passageway and realised he had lost Ubaid but did not panic and soon recovered him. The Afghan was taking a seat at a table and placing down a small pile of books that he had collected from the shelves.

Nikita swerved down a tall aisle of books and, confident that Ubaid was going nowhere for a while, distracted himself by perusing the volumes rising up either side of him. He expected to find himself in the science section of the library, or at a stretch, perhaps the history or religion section, but instead found himself more confused than ever. All of the books surrounding him were connected to the arts. Books on music, volumes on art and voluminous texts diving into theatre and cinema surrounded him, and it didn't make any sense. He tried to peer between the shelves to get sight of what Ubaid was reading, but his view was blocked by the man's back, who was poring over the books and entranced by their content.

With little else to do without making himself look conspicuous, Nikita browsed until he found some books that roused his interest and found himself a booth that afforded him a view of Ubaid from behind and sat down to look through them.

Nikita had never been much of a reader. Books were one of the many luxuries he had had to go without during his childhood in a shack on the edge of Kamenka in Southwest Russia. From then, he had been in the KGB with little things like surviving often taking up his time when others might enjoy sitting down with a good book. He had only been taught to read fluently once entering the KGB as part of his training and had proven an able student, quickly catching up with his peers, but those texts had been training manuals, communist government documents, strictly necessary learning materials and, at best, patriotic Soviet stories, none of which had excited him much. Now, he sat and opened a book about the rise in contemporary music in the sixties and quickly found himself entranced. So entranced, in fact, that he had to keep reminding himself to look up and check that the man he was following was still there. He was grateful that Ubaid seemed to be as absorbed by the books as he was. Nikita found that he wasn't reciting what he was reading but was really *learning* it. For a brief moment, he had a glimpse of what life must be like for normal twenty-three-year-olds, young people who could study and pursue interests. With a jolt, he realised he had never had an interest or hobby in his life. Everything he had done was for his family or for his country. Nothing had ever been for him. He didn't feel sad about it but noticed it curiously. After learning about bands that he had heard little about in his life so far, the Beatles, Rolling Stones, Bob Dylan and other artists who, the book suggested, had changed music forever. The only music Nikita had ever listened to in Russia was Soviet marching music and occasionally some classical music. During his time in the United States, he had been too busy staying in character to absorb any of the music. He remembered the music in the bar for the first time, only two nights ago, the Sam Cooke song that had triggered such feelings in him. Music and feelings, this was not the territory he had been trained to veer into. Finishing the book, he ambled around the library to see if there were any other books that caught his eye.

He found himself in the history section and, before he knew it, was nose-deep in a book on colonial history, which was a jarring change of pace from the birth of modern Western music. He was surprised so many of these books had survived the years of the oppressive communist government, but then, in a city that was almost impossible to leave, what were they going to do with the information? He found his way back to his booth, checking once more on Ubaid, and began to learn, to his horror, about the history of colonialism in Africa. The British, French, Portuguese, Spanish and Dutch had gone about pillaging West Africa, pillaging countries like Nigeria, the land of his parents, for slaves to ship across the Atlantic. Millions dying on the journey, living in horrendous conditions and enduring a life of appalling brutality while being made to work sugar and cotton crops. Nikita began to feel quite sick and again felt himself craving a drink. He pondered briefly about whether he could run to a shop, but his training prevented him from such amateur behaviour. He wondered if his father and sister, now living in Cuba, had learned anything of such horrors that had befallen their ancestors.

He put the book down, thirsty now to learn more of this history that had been so hidden from him for so long. He doubted he would find anything talking of any of the actions of the Soviet Union or Germany through history but was curious to see what else he could learn. His hopes were short-lived as he saw Ubaid rising from his table and walking slowly towards the exit. Nikita hurried over to the table the Afghan had been sitting at and looked at the books he'd left piled on the table. They were all on jazz music, which again hurt Nikita's head as he tried to understand the connection. He leafed through the books, looking for any hidden messages, but there was nothing there. He pocketed one of the books, looking guiltily around but veering through the history section and pocketing another as he angled back towards the exit to follow in Ubaid's footsteps.

Ubaid left the library and appeared to have a slight spring in his steps as he made his way into the city centre. Nikita noticed that all of the food shops seemed to have long queues of people outside them, hopping from foot to foot to stay warm and looking jealously at those who reappeared from the front of the line with a loaf of bread or a joint of meat. Ubaid walked past the lines to a despondent-looking café that had a sign saying that they had no food but to come inside for hot coffee.

Ubaid entered and ordered a drink, and Nikita leaned against a wall across the street, watching him from a distance. The man he was following was getting more and more curious. He did not behave like the bomber Nikita knew him to be. He had been into his apartment and had seen the equipment in his closet. Eventually, Ubaid made his way back to the library and picked up where he had left off -reading about jazz music.

It was a couple of hours later that he put down the books, and this time, Nikita felt like he might be getting somewhere. Ubaid walked away from the city centre this time and into a very run-down street that was thoroughly depressing. Concrete building after concrete building loomed over the narrow street, cutting out any sunlight. Rubbish littered the streets, and washing hung from greying balconies. It reminded Nikita strongly of some of the khrushchevkas, or concrete slums, developed by former Soviet General Secretary Nikita Khrushchev in the sixties that had spread across the Soviet Union like wildfire.

Ubaid kept looking down at his hands, clearly looking for a specific address, and when he found it, he approached cautiously. Nikita hid behind a rotting mattress which leaned against a graffiti-covered wall. Ubaid went down some steps that took him to what Nikita assumed was a basement apartment and cursed his luck that there was no way of following. His curses were short-lived, however, as little more than a minute later, the Afghan reappeared, looking nervous but excited and carrying a large bundle. He paused and tried to cram it into his backpack but quickly realised it wouldn't fit, so instead shoved it inside his coat. The result was a bulge that made him look somewhere between a pregnant woman and a man with a severe thyroid problem. Nikita shook his head in disbelief. The man was evidently not a professional, and it beggared belief why Kulu Alqasas, an organisation that had seemed so well organised in the Tora Bora caves, had selected someone so clumsy for such a major mission.

He continued to follow Ubaid as he returned to his apartment, whistling tunelessly as he went. Nikita decided he needed answers, regardless of the risks.

When Ubaid entered the apartment building, Nikita caught the door just as he had the night before and made his way up the stairwell, which had been scrupulously scrubbed clean of any sign of the fierce battle he had fought there only hours ago. The only suggestion that anything was different was the sour smell of fresh paint still lingering in the closed space.

He climbed the stairs, trying not to think about the men he had taken out the previous evening, hoping that the man who had pleaded with him had not been irreversibly hurt. These were not thoughts Nikita usually endured; they had been trained out of him, and he longed for the detachment he usually felt.

When he reached Ubaid's apartment, he could see that the Stasi had clearly had a harder time covering up the results of their bomb blast the night before here than in the stairwell. Fresh paint was visible everywhere, and the hallway carpet outside his door no longer matched that of the rest of the hallway. Nikita pressed his ear to the door and heard Ubaid's whistling continuing. He knocked, and the whistling instantly stopped. Keeping his ear to the door, he heard frantic movements and a rustling sound.

'Who is it?' shouted a heavily accented voice trembling with nerves from behind the door.

'Du hast Post,' Nikita replied calmly, trying to mirror the same 'postman' who had visited him at his apartment the day before. Ubaid, though, was not convinced.

'Nein! Nein post bitte,' he called in faltering German. Nikita pressed his eye to the spy hole and blurrily saw a warped version of Ubaid flailing around with a gun. He groaned inwardly. 'Just once, I wish things went the easy way,' he muttered to himself and kicked the door in.

But it wasn't just the door that fell inwards. It was the entire doorframe. The new door and doorframe had clearly not fully dried into place and had been screwed into broken and mangled wood and plaster. The entire thing had collapsed, leaving a gaping hole in the apartment.

Ubaid's will was already failing, and the gun hung limply at his side as he looked in shock at the young Black man appearing out of a cloud of plaster dust like an apparition into his apartment. Nikita walked up to him and took the gun out of his hands.

'Sorry about the door,' he said. He took Ubaid by the arm and led him into the living room, pushing him into a chair and drawing the curtains.

The man was trembling and looked on the verge of tears.

'Tell me everything, bomber,' Nikita said coldly, switching to English.

'W... what?' said Ubaid, his eyes wide and now laced with confusion.

'I do not have time for you to pretend to be stupid,' Nikita said. 'Coming back here is already a folly I can ill afford.'

'You were here before?' Ubaid said, looking drunk with confusion.

Nikita walked to him and struck him across the face with the back of his hand, causing the man to cry out.

'I do not want to do this the difficult way, Mr Ubaid, but I will if I have to. Tell me now, when and where are you planning to set off the bomb?'

'Bomb? What bomb?' Ubaid asked, and then held up his hands as Nikita raised his hand again. 'Please, sir, please no! I do not know anything about a bomb!'

'Do not play the fool!' roared Nikita. 'I know where your equipment is!' He marched to the bedroom and tore open the wardrobe to where he had found the equipment, but the closet was bare other than for a few shirts hanging up.

'Where is it? Where is all the equipment that was stored here last night? The equipment for your bomb?' Nikita said sharply, storming back into the living room.

'I do not know what you are talking about!' replied the terrified Ubaid.

Nikita looked at him and began to feel doubt creeping in. 'Where were you last night when the apartment was attacked?' Nikita asked him.

At this, Ubaid showed something resembling guilt and swallowed nervously. He looked down at the floor. 'I don't know what you mean,' he said, fidgeting in his chair.

Nikita pulled the dirk from his sleeve and approached Ubaid slowly. That menacing act alone was enough to make the man break.

'Okay, okay! They came and told me to stay away from the apartment. If I did not do as they said, they would deport me.'

'Who's they?' Nikita asked, raising an eyebrow.

'These terrifying white men! The secret police here. They did not give me a choice! They never do. But I swear to almighty God, I do not know anything about a bomb.'

Nikita was not, however, yet ready to be deterred.

'Today, you visited an apartment and came out with a package you clearly are not allowed to possess. I know you have it here. Show it to me.'

Ubaid pointed reluctantly to the kitchen table where the package, wrapped in brown paper, rested. Nikita tore it open and found it to be two records, one of Miles Davis and one of John Coltrane. Even Nikita knew enough to know they were famous jazz musicians. He pulled the vinyl discs out of the cardboard sleeves, inspecting it all for any hidden items or messages, but found none. He looked quizzically at Ubaid, his eyebrows raised in a question.

'I love the jazz music.' Ubaid shrugged, looking thoroughly miserable. 'We do not have this in Afghanistan.'

'Help me to understand this,' Nikita said in exasperation. 'You travel all the way from Afghanistan to Europe for jazz music, only to go to a country where jazz music is close to illegal, to then buy old records on the black market? You see why I'm struggling to believe you.'

'It was the best I could hope for, and it got me away from Afghanistan!' he exclaimed.

'You've swapped one hell for another, my friend,' Nikita said bitterly. 'Now tell me your story. If you do not, I will kill you where you sit. You have my word.' To demonstrate the point, Nikita took out a dagger and began grating it against the dirk.

Ubaid looked totally defeated, and his nose was running. 'It all began when the Russians came to my village in Afghanistan, just north of Kabul. They killed almost everyone there. I had no family, but they killed my friends and my neighbours. I did what I had to do to survive. I cooperated with them,' he said, a look of self-loathing upon his face. 'The place I lived, it had been beautiful, but they destroyed it all. The only thing I had was my life, which I now almost wish they had taken from me too.'

'How did you cooperate?' Nikita asked impatiently.

'I did some translation for them. I had worked as a language tutor at the university before they came and could speak Russian and English. They made me go to parlay with villages trying to defend themselves, and I was truly hated. But it kept me alive, and I began to earn their trust. I asked many times to be allowed to leave for Europe. They promised me much, and when they began to withdraw from my country this year, they took me with them, moving me to Ashgabat in Turkmenistan, using me as Soviet PR to show there were "no bad feelings" with the Afghan people. Finally, after my requests to be allowed to come to Europe, they told me that I could go to Berlin and that they would pay me for the pleasure. It seemed too good to be true; they just needed me to be in East Berlin. I do not really understand why. But even Berlin has felt like a freedom to me! I can never return to Afghanistan; I would be lynched. They said that all I would have to do is occasionally follow some instructions to go somewhere at a certain time, meet with some people or carry packages. The rest of the time would be my own.'

'And how's that going for you?' Nikita asked with a raised eyebrow.

'Are you serious? It is the most freedom I have had since their tanks rolled into Afghanistan in 1979.

I travelled here overland from Turkmenistan, and compared to some of the places I travelled through on the way, East Berlin feels luxurious. I just wish it was a little warmer, and also, you know, these other things they make me do. And my friends. I would like to have friends again.'

'Do not feel bad for surviving. Sometimes that is all we have,' Nikita said, switching to Russian and softening slightly. 'But do not look for friends in East Berlin. Trust and integrity have forsaken it,' he added, the hardness returning to his voice as his mind once again drifted to Elysia. He slumped into a chair opposite Ubaid and returned his knives to their sheathes.

'And do not think I trust you, Ghulum Ubaid, but I believe there is some truth somewhere in your words. You are a traitor and a survivor, and while I admire your will to survive, I think you would say whatever it is you think would keep you alive. There is more you have yet to tell me - what are the things they have made you do.'

'Not very much. I had to leave the apartment last night and stay away until they let me know to return. '

'And what else,' Nikita asked flatly.

Again, Ubaid shifted uncomfortably in his seat, licking his lips nervously.

'Do not make me unsheathe my knives again,' Nikita added threateningly. 'Who have you met with?'

'I was asked to carry a message to a very important man—'

'What man?' Nikita pressed.

Ubaid looked scared to his core. 'He will kill me if I tell you.'

'And I will kill you if you don't. You're a survivor, so I think you know which gives you a longer life expectancy.'

Ubaid looked imploringly up at Nikita through big brown eyes. 'Schleicher,' he said. 'Ernst Schleicher.'

'And what was the message?' Nikita asked sharply.

'It did not make any sense to me,' protested Ubaid. 'Just something about Rostock.'

Nikita's eyes bored into Ubaid, his mind working furiously and thinking of the address he had found at Schleicher's country retreat. At that moment, Nikita heard sirens in the distance. He wasn't sure, but he thought they were getting closer. He stood and began to walk towards the door. Before he left, he turned to look at the cowering Ubaid.

'Good luck,' he said simply and then left through the hole that had once been the front door. Pausing, he pulled up the frame and left it propped back in the hole, at least giving the Afghan some small sense of privacy to enjoy his jazz music.

He returned to the stairwell and began to descend, but as he reached the first floor, the entrance to the stairwell from the entrance foyer opened. Nikita's hand darted to the gun in the belt at his back, but he did not withdraw it when he saw that it was the blonde woman whose apartment he had passed through when escaping the previous night. When she looked up and saw him, she froze, her blue eyes wide. But not wide in fear, Nikita judged, but rather in surprise.

'Guten morgen, fräulein,' Nikita said, smiling gently at her, pausing where he was on the stairs.

'Guten morgen,' she replied, returning his smile. There was an awkward pause where neither knew what to say, but it was interrupted by the sound of a loud police siren outside the building.

'This is to do with you again, jah?' she asked reproachfully.

Nikita snorted slightly. 'Jah.' He nodded.

'Then you had better come with me again. At least you know how to escape from there,' she said quite matter-of-factly.

Now, it was Nikita's turn to look surprised, but he was confident he could overpower her if it was a ploy, and if not, he did know it to be a successful route of escape. He nodded and allowed her to pass him on the stairs as she walked to the first floor and her apartment.

This time, Nikita took in more of the apartment instead of looking to just pass straight through it. It was tidy, ordered and homely, with paintings on the wall and the smell of some kind of stew simmering on the stove in the kitchen. She closed the door behind him and invited him in, looking nervous, and Nikita moved with great caution. Random acts of kindness were rarely random or particularly kind in his experience.

Nikita walked around the apartment, looking out of all of the windows to see what the activity was outside. There appeared to be only a lone police car out the front and no sign of the kind of military operation he had been faced with the night before.

'What will you do?' the woman asked tentatively from behind him as he peered out of the living room window.

'If it is ok, I will wait here for a little while until they have gone,' Nikita replied.

She nodded. 'Would you like some tea?' she asked sweetly, taking off her coat. She was wearing a flannel shirt with a chequered skirt and thick, woolly tights.

'Do you have anything a little stronger?' he asked, rolling his shoulders.

She looked surprised, glancing up at the clock on the wall, which showed it to be only 11 a.m., but then shrugged. 'Why not?' she added with an impish grin.

She brought in a bottle of schnapps and two glasses and encouraged Nikita to take a seat on the flowery sofa as she perched on the other end. She poured two glasses and offered him one.

He took a drink of the peach-flavoured spirit. Not his favourite, but it was the staple of East Germany, and would get him there. She also offered him a cigarette, the same brand that Rosin had chain-smoked so furiously, but Nikita declined. She lit one herself, and Nikita noticed that he found it much less objectionable when it was her than the KGB station chief.

'What is your name?' he asked her.

'Heidi Liebers,' she said, 'and you?'

'Niki,' he said, giving no surname.

'Why are you helping me?' Nikita asked, sipping at the schnapps.

'I have lived long enough to know that the Stasi rarely chase the bad guys,' she said, looking at the floor. She looked up and held his gaze.

'You speak as if you do not fear them, as everyone else does,' Nikita said.

'There is little more they could take from me,' she said sadly, swallowing her schnapps whole. 'But you, you are not German, no?'

'No, I'm from a long way from here. For your sake, it is better that I do not tell you any more than that,' he added gently and refilled both of their glasses. 'What did you tell them about my visit the other night?' he asked curiously.

'Nothing at all,' she said, holding her chin high. 'I will tell those pigs nothing at all. Their time grows short.'

'What do you mean?' Nikita asked sharply.

Heidi stood and turned on the wood-panelled television set opposite the sofa. The news was showing the headline for November 7th, which announced the resignation of the East German prime minister and much of the Politburo. The news reader also reported that a new travel and emigration policy was due to be unveiled shortly.

'We are on the cusp of great change, Niki,' Heidi said, her face glowing with hope in the light of the TV, which was now showing protests and marches in Soviet satellite states across Eastern Europe. 'You are in Berlin at a historic moment.' She paused, then added, 'Or maybe it is a historic moment because you are in Berlin.'

'You have a good imagination,' Nikita said, chuckling. 'But in my experience, communism is a very reluctant overlord of change, so do not allow hope to overcome reality.'

'For one so young, you are not a very cheerful man,' she said playfully. 'At your age, I had no cynicism, only belief. You should allow yourself some hope.'

'Maybe some more schnapps will help with that,' he said gaily, topping their glasses up once more, even though she had barely started her second glass. He studied Heidi as he drank. She was at least fifteen years older than him, with gentle creases at the corner of her sad eyes and her mouth framed by lines that were beginning to deepen, but despite that, there was a certain proud beauty about her, not in the classical sense, but in the way she held herself. He could see on the finger of her left hand a thin white line where a ring had once been. They both relaxed as they sipped their schnapps, and he felt looser than he had done in someone else's company for a long time.

The more he drank, the more he found himself looking at her lips and wanting to kiss her, and the more they spoke the more he was sure she was thinking something similar. He thought of Elysia and felt guilty, but obstinate and reckless. He loved her, he couldn't deny it, but he no longer knew what that meant.

Emboldened by the alcohol, Nikita lifted Heidi's left hand, running his thumb around the place where a ring had once been.

'What happened?' he asked.

'As with so many others in this place, the Stasi happened,' she replied sadly. 'Joachim was a good man, a great man, but he flew too close to the sun. He was an artist, and East Germany does not like artists. He spoke just a little too loudly through his paintings. At first, they just tried to get in our heads, breaking into our house and moving things around or taking food from our refrigerator to make us think we were going crazy.'

'Zersetzung,' said Nikita, nodding. 'The Stasi's ritualistic and consistent destruction of people's self-confidence and sanity. They're the masters of it.

'It did not work on us. We soon realised what was happening. Then they moved to the next level of posting dead animals through our letterbox, slashing the tyres of our car and things like that. But still, Joachim would not stop his work, even though, by this point, I pleaded with him to. The fear and anxiety it provoked in me were quite terrible. Joachim just kept saying that our last sanctuary was our minds, and we could not let them invade that, too. But they are so good at it, Niki, so very good at it,' she said, almost shaking his arm. 'Then, one morning, he left for work and never returned. I found a suicide note, in his handwriting but it did not use his words, so it is clear they made him write it. They took our home from me, destroyed his paintings, and all I am left with is this apartment and the memories.'

'He may yet be alive,' Nikita said. 'I have heard of there being detention centres.'

'Torture centres, you mean,' Heidi said with a dry sob. 'I have no doubt they took him there first. But they do not leave suicide notes for men they intend to let live.'

'I am sorry,' Nikita said earnestly.

'Now you see why people must continue to fight, why change must come. Never has a country been so well silenced, but it is time we found our voice. The wall is ready to fall.'

'I was at Alexanderplatz on Saturday,' said Nikita. 'Something is happening in East Berlin right now, although I am still unclear what.'

He realised he was still holding her hand, and put it down tenderly before walking over to the window. He peered out from the edge: there was no longer any sign of the police, although he knew that did not mean that they weren't there. Leaving through the front door might not be an option, much as he didn't relish trying to climb down from the balcony again. He again thought briefly of Elysia, which gave him a sharp pang of nausea which he forced himself to ignore. He caught his reflection in the window and saw the scars spread across his muscular body. Whether the Cold War ended, the Soviet Union survived or fell, or the Berlin Wall crumbled he would always have the scars, he thought sadly.

'You're leaving?' Heidi asked, almost accusatorily, as he turned back and emptied his glass.

'Yes, I must. For your sake as much as my own,' he said, walking back to perch on the arm of the sofa.

She looked like she wanted to protest, but just nodded quietly, her brown furrowing.

Nikita didn't know what to say, so he said nothing.

Heidi sighed after a minute. 'I'm sorry, I know we have only just met and you do not owe me anything at all. It was nice to feel the warmth of a real human interaction, without fear,' she said, smiling at him now, her words slightly slurred from the schnapps.

He returned the smile and reached to hold her hand. 'I also had begun to forget the feeling of human warmth,' he admitted. 'Thank you for giving me a safe haven in a city that I thought kindness had long since forsaken,' he added.

'I'd tell you to come back to the safe haven anytime, but I suspect you rarely spend long enough anywhere to see a place more than once,' she said, her eyes questioning.

'And I suspect you're too sharp for your own good.' He winked and pulled on his clothes.

'Perhaps one day I'll see you when you aren't fleeing the authorities,' she added with a smile.

'That'll be the day!' he laughed. He kissed her gently on the cheek and then climbed out of the window again and out onto the balcony.

He tested his ankle. It was still sore but should be okay if he was careful. He looked back through the window one last time to where Heidi was standing watching him. She raised her hand in farewell.

Nikita's escape proved easier than the night before, with the presence of daylight and the absence of a military unit on his tail making life significantly easier. He made his way straight back to Kielhorn's apartment, being careful to check for any sign of a Stasi tail.

When he arrived at the apartment, he knocked on the door this time, but there was no answer, which didn't surprise him as he knew Kielhorn would be in the middle of his working day. But his intel on Ghulum Ubaid had been inaccurate; there was no way he was the bomber, but it was clear that the authorities wanted him to think he was, and if waiting was what he must do to get answers from Kielhorn, then so be it.

He tried the handle of the door and found it unsurprisingly locked, but when he went to pick the lock, he found that it was no longer there. The entire handle and keyhole had been destroyed, and the door jammed shut, held in place by a swelling of splinters that would have been obvious had the hall lights been on. He stepped back and charged it with his shoulder, and with a further splintering of wood, the door gave way. Nikita was not prepared for what he found inside.

CHAPTER 12

Kielhorn's apartment was in total disarray. The tidy, cosy apartment that Nikita had left only hours earlier was barely recognisable, with drawers upturned, cupboards emptied, and, more concerningly, there were clear signs of a struggle.

As Nikita moved into the apartment, with his gun held out in front of him, he saw drops of blood on the floor next to the bathroom door. He opened the door. The toilet was unflushed, and the seat was broken, alongside a lighter and packet of cigarettes, suggesting that Kielhorn had been enjoying a smoke with his morning ablutions when he was taken. There was some blood, but not so much as to suggest with any certainty that Kielhorn had been killed, but he had, without doubt, been taken violently and against his will.

Nikita continued his investigation of the apartment and found that Kielhorn's study was where the intruders' search had most focused. Papers were everywhere, shelves had been torn from the walls, and the desk was upturned. They had been looking for something, and Nikita wondered if they had found it.

He lifted the office chair up, setting it right, and slumped into it with a heavy exhale. To make doubly sure, he lifted the phone from the floor and dialled the operator, asking to be directed to the East Berlin Police Headquarters. Just after the phone was answered, there was a brief crackle on the line that Nikita knew all too well to be the sound of a wiretap. He nonetheless continued and asked the front desk to be put through to Polizeidirektor Kielhorn but was told that he had not shown up for work that day. Nikita hung up immediately.

Kielhorn had been telling the truth. They really had been listening. And if that was the case, Nikita needed to get out of there right now. As the realisation hit him, he jumped up, thinking of how foolish he had been to enter through the front door this time. They must know he was here. He made his way back to the rear of the apartment and climbed out the way he had entered the previous evening, making his escape, yet again, taking to the rooftops of East Berlin. Once atop the roof, he peered over the edge to the street below and saw the tell-tale vehicles of the Stasi pulling up outside. *Thank God for apartment buildings*, he thought to himself as he jumped from one high roof to another before descending a couple of blocks away from Kielhorn's building.

Nikita walked through the streets of the city, trying to piece together the puzzle that was unfolding in front of him. An Afghan sent to Berlin as a clear decoy, Stasi agents tailing - and attacking - a KGB agent who is meant to be their ally, a British assassin working on behalf of the head of the Stasi who was definitely not behaving as he should, and a police director being taken from his home in broad daylight. None of it made sense. And there were still the nagging thoughts of Elysia on his mind, concern for her recovery, guilt and hungover anxiety from his brief time with Heidi that left him somehow feeling like he had betrayed Elysia, followed by the feelings of anger at her betrayal of him.

He knew it defied logic, but he had to see her. He embarked on yet another rooftop jaunt and snuck back into his apartment to retrieve the passport and papers that Rosin had provided him with. He was in and out in under two minutes, the papers stored safely in his inside pocket. He made straight for Checkpoint Charlie.

The Allied checkpoint, located on the border of East Berlin and the American sector of West Berlin, loomed up menacingly in the middle of Friedrichstrasse, surrounded on both sides by armed soldiers. It was only a small white building raised in the centre of the street, largely hidden by piles of sandbags and barbed wire, but it nonetheless oozed a sense of foreboding, not helped by the stony-faced East German soldiers looking coldly at Nikita as he approached.

They searched him and asked for his papers. He handed them over, repeating the name Klaus Voller to himself over and over, memorising the details of the alias he had been given. Nikita knew it was a fool's errand to cross the wall, knew Rosin's spies and the Stasi would be instantly alerted, but he just knew he needed to see her.

After a brief interrogation, neither the East German nor American troops could find anything untoward in his papers, and he proceeded through the checkpoint with much greater ease than he had anticipated. *How many others have fared less well in trying to cross*, he thought to himself.

'You've been in the wars, son,' said the American official as he looked up from Nikita's passport and took in his face and hands, which still bore cuts and bruises from his gruelling few days in Berlin.

'I'm a Black man in East Berlin. Every day is a war,' Nikita said with a suitable level of glumness.

'Here's hoping the West is less of battle,' the soldier said with a genuine smile and waved him through.

Once through the militarised area, Nikita quickly made his way back to the large hospital that he had only left two days before, but that already felt like an age ago. Entering the hospital, he was about to enquire after Elysia but caught himself as he realised he had no idea what name she had given them. He proceeded to where he had last seen her but found that room now occupied by another. He chose to take that as a sign of her recovery progressing well rather than the other, unthinkable scenario.

He walked the corridors of the hospital, peering through windows and trying to look inconspicuous, but was soon lost in the maze of hallways in the enormous building. Eventually, he found his way to the inpatient ward, which was locked by a security system. Looking through the mottled glass, he could just about make out a vending machine and some seats but little else. Casting his eyes around, he saw an unmanned nurse station behind him, and behind it were some shelves. Upon them was an array of medical equipment, cleaning supplies and a very old toolbox, which he lifted. Returning to the door, he rang the bell, and a friendly-looking nurse opened it.

'How can I help?' she asked in German.

'I have been asked to come and fix the vending machine,' he said with a smile.

'I didn't even realise it was broken! But I hope you can fix it. Chocolate is the only thing that gets me through the day in this place,' she said cheerfully, letting him pass.

'We can't have you going without your chocolate,' he said with a wink and walked confidently towards the vending machine. Once the nurse had walked back into the nurses' office, he changed direction and walked through swinging double doors and onto an expansive, open ward. He quickly spotted Elysia, and his breath caught in his throat as it always seemed to when he saw her.

She was sat up in a bed at the far end of the ward plucking at a large bunch of grapes, looking pouty and bored, and Nikita thought with annoyance, quite beautiful. She looked up as he approached, and her face seemed to progress through every emotion, from delight right through to rage, and by the time he was within ten yards, she began throwing grapes at him. He caught one and popped it into his mouth with a grin, which only served to infuriate her more.

'You have some nerve to show up here—'

'After I saved your life?' he responded in a hushed voice while pulling the curtains closed around them, noticing that people in varying conditions were looking curiously over at the commotion.

'Only to leave me for dead,' she said, her anger moving swiftly into sadness as her eyes welled up. 'I woke up, and you were nowhere to be seen. Where were you? How could you leave me like that?' she added with a voice full of pain, also speaking quietly enough so that none but Nikita could hear.

Nikita tried to reply but felt a catch in his throat and took a deep breath. 'I'm sorry, Elysia. I did what I thought I had to, considering all of the circumstances. I'd hoped you would understand, given your newfound career.'

Elysia bit her lip, and Nikita could see her trying to fight back the tears. He tried not to crack, tried to stay cold, but he just couldn't. He reached over and wrapped her in his arms, and she then cracked herself, sobbing into his shoulder.

'I'm so sorry, Jake,' she said, which caused what felt like a dagger to stick in his belly full of guilt at the reminder of the CIA alias he used with her.

He buried his face in her hair, breathing in its sweet scent and trying to forget everything that had happened. For just that moment, he was in the safest place he'd ever known, and the pain in his body from the bombing, the fights, the escapes, and the pain in his heart from Elysia all melted away. For just that moment, he felt happy.

'Oh, Jake,' she said, pulling back and looking at him, her finger lacing its way over the cuts on his face and stopping with shock at the space where his full earlobe had once been. Nikita had almost forgotten about the injury to his ear. The pain from it had faded into insignificance compared to his other ailments, and he shrugged nonchalantly.

'All part of the job,' he said ruefully.

'Maybe these jobs of ours, maybe they aren't so good,' she said, rubbing her bandaged leg unconsciously.

'The difference between us is that you have a choice. You should get out now, Elysia. This life is not a long one,' he urged.

'So, it's okay for me to get out, but not you? Is it because I'm a woman?' she asked, her eyes flashing. 'You men are all the same. You think us meek little creatures—'

'Elysia, stop,' Nikita interrupted, trying to head off another of her rants, determined to not get into an argument with her. 'There are reasons why it is... less straightforward for me to leave this life behind. Nothing would make me happier than to find somewhere warm with my family and live in peace.'

'And do I feature in this dream of yours?' she asked, arching an eyebrow.

Nikita paused. 'Whether you are or not is irrelevant. It is only a dream. I've told you before not to look for any future worth living with me, and you know more now of why that is the case,' he said, feeling his heart begin to ache again.

'And do you remember what I told you last time you started speaking like that, back in Virginia?' she challenged, her eyes ablaze.

'You told me to get out of my head,' Nikita said with a sigh, looking down at his lap. 'To just enjoy the here and now.'

'And it's time you started listening to me. But there's only one way we can look forward together, and that is if you tell me the truth.'

Nikita looked up sharply. 'To do that would be to give you a death sentence,' he said. 'Especially here, in Berlin. There is a very high chance that one of these other beds is occupied by an East German spy. Have you arranged an extraction?' he asked, lowering his voice.

'Do not worry about me,' she said shortly, crossing her arms. 'I am just an interruption to your life in espionage, which you value so highly.'

'Elysia—'

She yanked the passport from his coat pocket and opened it up. 'Ah, so today you are Klaus. I don't think it suits you, but I'm sure you're very good at playing the part. I think you should go.'

'Elysia, please—'

'Tell me who you really are or leave,' she said coldly.

Nikita stood up and gazed at her with a look of complete sadness. 'If you spend enough time in this game of spies, Elysia, you will start to realise that nothing is so black and white as you see things now. Everything is a shade of cloudy grey.'

'What a cowardly answer,' she said, looking away from him. 'I think you should go,' she repeated, her voice failing to hide the wobble of impending tears.

Nikita stood for a moment, drinking her in, all the beauty, the pain, the things he loved and the things he loved to hate about her, and felt the hairs on his arms prickle with the thought that so often accompanied his departures from Elysia. The thought that he might never see her again.

Then, with a sigh, he turned and pushed the curtains aside, walking back out of the hospital ward and whispered so quietly that no one would hear. 'My name is Nikita.'

***

After he had returned back through the checkpoint, East Berlin felt bleaker than ever as clouds swept across the November sun. Certain that he would be followed once he re-entered the Soviet zone, he decided to pay Rosin an overdue visit and, for once, allow any Stasi or KGB agents to follow him. When he entered the innocuous-looking office building, he marched past the receptionist, whose objections he ignored, and walked straight through the open-plan room of surprised onlookers and into Rosin's office.

The weedy-looking man looked up from some papers he was writing on and produced a toothy smile, stretching his furry little moustache wider and thinner than ever.

'Ah, if it isn't our elusive Agent Allochka,' he said, spreading his arms.

'It has been, I think, two days, Rosin. You're needier than a newborn baby,' Nikita retorted, sitting heavily in the chair across the desk from the station chief.

'Please, take a seat,' Rosin said sarcastically.

'What's going on, Rosin?' Nikita asked directly.

'What do you mean?' Rosin replied, raising his eyebrows.

'Dispense with the performance, you aren't good at it. Why am I being followed? Why did the Stasi attack me? And why am I being thwarted at every attempt to do my job?' Nikita asked. He decided, for the moment, to keep his knowledge of Ubaid to himself.

'Good questions, Agent Allochka. Now let me respond with some questions of my own: why would I do anything to stop you from doing your job? We both answer to the same people. Why did you cross the wall for a couple of hours today when the job you are so keen on doing is very clearly in the East? And as for the Stasi following or attacking you, I know nothing of this.'

'As the KGB station chief in Berlin, you seem strangely uninformed.'

'As the KGB station chief in Berlin, I know exactly as much as I choose to. Knowing too much can get you killed, Allochka.'

'I've seen people get killed for a lot less than that,' Nikita replied dryly, leaning back in his chair. 'Rosin, I can't decide if you're much cleverer than you look or exactly as stupid,' he added as the smirk fell from the station chief's face. 'The Stasi would never dare to attack a KGB agent without expressly being told to by the KGB or a high-ranking Soviet official.'

'Believe it or not, Allochka, but Denisov and other high-ranking Soviet officials rarely deign to run their plans past me. I may be station chief of a key region, but you know as well as I do that in this game, one is only told what one needs to know. You appear to have landed on something that I did not need to know, and that is very unfortunate as I very much know something I am not meant to know. That puts me in a difficult position.'

'I didn't understand at first how you had come to such an important post as a station chief in East Berlin, but now I see it. You're a slippery worm of a man, aren't you, wriggling your way towards deniability wherever you can? I came here for answers but am left with more questions than ever.'

'That is a strange way to speak to a comrade,' Rosin said coldly.

'Comrade! Hah. There is a strange game afoot, and I know you have a part in it, Rosin. For someone who apparently did not know that the Stasi attacked me, you seem strangely blasé about them crossing such a line.'

'I would think that the Stasi have bigger problems than you right now. I suggest you take a look at the news; their government is on the brink of collapse.'

Nikita bit back the retort of 'lucky them' that had immediately sprung to mind. He stood to leave.

'Before you go, Allochka, I have a message for you from Denisov,' Rosin said, almost as an afterthought.

'You only say this now,' Nikita groaned, rolling his eyes. 'What is the message?'

Rosin opened a drawer on his desk and passed over a sealed envelope, which Nikita tore open to reveal a note. It simply said: Toropit'sya. *Hurry up.*

CHAPTER 13

Nikita watched from the window of the Deutsche Reichsbahn train as it trundled north from East Berlin towards Rostock. The carriage was almost empty, and on the table in front of him was a crumbled piece of paper, Schleicher's itinerary, which Nikita had tried to spread as flat as he could.

Schleicher's day-by-day was ordered and itemised down to the minute, with the man clearly liking to run a very tight ship. However, on this day, November 7th, his meetings ended mid-afternoon, with the rest of the day greyed out. What could he be doing? He didn't strike Nikita as someone who enjoyed kicking back and relaxing during a working day, especially when the East German government was on its knees. Unable to do anything other than speculate on Schleicher's activities, he folded the piece of paper back up and inserted it into his coat pocket and then stretched to the table across the aisle, where a newspaper had been left by a passenger.

Unfurling it, he saw that it was today's edition of *Neus Deutschland,* the official paper of the East German Socialist Party, which they used as one of their most powerful propaganda tools. Even they, however, were struggling to put a positive spin on the latest developments. They had given it their best go, however, lavishing praise on the integrity of prime minister Gerhart Bransch in refusing to buckle under the pressure of traitors to the socialist cause. *Printing time had not been kind to them,* Nikita thought with a smirk, *given that Bransch resigned shortly after the paper came out.* Nonetheless, Nikita read the paper front to back and was amazed at what a powerful tool the written word could be. He was reminded of so many of the things that made socialism great, equality for all, an absence of poverty, liberalness and openness. It was unfortunate that all of these things completely contradicted anything Nikita had so far seen in East Germany.

As the train snaked its way through the north German countryside, Nikita was struck by what a picturesque country it was once you got out of the city: forests, fields, and chocolate box houses spread out across a green vista, interspersed with the sparkling blue waters of lakes and rivers. He passed the time by flicking through the book on jazz music he had pocketed at the library, losing himself in a whole new world of music he had never known.

Eventually, the sparkling blue of the lakes was replaced by a steely grey that gradually took over the horizon as the train rattled towards the North Sea, and the coastal city of Rostock gradually came into focus ahead of it. The train ground to a halt as it entered Rostock HBF station, which stood south of the foot of the wide River Warnow estuary that led out to the sea.

Leaving the station, Nikita was greeted by a brightly coloured and lively city and a strong smell of salt in the air. But far from being drawn into the city centre, Nikita walked straight to the line of taxis at the front of the station. He jumped in the back of the one at the front before the driver had any chance to object and gave him the address that he had copied down from the papers in Schleicher's countryside study. The driver frowned but nodded and started the engine, pulling away. He drove east, joining a busy autobahn headed northeast, but was only on it for a few minutes when he took an exit, and soon they were in the quiet countryside. As they rounded a steep corner, a glorious view of the Bay of Mecklenburg opened up before them, and a beach with yellow sand so pale that it verged on being white, just visible beyond a dense, wooded area. The road grew narrower, which mirrored the taxi driver's expression as his brow became deeply furrowed.

'Are we almost there?' Nikita asked.

'Ten minutes,' grunted the driver, not bothering to try and hide his irritation.

'You can let me out here,' Nikita replied, wanting to escape the increasingly vexed driver and also keen to approach whatever was in store with some degree of stealth. He again remembered Balabanov's preparation mantra. The taxi driver visibly cheered up as the car slowed to a halt. Nikita paid him and began the walk along the track, which was hedged on either side, cutting off any view of the surrounding terrain. Rather than protecting him from the cold, it seemed to have become a wind tunnel, blowing heavy gusts of icy, moist wind right off the sea and into Nikita. He pulled his coat close around him and wished he had a Russian ushanka with him as the cold stabbed at his head.

After what seemed like an eternity, the track wound around a bend and opened up into a large clearing where a line of large, ornately built beach houses faced out directly onto the beach. As he entered the edge of the clearing, the force of the wind doubled, almost forcing him backwards. The sea was foaming angrily, with roiling waves crashing into a rock breaker, splitting the deserted beach in half. Nikita checked the address again, remembering how cheap the property purchase had been in Schleicher's notes, and he doubted any of these luxurious-looking homes would be available for such a low sum. It soon became clear as the track forked, and he followed the right path, which led him away from the beach, around the back of the houses and into a woodland of tall, pale trees stripped bare by the battering of wind and rain. Soon, a large barn became visible through the trees, made of wood, with large doors that were bolted shut at the front. It was well-kept and painted a deep burgundy colour, while cream-painted beams crisscrossed the panels that made up the walls.

This looked a lot more like what Nikita was looking for. A small sign in front of the property read Meeresfarm or Sea Farm. The building certainly wasn't a farm, but it could have been the barn for one. There was no sign of anything else around, and Nikita was certain that the sandy soil, dense woodland, and sea winds would be ill-equipped for any farming of note.

Nikita circled the building, looking for another entrance, but the only way in was through the front. He did find a small gap in the woodwork in a rear corner where a board had splintered slightly at the end and peered inside, but it was too dark to make anything out.

The rushing of the wind and waves was abruptly broken by the sound of a car engine, and Nikita hastily retreated into a series of bushes that lined the rear of the barn. Peering out from behind the leaves, Nikita saw that a car had just parked in front of the barn, and his eyes widened as he saw Ernst Schleicher himself step out of the vehicle alongside what looked to be a bodyguard: an oversized man with a closely cropped brown goatee and two very visible guns hanging in holsters strapped across both shoulders. They disappeared from view as they walked to the front of the barn, but then he heard the sound of the doors creaking open, and a glow emanated from inside as the lights were switched on. Nikita was about to venture back towards the rear of the building to look through the crack when another car appeared through the woods and ground to a halt alongside Schleicher's.

Out of the car stepped first a woman in a niqab and stiletto heels, followed by two men in headscarves wrapped into thick turbans, that from his time spent fighting them in the mountains of Afghanistan, could immediately identify as Mujahideen. They wore thick beards, shaved close over the top lip, tight-fitting jackets and baggy trousers. If that hadn't been a clue for Nikita, the AK47 slung over one of the men's shoulders nailed home his assessment. Combined with the firepower carried by Schleicher's bodyguard, this looked like a meeting that could go either way. It was also a meeting that went against everything that made sense, and one that Nikita knew he needed to hear.

Moving with absolute silence, he eased his way out of the bush and moved to the rear of the building, grateful for the sandy earth which dulled the sound of his footsteps. As he got closer, he began to hear voices and noticed that they were speaking in English.

'I am, as I am sure you know, Ernst Schleicher,' said the German, bowing formally to the woman as he shook her hand.

The woman replied in a meek voice, introducing herself as something that sounded like Rapa, but Nikita couldn't be sure, and she shook his hand timidly.

'This is a cold place, Mr Schleicher,' interrupted a well-spoken English accent that, when Nikita peered through the gap in the wall, saw was spoken by one of the Afghan men.

'It is a quiet, hidden place, Mr Al-Zalmay, and that, I think, would be the preference for both of us for this meeting?' Schleicher said, his voice dripping with disdain. Nikita turned and leaned his back against the wooden panelling of the wall and tried to digest what he had just heard. Bedar Al-Zalmay, the leader of Kulu Alqasas, was here in a deserted place on the northern coast of East Germany, meeting with the infamous head of the Stasi.

This wasn't just big; this was nuclear.

He turned and pressed his eye up to the gap once more. The two men had taken seats at a round table, while the two armed men stood behind their own man, gazing fiercely at one another and firmly holding their weapons, while the woman in the niqab sat at a chair to one side, looking bored.

'Be that as it may, let us get this meeting over with as quickly as possible so I can return home. It is a poor time for us to have left our country.'

'But it is a good time for us to change the world, is it not?'

'If God wills it,' Al-Zalmay said, inclining his head.

'God does not belong in East Germany,' Schleicher said with a grimace. Al-Zalmay looked unimpressed with the remark, and his companion shuffled nervously on his feet and said something in Pashto to Al-Zalmay, who snapped off a sharp reply, causing his man to fall silent.

'Where is your previous bodyguard? The skinny one who looked like a rat.' Al-Zalmay asked cautiously, eyeing the enormous bodyguard behind Schleicher.

'You are well informed, Mr Zalmay,' Schleicher said, showing surprise that Al-Zalmay knew such a thing. 'It is quite curious, but he seems to have left my employ,' Schleicher said, spreading his hands. 'But Sebastian here is more than an able deputy.'

'To lose your bodyguard seems careless, Mr Schleicher. I hope you will take more care with our business dealings,' the Afghan warlord said sternly.

'I would not allow yourself to lose too much sleep over the loss of Mr Muller. He was planted in my services by British Secret Services,' Schleicher said with a slow smile.

'What is this? MI6 work for you?' Al-Zalmay gasped, looking around him as if expecting spies to melt out of the walls of the barn.

'My, you are a nervous one, aren't you,' Schleicher said, his voice dripping condescension. 'Do not worry, I knew who and what he was from the beginning, but he served my purposes. The British are very keen that I, and you for that matter, join forces with them to help facilitate the dissolution of the USSR.'

Al-Zalmay began absently stroking his beard, deep in thought, gazing distractedly at the woman. 'This is a most interesting proposal,' he said.

'Indeed, but not what we are here to discuss. Are we ready to talk about the business at hand now?' Schleicher said coldly.

'For a man who asks for much, you do not show a great deal of respect,' Al-Zalmay said.

'Do you understand who I am? I have earned the respect and admiration of all from a lifetime of service, while you have only just begun. Speak to me of respect in thirty years' time. Now, what of my proposal?'

The woman cleared her throat, and Al-Zalmay glared at her as if daring her to make another sound. 'Your proposal is... acceptable,' Al-Zalmay said hesitantly, turning to face Schleicher again. 'You have arranged the Black Sea shipping?'

Nikita noticed he had stopped breathing and urged the men to name what they were talking about.

'Yes, yes, do not worry about this. It is all in hand. I have shipping lines and transport routes arranged across Moldova and into Eastern Europe. Moldova is a hotbed of anti-Soviet revolution at the moment. It is the perfect place to smuggle through. Tell me of your production and supplies.'

'I have many poppy fields in the Helmand Province. Production is not a problem. You will have access to an unending supply of the finest opium in the world.'

'And you would give me exclusive rights to this, why?'

Al-Zalmay leant forward on the table, looking intensely at Schleicher. 'If you had seen what your beloved Soviet Union has done to my country, my people, you would understand. East Germany is their beacon in the West. Let them see how brightly it shines when its people, the infidels, are slaves to addiction,' he finished, spittle on his lips as he looked full of righteous fervour. 'And now for your side of the deal, Mr Schleicher,' he finished, leaning back in his chair and breathing deeply. 'Tell me of the bomb. You know there are powers far greater than you or I that have demanded it.'

Schleicher had remained impassive and unmoved by Al-Zalmay's words. 'I have found just the man to carry out this operation.'

'Who?'

'Do not concern yourself with such details, but feel confident that it will be done. Berlin will burn, and it will happen in two days. It is a sickly city that needs to be put out of its misery. I suggest you do the same as me and make sure you are far away from the place when the bomb goes off.'

'We will need to take some precautions,' Al-Zalmay said coldly, 'to ensure some leverage.'

Throughout his KGB training, Nikita had always prided himself on his vigilance, preparation and, above all, a sixth sense and alertness that had ensured his survival. But today, he had let himself down, such was his eagerness to hear everything being discussed between the head of the Stasi and the leader of Kulu Alqasas, two men central to horrors he had endured on two sides of the world, meeting in the most unlikely of places. His eagerness to listen had stopped him from paying attention to his surroundings, had stopped him from noticing the soft, sandy footsteps as they approached him from behind, and had meant that just as Schleicher revealed his plans for the bomb, Nikita entered a world of pain.

***

SLUTSK, BYELORUSSIAN SSR (SOVIET BELARUS). 1984.

Nikita sat against the wall in the low cell that prevented him from being able to stand up, which was not wide enough to lie down in. His muscles screamed from being cramped and unable to stretch for the past forty-eight hours. Blindingly bright halogen lamps glowed from all corners of the room, burning his eyes every time he involuntarily glanced at them. The days since Balabanov had sent him for interrogation resistance training had become a blur of horrors. First, in Leningrad, they had begun the sleep deprivation, not allowing him to sleep for days on end. Next, he had been taken south to Byelorussia, a constituent republic of the Soviet Union bordering Poland. They had taken him, still awake, to the city of Slutsk in the centre of the country, where he was now being confined in a secret KGB holding facility. He had no idea how long he had been there, but he had at least then been allowed to get moments of sleep, although the cramped conditions and bright lights made any meaningful rest impossible, and instead, the time passed in a trance-like slumber.

Nikita was in one such semi-awake doze when the low, squat door to his cell was abruptly opened, and he was dragged out by the ankles. He was taken into a bare room that smelled of antiseptic, with white walls and a metal table in the centre. He could barely make out those handling him due to the spots swimming across his eyes from looking at the halogen lights. His captors stripped him of his clothes, chained him naked to the bare steel table, and then left the room. Slowly, his vision returned to him, and looking sideways, he saw that there was a wide window on one side of the room. Behind it were a number of women who were pointing at his body and laughing cruelly, mocking and making crude gestures towards him. He knew humiliation was a classic torture tactic to make the victim feel small and vulnerable, but he nonetheless felt shame burn through him and instinctively tried to cover himself, but the chains around his wrists bit into his skin and prevented him from doing so. Suddenly, the sounds of the women came through speakers into the room, and Nikita was forced to endure all the cruel taunts they made about his body. Then, as suddenly as the women and the sound had appeared, they disappeared from view, darkness filling the room they had been in. The lights buzzed back on for a second, and Nikita thought he saw the grinning face of Colonel Klitchkov, the man who had forced him to join the KGB. And then both rooms went entirely dark, and he was not sure if Klitchkov had really been there at all. At first, Nikita did not realise what was happening, and his head whipped side to side, trying to see anything coming towards him, his nerves frayed to the point of snapping and his teeth chattering from fear.

But then he realised that his teeth weren't chattering due to fear but due to the cold that was growing throughout the room, sinking into his body like ghostly tendrils. His ears picked up the very soft sound of air coming through vents into the room, and the temperature rapidly plummeted. He tried to compact his body, draw his shoulders in or bring his knees up a little, anything to retain some warmth, but the cruel chains held him in place, making it impossible to resist in any way. The cold quickly became so intense that he stopped being able to feel his fingers and toes, and the freezing metal table below him sent daggers of cold into his shoulder blades and spine. Within minutes, he began to stop feeling anything at all.

At that moment, the lights came on, and a figure walked into the room. A man in a balaclava, KGB uniform and a thick coat entered, and although Nikita couldn't see his face, he could see the glee in the eyes. Nikita felt frost on his eyelids and struggled to keep them open.

'Kak bac zavyt?' barked the KGB officer. What is your name?

Nikita said nothing. He was no longer sure he could if he wanted to.

'Who do you work for?' the officer continued in Russian.

Once more, the officer was met with silence. He withdrew some keys from his coat pocket and unchained Nikita. Then, with the help of another masked man who joined him, they flipped Nikita over. Nikita let out an inhuman roar as the skin on his back, which had stuck frozen to the table, was torn from him, and he lay curled up in a ball on the table, sobbing soundlessly but refusing to allow a single tear to leave his eyes. Heat began to return to the room, and chilblains tingled uncomfortably through his body. Then, hot water, just shy of burning, was poured over his body, forcing him to scream involuntarily once more as the heat sent shockwaves through his body. The sobs were replaced by shudders and shaking as his body protested against the barbaric treatment.

Then, all at once, everything went dark once more as a hood was forced over his head, and he was flipped back onto his back. He was pulled roughly so that his head hung over the end of the table, and his body was pinned down forcefully.

'Let me ask you again. Who do you work for!' roared the man, who gripped Nikita's head roughly. Nikita knew what was coming, and he wanted to break. But a tiny voice in his head was shouting at him from a distance. As the water was slowly poured over the sack above his face, he began to choke, to feel as if he was drowning, his lungs screaming, and the tiny voice got louder and louder until it was a roaring filling his head.

DO NOT LET THEM BREAK YOU! roared the voice and repeated it over and over. It was a voice filled with love and support, a voice that would be with him forever. Just before he lost consciousness, he realised it was the voice of his mother.

***

Nikita heard the clinking of chains and felt the cold metal against his skin before his eyes opened, and he fully regained consciousness. The back of his head felt sticky with blood, and waves of pain were radiating through it. His mind slowly pieced together what had happened, and he cursed himself for the laxity outside the barn. He could not remember a time he had allowed someone to sneak up on him, at least not when he was sober, and as he opened his eyes, he realised that the first time he had slipped might be the last time.

He was immediately transported back to that hidden KGB facility in Belarus. The sterile, clinical smell of bleach filled his nostrils, and the bare walls and metal table made it impossible not to be consumed by the memories of his interrogation resistance training. Once again, he was handcuffed to a surgical table, although this one at least had some cushioning for his head, and his legs had been strapped down rather than manacled, all of which made it feel like a luxury compared to his experience in Slutsk.

CHAPTER 14

This time, his torturers were unmasked, and two men stood above Nikita, both with almost identically nondescript faces, militarily sharp side partings, and straight noses. The only thing separating them was the eyes: one had large frog-like eyes that were wide apart on his face, while the other was the exact opposite, almost cross-eyed with them unusually close together. Both showed no emotion, just the workmanlike poise of two professionals going about their business. There was another table in the room, and the man with narrow eyes picked up a long, steel, needle-like implement from it and walked over to Nikita.

'Before we begin, you should know, Mr Allochka, that Wolfgang and I are very good at keeping people alive while in a maximum amount of pain,' he said in a nasal voice.

'If you know who I am, then you know I won't talk,' Nikita said with as much confidence as he could muster, already beginning to detach himself from his body, mentally preparing himself to ignore whatever pain was inflicted upon him.

'Talk? Who said anything about getting you to talk?' said the frog-eyed Wolfgang, smiling now as he also approached the bench, holding a pair of pliers.

It was then that Nikita began to feel afraid. Resisting interrogation was something he had been trained for, something he knew he could do. Resisting mindless torture with no hint of interrogation was something else. They would not stop, and they would break him. He felt a cold sweat begin to gather on his upper lip.

The narrow-eyed interrogator smiled congenially, then held the needle into the top of Nikita's left foot. With his eyes fixed on Nikita's, he began to push down. Nikita did not look, instead trying to get lost in the eyes of the man, trying to let them transport him somewhere else, but they had already managed to get into his head. He felt the spike, like a sharpened knitting needle, pierce the skin of his foot and felt it move agonisingly slowly through flesh and sinew until it reappeared through the sole of his foot. Narrow-eyes then left it there, his foot completely skewered with the needle, and moved to one side. Nikita refused to roar or shout and instead lay back with his eyes closed and teeth gritted as Wolfgang moved to the fore.

'Niet, niet, my Russian friend. None of this can be done with eyes closed,' he said in a croaky voice that matched his toady eyes, and Nikita's eyelids were forced open and held there by Narrow-eyes. 'I was going to do this with your hand tied back, but now I think we shall make you watch,' he continued and undid the handcuff on Nikita's left hand.

Huge mistake, frog-eyes, Nikita thought to himself, but allowed the Stasi torturer to think him more malleable than he was.

Nikita began to moan. 'Please, no, please. I will tell you anything you want to know, anything at all,' he protested as frog-eyes lifted Nikita's hand in front of his face with one hand firmly clasped around his wrist. With his other hand, the torturer brandished the pliers and fastened them to the nail of his little finger.

'Eins?' he said with a malicious smile, which forced his eyes even further out of his head.

Nikita began frantically shaking his head.

'Zwei?' he said, grinning toothily now. And then he pulled. Nikita, allowing himself to be more present than any of his training would have allowed, roared as he felt his entire nail be ripped out of the finger. Wolfgang held up the nail right in front of Nikita's face so that blood dripped onto his face.

'What happened to drei?' Nikita protested, unable to help himself. The fist of Narrow-eyes promptly smashed into his mouth, and Nikita felt the hot metal taste of blood fill his mouth.

'You think this is funny?' he asked, looking furiously at Nikita. Nikita said nothing and just allowed his unfettered hand to dangle uselessly to one side, but he was pleased that he had got under the skin of the previously expressionless man. Narrow-eyes walked back over to the table and, this time returned with an instrument that turned Nikita's blood cold. A butcher's bone saw. In his other hand, he held a filleting knife.

'I see your jokes have stopped, Mr Allochka,' he said coldly, his eyes gleaming. 'Do you know what it is like to have no skin? I don't suppose you do, but soon you will experience this, and you can tell me how it feels. Then, perhaps, you can tell me what it is like to have no arms.'

Nikita spat blood onto the shiny black shoes of Wolfgang, who slapped Nikita hard. 'You have the uncontrolled insolence that typifies your race. The only way to train you people is to break you!' he shouted, grabbed Nikita's hand again, and picked up his pliers.

Nikita started screaming and began to writhe on the table, making it difficult for Wolfgang to keep a grip. He motioned to Narrow-eyes to help, and his associate placed the bone saw and the filleting knife down in front of Nikita's face to leave him in no doubt about what was coming, and then grabbed Nikita's hand, keeping it in place in front of his face, while Wolfgang picked the pliers back up. It was exactly what Nikita had wanted, and as they both focused on the nail of his middle finger, he began to just slightly bend the leg of the foot that had been run through with the oversized needle.

Wolfgang yanked the next nail out of Nikita's finger, this time doing it even more slowly to prolong the agony, and once more brandished it in front of his face as they allowed his hand to fall. This was the moment Nikita had been waiting for. He flopped his hand down and then, quick as a flash, grabbed the filleting knife and stabbed the long, thin blade straight into one of Wolfgang's bulbous eyes. He swiftly withdrew it, and to Nikita's surprise, the eye came out with the blade. Then, without hesitating, he swiped across the face of Narrow-eyes. They had taken care to keep their torture implements sharp, and the blade, despite carrying globules of the eye with it, cut a deep lesion across the middle of the man's face, with a particularly deep cut through the centre of his nose. Both men screamed and fell backwards, which gave Nikita just long enough to slice through the straps holding down his legs, and then he began cutting through the remaining handcuff with the bone saw.

He saw Narrow-eyes fumbling around on the table and reappearing, brandishing an eight-inch chef-style knife. Blood was pouring down the bottom half of his face, and he looked far from expressionless now as his eyes were filled with a crazed mania. Wolfgang was continuing to stomp around, his hands over his empty eye socket.

Nikita frantically sawed at his handcuff, but the saw was designed for bone, not metal and was making painfully slow progress through the thin steel. Narrow-eyes fell upon him, stabbing downwards, and Nikita rolled to one side as the knife struck the metal table with an almighty clang, missing Nikita's throat by inches. Nikita swung his legs down to the floor and, with a roar of pain, felt the long needle hit the ground first and slide back through his foot. Before it was fully extricated, Nikita swung the foot up, yanked the needle out the rest of the way, and blindly stabbed behind him. Tempered metal struck flesh, and flesh struck blade, as both Nikita and Narrow-eyes hit their target, and both crashed to the ground. One got up. One didn't.

The torturer climbed to his feet while Nikita lay face down on the cold, concrete floor, the knife rising up from his back. But while the Stasi interrogator's mouth was opening and closing, it wasn't making any sound, and the long, metal needle that had only seconds ago been through the middle of Nikita's foot was now buried deep into his throat. His arms flailed around, and he grabbed Wolfgang, his eyes wide in terror, trying to shake his associate from his own torment. Wolfgang's hands dropped to reveal a bloody, dark hole where his oversized eye had once been. His mouth hung open upon seeing the shiny dart protruding from the neck of his companion, who was now shaking him, his eyes beseeching. Wolfgang tentatively raised his hands and pulled the needle out, which, it turned out, was the worst thing he could have done. Blood sprayed from the wound like a corked bottle, and a gurgling sound began to emanate from it as air bubbles appeared. He began to drool blood, and his movements became slower as Wolfgang frantically tried to stem the bleeding with his hands while looking wildly around the room for something that could help and yelling for aid. But this was a room for inflicting pain, not easing it. It was a room built to ensure cries for help remained unanswered.

Nikita watched the scene from the floor and then grimaced and noiselessly sat up, reaching over his back to try and gain a purchase on the knife handle. It took some time to get a hold, and he felt his way along the handle to the blade. To his relief, it had not buried itself as deeply as he had feared, as it appeared to have struck the bone of his shoulder blade. But pulling it out was still not something he relished.

'Adin, dva, tri,' he counted to three in Russian and then pulled with all his might. The knife moved but only a centimetre and remained lodged in his back. The pain was incredible as it seared right across his broad back and down his spine.

'Nu zhe,' he continued in Russian. *Come on.*

With a pull that felt like it took everything he had in him, he tugged the knife with the last of his strength and felt it come out, triggering pain sensors that sent waves through his whole body. Without stopping to dwell on it, he jumped up and saw that Narrow-eyes was now lying on his back on the floor, his eyes wide and staring, and a growing pool of blood spreading around him as blood continued to dribble feebly from the hole in his neck.

But then Wolfgang was upon him, swinging the bone saw wildly at Nikita, spluttering and swearing with a mad fervour.

'You killed him!' he shouted at Nikita as he swung the saw in a wide arc that Nikita easily dodged. 'Now I will kill you!'

Again, Nikita sidestepped a swing and rolled his shoulder to try to loosen it but felt blood dripping down his back from the knife wound.

'Do Stasi torturers not like having the tables turned upon them?' Nikita said as the two began slowly circling. 'You can give it, but you cannot take it, eh?' he said, trying to goad Wolfgang into making a rash move. But it was becoming increasingly obvious to Nikita that these were not fighting men. They were psychopaths who enjoyed inflicting pain on people who were tied up and strapped down. Dispatching his one-eyed opponent would ordinarily be no problem, but Nikita was struggling to put any weight on his foot, and any time he tried to lift his right arm, it sent such pain through his entire shoulder blade that it made his eyes water. He could feel blood being squeezed out of the hole every time. He allowed it to hang limply at his side and hobbled around Wolfgang, trying to only use the heel of his foot. His head felt dizzy, and as if sensing his weakness, Wolfgang leapt forward. The teeth of the bone saw bit into Nikita's weak arm as Nikita struggled to turn quick enough to get out of the way, and Wolfgang jumped back again before Nikita could get a shot at him. The torturer grinned a horrible sight on his one-eyed, blood-stained face, his hair sticking out at odd angles like a mad professor. Before Nikita had time to recover, Wolfgang leapt forward once more, this time ducking low and slamming the saw into the thigh of Nikita's good leg.

Nikita couldn't stop himself from falling to one knee with a grunt. The room was beginning to spin, and his hands were shaking as his body showed signs of going into shock from the multiple wounds that had been inflicted upon it.

Not by his hand, Nikita thought to himself. *If I am to die, it will not be at the hands of this man, and it definitely will not be from being bitten to death by a bone saw.*

Tensing his whole body, he readied himself to spring, for a last hurrah, to use every ounce that he had to finish it. And then the lights went out.

'Turn the lights back on!' he heard Wolfgang scream, but then he heard the familiar *phut phut* of a silenced pistol and the thump of a body hitting the ground.

Nikita couldn't see a thing but tried to make himself as small as possible and ran his hands around blindly on the floor, trying to find a weapon with which he could take on this hidden new enemy. But consciousness was beginning to feel elusive, and the blackness of the room mingled with a deeper darkness that was beginning to cross his eyes. He blinked rapidly and flexed his fingers, forcing his body to keep going, to stay awake. To stay alive.

But then he felt hands roughly grabbing him. He was lifted and tossed over the shoulder of his new captor.

'Who are you?' he asked, but other than a hush from a gentle and vaguely familiar voice nearby, he was afforded no response.

As he was carried out of the room, he briefly saw the bodies of guards lying dead on the floor, illuminated by the flickering security lighting of the hallway. And then, finally, he allowed his consciousness to fade.

CHAPTER 15

Nikita awoke to the sound of unmistakably British voices in the distance, the clipped sort of voice that belonged to Etonians and the upper classes. As he forced his eyes open, he found himself in a world of pain. He was in a bed surrounded by humming machines with various devices attached to him.

No matter how he moved, his back was on fire. Any time his hand brushed the sheets, the now hypersensitive fingers with no nails sent deeply unpleasant sensations through his hand, and his arm, leg and foot were doing their best to remind him of the wounds inflicted there, too. His mouth felt like it had been stuffed with sand, and when he tried to make a sound, his dry throat only rustled painfully.

Ignoring the pain, he pushed himself up slightly and tried to take in the room and process what was going on. It wasn't a hospital, more a bedroom that had been turned over to medical care. It screamed of government to Nikita, and the last place he could afford to be seen was in some sort of British government building. He yanked a long IV drip needle out the back of his hand and pulled off a pad that had been stuck to his chest. Immediately, one of the machines started beeping loudly, and when he tried to lean over to switch the machine off, he lost his balance and crashed to the floor. He could not help but emit a low moan as his wounds simultaneously protested against the treatment. He heard a door and running footsteps as a doctor hurried over to him.

'What on earth are you doing, young man?' asked the clipped British voice that he had heard in the distance. 'You need to rest, not roll around on the floor.'

Nikita rolled onto his back and looked up. He had not been called a young man in many years, and despite being only twenty-three, he found it patronising, which was not helped by the condescending, raised eyebrows look that the doctor had fixed upon him.

'Who are you?' Nikita said in a low voice.

'I am Doctor Bothwell-Monro, and I have been charged with healing your many, many wounds,' he said with a shake of his head as if Nikita had simply been careless.

Where am I?' Nikita said through gritted teeth as he tried to push himself, unsuccessfully, up.

'Let me guess, he's being difficult and answering your questions with questions,' sounded an all too familiar voice from the other side of the bed. Nikita closed his eyes and let his head fall back with a groan. When he opened his eyes, Elysia's face swam into view.

'What are you doing here?' he demanded, trying to hold his American accent.

'Friendly fellow, isn't he?' commented Doctor Bothwell-Monro to Elysia as he gazed down over his half-moon spectacles.

'You have no idea,' Elysia said, shaking her magnificent curls. 'Let's get him back into bed.'

The doctor grabbed Nikita gently under the arms while Elysia lifted his feet in a far less gentle fashion, and they put him back onto the bed. Nikita wanted to protest at being treated like an invalid but had long ago learned that some battles were not worth fighting.

The doctor checked some of the machines, switched off the one that was bleeping, and looked at Nikita with a faint cluck of disapproval. 'I would like to give you some morphine for the pain,' he said, looking at Nikita.

'No, no drugs,' Nikita said sharply, holding up his good arm. There was no way he was letting anyone drug him, especially while he had no idea where he was or what was going on.

'Oh yes, your body is a real temple, isn't it,' Elysia said, rolling her eyes.

'Very well, if you wish to suffer, that is your choice,' the doctor shrugged. 'I shall leave you two to get reacquainted, but he must rest, Agent Nightshade, so be brief,' he said before checking a pocket watch in his breast pocket and walking out.

'Agent Nightshade?' Nikita said disbelievingly. 'That's a terrible codename.'

Elysia sat down on the chair next to him. 'Yet somehow it feels more plausible than you being Klaus Voller. Feel free to thank me any time you want, by the way,' she added, looking at him reproachfully.

'What for?' Nikita asked, surprised.

'For saving your life!' she exclaimed.

'You?' he replied dumbly.

'Yes, it was me and another agent that rescued you from that torture chamber. Do you not remember?'

'I had one or two other things on my mind.'

'So I saw,' agreed Elysia. 'I thought you were dead. There was so much blood,' a small crack in her voice the only sign of any emotion.

'You seem changed,' said Nikita, concerned.

Elysia shrugged and looked away.

Nikita leaned forward and grabbed her hand. She looked up at him. 'Thank you,' he said with total sincerity. 'For saving my life.' He tried to put as much feeling into his words and eyes as he could to bring her back from the path she was going down.

She smiled and blinked back the tears forming there. Nikita allowed himself to drop back onto his pillow but continued to hold her hand.

'How did you find me?' he asked.

'When you left the hospital, I decided to come after you. I feared you would melt away again and that I would never find you this time. I wanted to make amends, but then you crossed the wall, and I lost your trail.'

'How did you pick it up again?'

'I crossed the wall in the only way I know how,' she said, winking at him.

'What about your leg wound?' Nikita asked.

'It is painful but useable,' she said dismissively.

'The mantra of the spy,' Nikita laughed bitterly.

'Once I crossed, I elicited the help of some of my contacts to help track you down. A Black guy in East Berlin is not difficult to find, you know. Kinda strange that you got posted there when you think about it.'

Nikita said nothing, as it was a thought that had also occurred to him more than once.

'Anyway, I tracked you down and followed you up to Rostock, but when you got in a taxi, it was hard to follow you. I stole a motorcycle, but there was no way I could follow you down those narrow country roads without you seeing me or your driver getting suspicious. I left the bike on the beach and watched from a distance as you were dragged to a car, and then I saw Schleicher which I had certainly not expected. What have you gotten into?'

'Something much bigger than I could ever have guessed,' muttered Nikita.

'When they bundled you into the trunk of the car, I followed on all the way south back towards Berlin, and when I saw them take you into that facility near Potsdam, I knew I would need backup. I don't have any Greek support on that side of the wall, so I had to go to the British.'

'You're crazy,' Nikita said, shaking his head. 'You got the British to risk a diplomatic nightmare by extracting an agent who doesn't even belong to them? How?' he asked, dumbfounded.

'I can be pretty persuasive when I need to be,' she said, looking defiant. 'Besides, it was a black op, full deniability for the British, and the Greeks for that matter. And the East Germans aren't likely to shout to the world about their secret torture bunker, so I'd say we're all good.'

'All good,' mouthed Nikita, wide-eyed and shaking his head. 'You're actually insane.'

'Well... you know they say there's no such thing as a free lunch?' Elysia said tentatively. Nikita closed his eyes in a silent prayer.

'What do they expect me to do for them?' he asked, keeping his eyes closed.

'Nothing really, just check in with them from time to time. Let them know if you come across anything that might be of interest in East Berlin.'

'The hope is that I'm not in Germany for much longer, let alone East Berlin,' he said flatly. 'But I bet the deal with them doesn't end then, huh?'

'There is no deal, old boy,' said another voice, interrupting the privacy Nikita and Elysia thought they'd been afforded. Into the room walked a rakishly good-looking man with curly grey hair, combed back in a quiff and side parting, and a silk scarf draped around his neck. He had a strong, clean-shaven jaw and bright eyes. He walked with a slight limp and a brass cane. Elysia whipped her hand away from Nikita's. 'Only two chaps becoming a little better acquainted with one another.' He smiled toothily, showing straight, white teeth. He had the same clipped, Oxbridge accent as the doctor.

He walked to the bed and held out his hand to Nikita. 'Miles Curbishley, at your service,' he said, grinning once more. Nikita took the hand reluctantly.

'I'd give you my name, but I'm sure you know all about me,' Nikita said, ensuring the handshake was a very brief one.

'Ah, you have the staple cynicism of our friends at Langley, Mr Marshall.' Nikita inwardly breathed a sigh of relief; they did not know he was KGB; they did not know his real name. Yet.

'It is a cynicism that has been well earned with our British friends,' Nikita replied. 'You know, that little thing called the War of Independence.'

'Ancient history, old boy, all ancient history as far as I'm concerned. I find myself far more interested in the present day, particularly when it comes to Berlin.'

'Now that I can agree with. What day is it? How long was I out?' Nikita asked, realising he had no idea how long he had been unconscious.

'It is Wednesday, November 8th,' replied Curbishley, rapping his cane on the hardwood floor. 'You enjoyed a fine night's sleep with the best care we had at our disposal. You were in jolly bad shape. Agent Nightshade here seemed quite concerned about you. She did rather well to rally the troops when she did. I suspect your days, or perhaps minutes, would otherwise have been numbered.'

'I was doing ok,' Nikita said defiantly, setting his shoulders slightly, which caused a pang of pain through his back.

'Well, you were certainly doing better than your tormentors, who did not seem to have ended their days with a smile,' chuckled Curbishley darkly. 'But I prefer not to dwell on such grisly details. I am curious to know, however, what had taken you to Rostock and what Schleicher was doing up there. He doesn't strike me as the type to enjoy lying on a beach, particularly in November.'

Nikita said nothing, his jaw tightening as his mind worked overtime.

'Jake, maybe they can help you,' Elysia said softly.

Nikita ignored her and looked instead at Curbishley. 'I am grateful for the care you have provided for me and for the lengths you went to in salvaging me from Schleicher's men. But you strike me as a man who knows the game, and you know the rules.'

Curbishley laughed. 'I not only know the game; I delight in it! But let me tell you something about the game; it is one in which one must write one's own rules. It is what makes it so fabulously entertaining.'

'I don't find a game that deals in death and destruction particularly entertaining,' Nikita said, noting that Elysia looked down at the floor.

'Yet here you are living it nonetheless, and you seem particularly adept at surviving it, which is no mean feat for a field agent such as yourself,' Curbishley said, no longer smiling. 'I know your position, agent, but do not expect sympathy from me. This game does not allow for emotion; it requires only logic to find the best route to survival. Let me explain to you the facts: The Berlin Wall is ready to fall, and the Iron Curtain is not far behind it. I know something of the game that your friend Schleicher is playing; until very recently, we had a man close to him, but he appears to have dropped off the map, so to speak.'

'Yes, I know all about your plans for Schleicher, the tyrant who has terrorised the lives of East Germans for decades. Not forgetting, of course, your hopes to bring the leader of an Afghan terrorist cell into your warm British embrace.' He turned his head to Elysia. 'These are the people you align yourself with, Elysia,' Nikita said to her, nodding towards Curbishley with disdain. Her mouth tightened, but she said nothing.

'You are well drilled, and you say all the right things, old boy, but I'm afraid I don't find myself believing a word of it. I know for certain that you are not so naïve as to not know that sometimes, in this chess match, we must align ourselves with some unsavoury characters. It is very much the nature of the beast,' Curbishley retorted. 'Now, you see, you have already given me something of what you know, and it required no betrayal on your behalf whatsoever,' he finished with aplomb.

'All I've done is confirm that I know something of what you're up to. I don't imagine for a second that I have the full picture.'

Curbishley only winked in response. Despite himself, Nikita couldn't help but like the man, but he knew that was exactly why he had been picked to do what he did.

'I think I might surmise one or two things about your position, Mr Marshall. You have been abandoned a little by your employers, even, dare I say it, hung out to dry on this crusade of yours around East Berlin. It is not the first time I have seen your employers do this. You have, however, been highly effective in irritating the Stasi, which, while entertaining, may be ill-advised; they really are quite ruthless, you know. It is nonetheless impressive, but consider this: why would they send you here, to a place where you stick out like a sore thumb, if you don't mind my saying so? I don't profess to know your mission, but I suspect it is not going to plan. With my organisation—'

'Which organisation is that?' Nikita asked, wanting to hear him say it.

'We go by many names, but you would best know us as MI6, and we are in a position to offer you a level of support that it seems you are not receiving elsewhere.'

Nikita couldn't help himself, and he laughed out loud.

'Something amusing, old boy?'

'I've heard it all before. It'll be better with us… we can look after you… we'll keep you safer than anyone else. Then when push comes to shove, it's every man or woman,' he said with a glance at Elysia, 'for themselves. Don't try and pretend to me that MI6 is a nice and cuddly spy organisation; no such thing exists, and you're more of a fool than I thought if you believe otherwise.'

'Nightshade, I think you're needed for a debrief downstairs,' Curbishley said with a meaningful look at Elysia. Elysia looked as if she wanted to protest, but an uncharacteristically commanding look from the Brit silenced her and, with a brief glance and half smile at Nikita, turned and walked out of the room. Curbishley watched her leave the room and, once the door was closed, turned back to Nikita.

'I think it is time we were a trifle more direct with one another, wouldn't you agree?' he asked Nikita with an arched eyebrow.

Nikita nodded slowly.

'I know that the Yanks have all but left you for dead out here, and I have reason to believe your fingers may be in other pies as well. I don't expect you to answer that,' he added, holding up a hand as Nikita opened his mouth to respond. 'But let me explain your position a little more clearly.' He withdrew some photographs from his pocket, which showed intimate photos of him and Elysia together back at his house in Langley, Virginia, from when Nikita had been stationed by the KGB as an embedded agent within the CIA. Nikita looked at them briefly and felt a cold rage beginning to spread through his body as he looked up at Curbishley.

'I have my suspicions that it would behove you to keep these photos under wraps. A CIA operative canoodling with a Greek Secret Service and MI6 agent would most certainly be frowned upon. But I suspect there are others in your world who would frown on it even further.' Curbishley gave a pained look. 'I actually despise methods such as these. That is the honest truth. But the game is reaching a dangerous conclusion and unfortunately needs must.'

'What do you want from me,' Nikita said through gritted teeth.

'It is as I already said; I want only a little cooperation. It is fair to say there is nobody quite like you in operation at the moment. As you seem to already know, we are working to bring Schleicher over to our side. He is one of the worst people I've ever had to deal with, but a little immunity for him in return for what he knows could save an untold number of lives and stop the spread of communism dead in its tracks.'

'From what you said, the spread of communism is already about to stop in its tracks, so what difference does Schleicher make?'

'You know the story of Hydra in Greek Mythology, I presume?' Curbishley asked.

'The many-headed serpent,' Nikita replied. 'When one head was cut off, another two grew in its place.'

'Precisely. Communism is the Hydra of the modern world. We may cut off one head, but it will only regenerate elsewhere. Schleicher could be our

Heracles, our way of burning all of the heads off at the neck.'

'And the Afghan?'

Curbishley shrugged. 'The enemy of my enemy is my friend. For now.'

'Do you have any agents behind the curtain?' Nikita asked, knowing the answer.

Curbishley laughed. 'I can't imagine for a second that you expect me to answer that.'

'Never hurts to try,' Nikita answered ruefully. He closed his eyes and lay back on his pillow. He ran through his options and quickly realised that there were few choices. He didn't care if Deputy Director Barker knew who he slept with or even Denisov. But he did care about Elysia and knew that she would quickly be killed or used against him if either found out. He must become a triple agent, and the thought made him feel quite sick.

'Burn those pictures right now, and any other copies, and I will help you. And if you attempt to blackmail me again, I will kill you where you stand,' Nikita said coldly.

'Deal,' said Curbishley, immediately withdrawing an ostentatiously large lighter from his pocket and setting fire to the photos, dropping them into a metal rubbish bin in the corner of the room. He withdrew the negatives from his pocket and wiggled them flamboyantly at Nikita before dropping them into the flames. Tendrils of sickly acrylic smoke laced their way around the room.

'What protection can I receive?' Nikita asked.

'Principally, none,' Curbishley said. 'You are not on our books, and only myself and your very lovely, if rather green, friend Agent Nightshade know of your involvement. But I do have it within my power to provide you with a degree of support where possible. But that support will only last as long as you are cooperating and providing information. You can begin by telling me what you are looking for in East Berlin.'

'A bomber,' said Nikita curtly. 'Schleicher and Bedar Al-Zalmay have plans to set off a bomb in East Berlin. I thought I had found the bomber, but it was a red herring. Before I was captured, I heard Schleicher tell Al-Zalmay that *he* had sourced a bomber rather than the other way round, which is not what I had expected.'

'That is most interesting and most disquieting. A bomb, you say? I knew Schleicher was a bastard, but to bomb his own people... he really must be as ruthless as they said,' said Curbishley, distractedly stroking his chin. 'What are those two up to?' he added, almost to himself. Eventually, he seemed to snap out of his reverie. 'What do you need in order to continue to pursue this line of investigation?' he asked Nikita.

'A drink would be a good start,' said Nikita, spitting out what had been on his mind since the conversation began.

'An excellent idea. Scotch okay?' asked Curbishley as he opened a hidden panel in the wall to reveal a whisky decanter and glasses. 'This is my office that you have taken over, but I left a few small comforts behind.'

'Scotch always sounds okay to me,' said Nikita. He took the glass with a nod, unconsciously sniffing it for any sign of tampering and waiting to see Curbishley sip his own before he followed suit. The moment the whisky hit his tongue, he instantly felt more relaxed.

'I needed this,' Nikita said absently.

'I shouldn't wonder. Those Stasi bastards did quite the number on you,' Curbishley said, taking a seat.

'I've endured worse,' Nikita said through closed eyes.

'I have seen your scars,' confirmed the Englishman.

'I have one request,' Nikita said, ignoring the remark.

'Prithee tell,' Curbishley replied sarcastically.

'Keep Ely—ah, Agent Nightshade, out of this.'

'That, I'm afraid, dear boy, is not the call of either of us to make.'

'Bullshit,' said Nikita. 'You want my help, you get her out.'

'She is a very strong-willed woman, as I have no doubt you are aware, and incredibly bright...'

'Just sort it, Curbishley. I don't know what game you're playing with her, but MI6 has no need for Greek Secret Service agents.'

'MI6 always has a need for very good agents, though,' Curbishley said, smirking. 'I promise you there is no way I can get her removed from active duty. She is merely on loan to us from the Greeks, but I can try to encourage them to recall her.'

'Good, now get me out of here,' Nikita said.

Curbishley nodded. 'I'll fetch the good doctor and encourage him to discharge you. It will be nice to have my office back. Let Agent Nightshade know of any hardware you require, and she will ensure you have what you need. If you require me, you can reach me here,' he said, handing a card to Nikita. With that, he walked out, and moments later, Doctor Bothwell-Monro returned, looking unimpressed.

Nikita had swung his legs off the bed and was in the process of peeling off various bandages to peer underneath.

'Leave those,' snapped the doctor, pushing Nikita's hands aside and gently pressing the bandages back into place.

'I'm leaving,' said Nikita.

'So I hear.'

'You disapprove?' Nikita asked with a raised eyebrow.

The doctor snorted. 'What do you think? You shouldn't be going anywhere for at least a week at the bare minimum.'

'Needs must, Doc,' Nikita said with a wink. He tried to stand, but a sharp pain shot through his foot.

'Yes, that was a particularly nasty one. There's a real danger of infection there,' said Bothwell-Monro. 'Thankfully, the Stasi kept their implements nicely sterile. Otherwise, you'd be in real trouble. I'll pack it out with as much dressing as possible, which should lessen the pain, but you will need to change the dressings at least twice a day if you're walking on it. It will not heal until you do not use it for several days.'

'Yes, Doc,' Nikita replied, thinking there was more chance of the Berlin Wall collapsing than there was of him getting several days to put his feet up. 'What about my back?'

'That will heal quicker if you look after yourself. It took some flesh, though, so you must keep it dry. No pull-ups any time soon,' the doctor added, softening slightly. 'Your nails will grow back eventually, but will unlikely ever be the same again, but everything else was just cuts and bruises, albeit nasty ones. Your ear will be forever changed though, but it did not look like that had just happened...' he said, leaving it hanging.

Nikita looked at him with raised eyebrows, and the doctor fell silent. 'Thanks for patching me up,' he said and moved to where some clothes and a suit had been left out for him.

'Yes, well, I expect I will see you back here sooner rather than later.'

'Thanks for the reassuring words,' Nikita said with a grimace. The doctor left and was replaced by Elysia, whose face showed a mixture of irritation and concern.

'It's crazy you're going back out there right away,' she said. 'You look a complete mess.'

'You always did have a way with words,' said Nikita as he tried in vain to pull a shirt on over his scabbing back.'

Elysia walked over and helped him to pull the shirt on. He could smell her perfume, and with the whisky on an empty stomach, it made his head spin, making him not care about what had broken between them. Without thinking, he pulled her to him and then groaned slightly as it stretched the deep cut in his back. They were face-to-face, only centimetres apart, and unable to resist anymore, Nikita leant forward to kiss her.

His lips barely brushed hers when she pulled away and stepped back. His arm absently reached out for her in longing before he noticed it and let it drop, embarrassed. Her face was a welter of emotions, none of which Nikita could read.

'Jake... I... I'm sorry, I can't,' she said.

'Oh yeah, right. Of course. Sorry,' Nikita said, turning away and feeling the hurt of the betrayal all over again.

'It's not that I don't... can you look at me?' she said, spinning him round. He landed on his wounded foot and lost his balance, falling onto the bed clumsily.

'I'm looking at you, Elysia,' he said, looking up at her. 'Say what you have to say,' he added, bracing himself sadly.

'You know I love you—'

'But,' interrupted Nikita.

'But I don't know who I'm in love with anymore. I don't know your real name or where you're really from. I don't know anything about you.'

'You know everything that's important. You know what really matters, which is this,' he said, gesturing between them. 'What we *feel,*' he added.

'That's not enough for me,' she said. 'I have a job to do now, a job that is bigger than what we have. The only way I can stay alive is to only focus on that,' she said, her lower lip wobbling slightly. 'Let's call it what it is; we're spies. Like you said, what sort of future would there be for us?'

Nikita wished he could walk out, but he needed to finish dressing and knew he was incapable of doing it either quickly or gracefully.

'Say something,' she implored.

'I think you've said it all,' he answered shortly. 'I'll be seeing you, Agent Nightshade,' he said and began pulling on the suit trousers, now feeling self-conscious at his state of undress.

Elysia moved towards him. 'Let me help you,' she said.

'I'll be seeing you,' Nikita repeated, gritting his teeth and tugging the trousers over his bandaged foot. He lurched to his feet and began pulling on the suit jacket and ignoring the screaming from his back. He wanted Elysia to remember him in a sharp suit rather than floundering around with his trousers around his ankles.

When he turned around, Elysia was gone.

CHAPTER 16

Ernst Schleicher stood at the window of his office at the Stasi headquarters in Berlin-Lichtenberg and stared into the middle distance, taking nothing in other than the words of his lieutenant, Gerhard Schenke, who was in the process of detailing the escape of the prisoner from their interrogation facility.

'This is a problem for me, Schenke,' Schleicher said, turning to face the man sitting in front of his desk, who was almost cowering now he had finished delivering the news of Nikita's escape.

'Yes sir,' he replied feebly.

'And a problem for me is very much a problem for you,' he continued, taking a seat at his desk. Like so many lieutenants who had come and gone, Schenke had the near-religious fervour of one dedicated to the cause but had the total inability to see the bigger picture. 'What of our other prisoner?'

'He is still in the facility. As requested, he has been kept alive but nicely malleable. I don't think he will be any further risk to the state.'

'And are those overseeing him aware of his identity?'

'No, to them, he is just another dissident.'

'Then you have at least not failed in one of your tasks. However, you did fail in your other.' Schleicher picked up the phone on his desk and simply said, 'Send him in.'

A burly man with a shaven head came in. Schenke turned to see the man who entered and smiled at him, 'Leonard, good to see—' the lieutenant was cut off in mid-flow as the large man walked up to him and, without blinking, covered his mouth with a rag. Schenke's eyes gave a terrified look and then a look of realisation, a realisation that he had been betrayed by the cause he had utterly dedicated himself to. Then, unable to resist, he inhaled and fell silent.

Schleicher picked up his phone and dialled a familiar number, holding up a hand to Leonard and instructing him to stay put. 'What are the names of the officers working with prisoner, ah' - he checked a form in front of him - '511312?'

The voice at the other end gave him three names, which Schleicher jotted down on a Post-it in front of him. He passed it to Leonard, drew his finger across his neck and then shooed the man with a dismissive wave of his hand, swivelling his chair to the side so he didn't have to see his former lieutenant be dragged away. There could be no loose ends for this. Nobody could so much as suspect the truth. The only anomaly now was Allochka.

***

The large quantity of Scotch he had consumed was doing little more than take the edge off the pain zigzagging its way through Nikita's body, but it did at least ward off the cold. He had imbibed what remained in the decanter in Curbishley's secret cupboard and had no intention of stopping there. He wanted to forget. He wanted to not think about Elysia. More than anything, he wanted to go back to before he had known her. But then the thought of losing the memories they had shared caused him to doubt that, too. He cursed the KGB. For all the years of training he had been through, he had learned how to attract, to seduce, and been told to never get too close. But never once had they taught him how to cope with what happens if you made a mistake or if you *did* get too close.

He walked down a quiet West Berlin street and threw the empty bottle of whisky to the floor, enjoying the destructive smash of glass as it hit the tarmac. As he moved, and as he began to get angrier at the situation he found himself in, he found that his body began to loosen. The padding Bothwell-Monro had wrapped around his foot and the smart, well-made shoes he'd provided did much to cushion the pain, and his back felt like it was benefiting from being up and about. He rolled his shoulders under the thick, wool-blend overcoat and glared at anyone who walked past, almost daring them to start a fight. He found not caring quite liberating; he was used to having to make himself the quiet, apologetic Black man so as not to make any nervous white folk feel threatened by someone of colour with so much as a raised voice.

As he walked past a phone box, he impulsively decided to check in with one of his many bosses, this time the CIA. The receptionist directed him to a nearby hotel where there was a secure line. The hotel was a grand affair, with a large, airy reception area that was busy with people milling around and waiting in line. Nikita walked straight past them to where there were three phone booths set into the wall to the left of the front desk, and the moment he closed the door behind him in the middle one, the phone rang.

'Agent 28. We don't hear from you for two years, and now twice in the space of a week,' came the voice of CIA Deputy Director Barker.

'What can I say? I missed you, Deputy Director,' said Nikita dryly. 'Are you my handler now?'

'Hardly,' said Barker with a dismissive snort. 'But you've reported a few things that could have some fairly significant national security implications.'

'You've changed your tune, I thought you didn't trust me, were convinced I'd gone rogue, and had no interest in what I'd been sent here to do.'

'All of which may very well still be the case, so I suggest you remember who you're talking to, show some respect and give me whatever intel it is you have to share.'

'You don't need me to tell you that the entire Eastern Bloc is on the verge of revolt at the moment. There are a lot of nerves about, in East Berlin. Since I last spoke to you, I've been attacked by a Stasi military unit, seen a director of the East German Police Force, who not only fed me what was, apparently unknowingly, a deliberately false trail for an Afghan bomber but also has definite ties to the Soviet Union, and has been taken and presumably killed by the Stasi.'

'My my, you have been busy,' said Barker, almost sounding impressed.

'Oh, there is more, mein führer,' Nikita said, no longer caring what Barker thought of him. Perhaps it was the whisky, but he found he no longer cared about very much at all.

'Thin ice, Agent 28. I'm not above pulling you in.'

'Go for it,' Nikita said with a shrug. 'In fact, please do pull me out of this hellhole. But you'll want to hear this next part first.'

'Go on.'

'I also learned that the seemingly unimpeachable servant of communism, Ernst Schleicher, is in cahoots with an Afghan warlord to ship heroin into East Germany, and they're also working together on the bomb. I didn't get too much more information than that, though, as I was then captured, taken to a secure facility, and brutally tortured,' Nikita said buoyantly, working hard not to slur his words.

'And what did you tell them?' Barker asked sharply.

'I'm fine, thanks for asking. Well, not fine, I'm in excruciating amounts of p—'

'28!' shouted Barker, losing his temper.

'I didn't tell them a damn thing,' Nikita retorted. 'I was able to take out the two guys torturing me and escaped, just about,' he finished. 'They were more interested in causing pain than in extracting any information. They'll know I'm some sort of agent, but I'm pretty sure they don't know for whom,' Nikita said, deliberately leaving out some key information.

Barker was silent for a moment as he tried to process what Nikita was telling him. 'This bomb, you got any further with it?' he asked, breaking his reverie.

'No, only that it's happening, and Schleicher is sourcing a bomber for Al-Zalmay.'

'I'm finding this Schleicher line of intel pretty hard to believe. The man *is* the Stasi. Him turning against the cause doesn't make any sense.'

'It would if you were here. It's like rats jumping from a drowning ship. People are manoeuvring for life after the Iron Curtain. You must have seen the news. East Berlin is right on the brink, and if it falls, so will the rest of the Eastern Bloc.'

'Yes, of course. But *Schleicher?*' exclaimed Barker. 'I would have thought the only way for him to stay alive would be to head east to Moscow. I wouldn't be surprised if he was lynched if the wall comes down.'

'I get the feeling people are more interested in their freedom than they are in lynching.'

'The lynching will come, believe me, it always comes sooner or later in these situations, but then I suppose you'd know about lynchings, wouldn't you. One way or the other, 28, you've found yourself right in the heart of the action. Our analysts will investigate your intel.'

'That's it?' said Nikita furiously. 'You're asking an awful lot of me here, and in return, all I'm getting is some casual racism. Any instructions? Some support or advice?'

'Stay alive,' said Barker simply, and the line went dead.

Nikita slammed the phone back into the holder and leaned his head against the cold metal, breathing deeply with his eyes closed. Between the CIA, who didn't seem to care if he, or the people of East Berlin, lived or died, and the KGB, who seemed to be actively overlooking the Stasi trying to kill him, the blackmailing British were starting to look quite warm and friendly. He had never felt so lonely. More than anything, he wished he could be in Cuba with his father and his little sister Milena. He hadn't seen them since the death of his mother in Siberia, when he had negotiated with Denisov for them to be sent to the much more pleasant ally, Cuba, in exchange for him going to Afghanistan. He sighed. Even as far away as Cuba, they wouldn't be safe if he abandoned his mission.

The thought brought him back to his senses a little, and he slapped his face hard. 'Toughen up, Niki, you're getting soft,' he said harshly to himself. He gave himself another slap, doubly hard this time. 'No more emotions, just finish the fucking job.' He clenched his fists and his teeth, bristling with a new determination to get it done and get the hell out of Berlin.

First stop, Schleicher, he thought to himself.

CHAPTER 17

Nikita knew he could no longer afford to cross the wall via a checkpoint, so he had been forced to return via Elysia's hair-raising underground train route, something he had been keen to avoid doing again. It had the unfortunate effect of both sobering him up and tearing the freshly formed scab on his back, neither of which were things he wanted right now. As he walked back along Eberswalder Straße, he could feel his shirt getting sticky from the seeping wound, and his head began to throb, not helped by the low autumn sun that had appeared in the early afternoon and forced him to squint.

It wasn't until he had been walking for perhaps ten minutes that he began to absorb that something felt different from when he had last been here a few days ago. Back then, the streets were quiet, people were walking with their heads down, and front doors were firmly closed. But now, there was an energy present on the streets that Nikita had not experienced in East Berlin before. People were standing, doors open, chatting with neighbours, groups of people were conversing on street corners, and Nikita even heard the sound of laughter, which had been a rare commodity during his time in Berlin. It felt as if the city was exhaling slowly after a long, deep breath. For a moment, Nikita remembered the words of the Sam Cooke song he had heard days before. The words that told him it had been a long time coming, but that change was on its way, and how apt it felt to the people of this city. But then he remembered the beating he had taken in the bar, and the real meaning of the song came flooding back.

As he walked, for the first time, Nikita felt like the people here were more interested in each other than they were in ogling him. He found it liberating and helpful as he wanted now more than ever to operate unnoticed. He strode purposefully down the road, and it turned into Husemannstraße. He heard the sound of a tram rattling along from behind him and jogged to the Husemannstraße stop ahead of him, just reaching it as the old tram rattled to a stop. What East Berlin had lost in the U-Bahn when the wall went up, it had made up for with its tram system, which it had largely kept at the expense of the western side of the city. The tram was busy, with no seats available, forcing Nikita to be the only passenger standing, which made it impossible for him to be invisible as all eyes turned on him, some out of curiosity, others with undisguised distaste. He turned to face the foggy glass door, ignoring the other passengers, and watched as the city passed by, the high old buildings on one side, the huge green of Volkspark Friedrichshain on the other. The tram ground to a stop at the junction with Landsberger Allee, and Nikita disembarked with several other passengers and stepped back out into the chilly Berlin afternoon. He walked over to a phone box next to a post office and dialled Moscow.

There was a series of clicks as the undoubtedly wire-tapped line connected to the Lubyanka Building in Moscow, which was the huge baroque building that served as the headquarters for the KGB.

'Da, zdravstvuyte, Lubyanka,' answered a stern female voice. Nikita always enjoyed hearing his native tongue, even if it was from the KGB building.

'This is Agent Allochka. I need to be put through to Denisov at once,' Nikita replied in Russian.

'One moment, please.'

Nikita was put on hold for what felt like an age as the coins he had quickly began to diminish. Eventually, the flat, reedy voice that he had known for years came to the line.

'Is the line secure?' he asked.

'Almost certainly not. Nowhere is secure in East Berlin,' Nikita replied, 'but I don't think getting the

Stasi to strike the call from their records would be any problem for you.'

'This is beyond amateur. If you were in Moscow, I would have you shot,' Denisov admonished.

'Or, you know, send me on an insane mission to East Berlin and let the Stasi wolves have me...' countered Nikita, leaving it hanging.

'What?' snapped Denisov, sounding convincingly in the dark.

'Why am I here?' Nikita demanded.

'Yet again, you forget yourself, Allochka. This is not some third-world operation; this is the finest agency in the world. Here insubordination has unpleasant consequences.'

'Am I disposable?' Nikita retorted.

'Everyone is disposable,' wheezed the reedy voice.

'Let me rephrase. Am I to be disposed of?' Nikita asked.

'Why would I dispose of one of my most important agents?' Denisov responded. Nikita thought almost too quickly. 'What is this line of questioning? I have more important things to do than bandy words with an insubordinate chernozhopy,' spat the leader of the KGB.

Nikita slammed the phone down and took a deep breath, livid at being labelled with the hugely disparaging insult usually reserved in Russia for indigenous people from the Caucasus. This didn't feel right. Since Denisov had ascended the KGB throne, Nikita had been in his favour, more so than many other agents, yet something was different now. Denisov's whole demeanour was different, and Nikita's sixth sense was tingling with suspicion. Everything about this mission felt increasingly suspicious.

The phone started to ring, but Nikita turned and walked away.

Fifteen minutes later, Nikita stepped off another tram that had led him into the heart of the Hohenschönhausen Borough east of the city centre. He was in the epicentre of Stasi Germany now, with both the infamous Stasi prison and also their headquarters based in the region. Nikita had memorised Schleicher's itinerary, but he had a feeling that it may have changed, and he was prepared to smoke out the head of the Stasi quite literally like a fox in a hole.

He stole a woolly hat and scarf from the washing line of a ground-floor apartment and pulled the hat down low over his head. He wrapped the scarf around the bottom half of his face, walking head bowed. He then began circling the Stasi headquarters, one of the ugliest buildings he had ever seen. It sprawled out in a rectangle, with an L-shaped extension stretching off to the side. It rose up, fifteen stories of concrete bleakness as if it was paying tribute to Stalin's concrete factories that had spread across the Soviet Union throughout the twenties and thirties. Not only was it ugly and cold, it was also terrifying. The ruthless, emotionless efficiency of the Stasi was reflected in the grey uniformity of the building, and Nikita knew that was nothing compared to what went on within its walls. It took some time to make his way around the entire complex without arousing any suspicion, and with no obvious entry point, Nikita decided, perhaps egged on by the whisky still making its way through his veins, that in this case, attack was the best form of defence. This wasn't Estonia, and he was feeling impatient to get things done.

He discarded the hat and scarf, drew himself up to his full height, and checked his reflection in a car wing mirror, ensuring he was clean and looked the part he was about to play.

With that, he marched confidently up the main steps of the building and into the main entrance. The hall he entered was as brutalist as it had looked from the outside but was busy with people milling about. He strode up to the main desk, which sat beneath a large black and white sign announcing that it was the Ministry for State Security and nudged a young man out of the way.

'I am from the Angolan delegation. Schmidt is expecting me,' he said loudly in English, in his best effort with a vaguely African accent, causing some to look around at him curiously. Angola had been a socialist state since 1975, and Nikita fervently hoped they had some relationship with East Germany.

The mousy-looking German woman on the desk looked terrified at the tall presence looming threateningly over her. 'Your name?' she squeaked.

'Mafula de Sousa. I am here on behalf of the ambassador,' he said, sounding both irritated and proud, unbuttoning his coat and looking resplendent in his suit.

The meek receptionist flicked through the papers in front of her and, after clearly not finding his name and looking despondent at the thought of having to report it back to Nikita, checked them again. Eventually, she gave in. 'I am very sorry, Herr De Sousa, but I do not have any record of your visit.'

'What is this? I have travelled a long way for this meeting with Schmidt, and this is the welcome I get. Where is his office? I will reprimand him myself.'

'Can I see your papers, please?' asked the receptionist, sliding lower and lower into her chair.

'My papers?' roared Nikita. 'What insult is this? Where is Schmidt?' he demanded. When the receptionist didn't answer, he started calling out his name loudly, praying to God that there was a Schmidt in the building, having just picked the most common surname he knew of. People were openly staring at him now with undisguised distaste. 'WHERE IS HE?' Nikita roared at the receptionist. 'Or should I go to Ernst himself? I'm sure he would love to hear of my treatment! Is he in today? Perhaps I will pay him a visit also.'

She looked on the verge of tears, nodded, handed him a name tag on a lanyard, and pointed in the direction of a door on the far side of the hall. He turned with great arrogance and stormed off towards the door, people clearing a path for him, his eyes ablaze with apparent fury. He just about heard a voice from the front desk squeak, 'Second floor, Herr De Sousa,' and then he was through the door.

It opened to an atrium where there were several elevators and a stairwell leading off to the right. Nikita aimed straight for an open elevator door and stepped inside, mashing buttons to get the door closed before anyone else could enter, and exhaled heavily. He couldn't quite believe it had worked, and what was more, now he knew that Schleicher was in. He inspected the labels running down the elevator, identifying each floor. He doubted that Schleicher's office would be difficult to find; men like him always wanted the top floor with the best view, and it was all but confirmed by a label against the top floor saying simply *Büro des Präsidenten.*

Moving up the floors took time after mashing all the buttons, but when he reached the thirteenth floor, two below Schleicher, he stepped out. A corridor stretched out in front of him, with offices lining either side and a smattering of people moving from one room to the other. Nikita had spent time working in an office as an analyst in the CIA, and there had always been a steady drone of background noise and conversation, but that was not present here, as everyone focused only on their job; to monitor the people of East Germany and maintain the government's absolute control of its people. Nikita waited until the corridor was deserted and hurried along it, glancing into offices as he walked past them. As soon as he saw an empty office, he darted inside it and quickly closed the door.

It was a featureless, boxy room with a small window looking out onto the wall of a neighbouring section of the building. There was a neat and tidy desk with several orderly piles of papers stacked up. Nikita pulled open the drawers and found what he was looking for, a lighter shoved inside a packet of cigarettes. He grabbed some of the papers, lit them and tossed them into a small metal bin in the corner of the room, where the flames started licking higher. He fed the flames with more paper from the desk and then spread the burning paper across the desk, which looked to be made of MDF. The room quickly began to fill with white smoke. He pocketed the lighter and as much paper as he could fit inside his coat and left the room, closing the door behind him. He did the same again in an office further along the corridor.

He quickly moved back to the stairwell, hurried up the steps to the next floor, and repeated the procedure in another three offices, building as many smoky fires as he could manage. Smoke was beginning to creep into the hallway as he finally moved up to the top floor. This floor of the building was a little more lavish than the others, with some glass-fronted offices giving a glimpse of equally uniform offices to those below, but with larger, comfier chairs and some with computer screens whirring away. But Nikita paid little attention to them as he almost ran to the office at the end of the corridor. It was as big as three of the other offices pushed together and was not glass-fronted. Schleicher definitely did not want people to see what he was up to.

Nikita walked up to the door and, with a swift twist and a grunt, broke off the handle to the door, effectively locking the head of state security in his office. Nikita then hurried along the corridor and stationed himself in an empty office. No sooner had he closed the door than the fire alarm went off.

There was little protest from staff as smoke trailed into the corridor from the stairwell, and instead, there were some cries of alarm. People pulled suit jackets over their heads and began running to get out of the building as quickly as possible. Once it looked as if everyone had left, Nikita exited his office and walked back towards Schleicher's.

The door was rattling with a panicked frenzy but not budging. Nikita rapped on the door.

'Guten abend,' he said just loud enough to be heard through the door.

'Who's there? Get me out of here!' commanded Schleicher's unmistakable voice.

'It seems the handle is broken,' Nikita said calmly. He lit a piece of paper with the lighter and held it to the bottom of the door so that the smoke began to feed its way into the room. The rattling of the door became frenzied.

'Break down the door!' ordered the head of the Stasi. 'Get me out; otherwise, we'll both be trapped.'

'I can think of worse ways to go,' Nikita said slowly. 'Like being taken apart piece by piece in a torture chamber, for instance.'

The rattling stopped, and Nikita could hear Schleicher's ragged breathing; he was not a young man.

'Who are you?' he asked, sounding afraid now.

'This is the problem, isn't it, Herr Schleicher. Suggesting I've been tortured by your men doesn't really narrow it down, does it?'

'Whoever you are, you will pay a heavy price for this,' Schleicher said, recovering some of his commanding tone.

'Listen closely,' Nikita said just loud enough to be heard and almost sensed Schleicher press his ear to the door to hear. Nikita stepped back and kicked with all his might, with his uninjured foot, into the door, smashing it into Schleicher's face and sending him sprawling to the ground, with the door landing on top of him. Nikita grunted in pain, forgetting that while his foot was uninjured, his ankle still had not fully recovered from his encounter with the Stasi militia. The memory only increased his feelings towards Schleicher, and he hobbled into the room, making sure to step heavily upon the office door with the old man beneath it. Schleicher groaned, a feeble croaking sound, and Nikita slid the door off him. Up close, he looked every inch of his eighty-two years; his bald crown was surrounded by grey hair, carefully combed backwards, and his skin was a creamy grey, almost puffy texture. Blood was coming from his ear, where Nikita had slammed the door into him, and with his breathing ragged, Nikita suspected there were some broken ribs, too.

Schleicher's eyes widened slightly when he saw Nikita, but to his credit, he did not look afraid.

'Ah, the Black Russian,' he said with a sigh and pushed himself into a sitting position, confirming the broken ribs by gasping with pain and holding his side as he moved. 'I had hoped you would be captured by now.'

'The Stasi are good, but they're no KGB,' Nikita responded while screwing a silencer into the barrel of one of the guns Elysia had furnished him with from Curbishley's stores. Schleicher said nothing.

'Now, what was it that your friends in Potsdam said? Ah yes, before I begin, you should know, Mr

Schleicher, that I am very good at keeping people alive while in a maximum amount of pain,' he said, trying to mimic the nasal voice of Narrow-eyes.

Schleicher's face remained stoical. 'You seem to think you have a lot of time, Mr Allochka, but of all people in this building, I am the first that would be noticed if I do not leave when there's a fire.'

'You know what, you are absolutely right,' Nikita said and shot him in the knee. The stubby Walther PP barely made a sound as the bullet flew through the silencer and tore through the cartilage and bone of Schleicher's knee. Schleicher was clearly not wearing a silencer, however, as he let out a bloodcurdling wail. Nikita walked past him and lifted the door back into place to block out any noise from anyone coming down the corridor. He could hear the sound of sirens outside as the East German Feuerwehr came speeding towards the building.

'Did that hurt?' Nikita asked, but Schleicher only whimpered. He walked across the office to where there was a drinks cabinet. He pulled it open and was delighted to see a bottle of bourbon in there, his personal favourite developed from his time in the US.

'Good to see you continuing the theme of the rules only applying to others,' Nikita said, pulling the cork out of the bottle with his teeth and taking a long swig, enjoying the taste, which was much sweeter than the peaty Scotch he had drunk only earlier that day.

'What do you want?' cried Schleicher, his hands frantically trying to stem the bleeding from his knee.

'Well, I'm glad you asked,' Nikita said, 'because I do have one or two questions.' Nikita normally despised this sort of work, but in the case of Schleicher, he found not enjoyment but a definite absence of sympathy. 'As you pointed out, I don't really have time for the psychological decomposition that your secret police are so effective at, so I'd ask you to be cooperative; otherwise, this will get very bloody very quickly, which neither of us really wants. You seem to be playing a dangerous game; the Stasi, the USSR, MI6 and the Mujahideen. Not the most compatible list of allies.'

'You don't know a thing,' Schleicher said, spitting blood in Nikita's direction. Nikita let off another shot, this one thudding into the wall just an inch from Schleicher's head. The man's face paled even further, and his eyes grew wide in fright. Nikita noticed that he had soiled himself.

'You've murdered untold thousands over the past few decades and inflicted unimaginable terror upon your own people, all to prop up the communist regime in this country. Why would you then want to destroy it with heroin and a bomb?' Nikita asked, raising the gun threateningly again.

'It is all failing,' Schleicher said miserably. 'The wall will fall, maybe in months, maybe even in days. There will be a price on my head when it does. It only makes sense to prepare for that eventuality,' he shrugged.

'You would turn Berlin into an opium den to make a profit for the few years you have left rather than go down honourably?' Nikita asked.

'I have seen a lot of men and women die for honour,' Schleicher said. 'And where are they now? Buried underground, forgotten and useless.'

'That's one way of looking at it, I suppose,' Nikita replied. 'But tell me this, in your meeting with Al-Zalmay, you discussed that orders for a bombing had come from much higher up. Explain.'

At this, Schleicher began to cackle, a rasping sound from the lungs of a man who had spent a lifetime smoking unfiltered Soviet Bloc cigarettes. 'You're crazier than I thought if you believe I would tell you that,' Schleicher said.

'Oh, I think you'll tell me, for two reasons,' Nikita held up two fingers. 'Firstly, you are a man whose first priority is clearly self-preservation, and secondly, if you don't, I shall put away the gun and begin work with my knife,' he finished with a chilling calm.

Schleicher shook his head, remaining defiant. Nikita slowly withdrew the knife he had selected from Curbishley's weapons room from a sheath at his belt, letting the serrated edge grind off his belt buckle for extra effect. Then he strode over to Schleicher, who crumpled before he was within a metre.

'Okay! Okay!' he cried, holding his hand up, which was dripping with the blood he had been trying to stop flowing out of his knee. 'It's all Denisov!'

'What?' said Nikita, stumbling backwards slightly in shock. 'What is Denisov?'

'All of it, even more than you might think,' Schleicher said. 'He is playing both sides, just as I am, in preparation for the end, only his game has been longer in the making. Who do you think financed the Pamyat Neo-Nazi operation that attacked your family?'

'No!' cried Nikita, dropping the knife and clawing at his face, remembering how his mother had died at the hands of Vasilevsky and then recalling how, just before he had killed Vasilevsky, he had revealed that there was someone with great power who was closing in on a new Russia.

'Oh yes,' said Schleicher with a hideous grin as he saw Nikita suffer. 'He has been building ties with the Russian oligarchs who will move to own all of the oil wealth when the Union falls. They all stand to become very rich men on the back of Denisov's promises.'

'But the Afghanistan bombs—' Nikita started, talking more to himself.

'Oh yes, I know all about that too. As I said, Maxim plays both sides and plans for every outcome. If Petrenko saves the Soviet Union and turns their fortunes around, Maxim wants to be on the side with a hidden nuclear arsenal. He suspects the Union has to fall apart for a little while, but in time, if he accumulates enough wealth, power and allies, he can take it all back. This time as President. He is quite brilliant,' Schleicher added with the fevered glow of a disciple.

'And I suppose you stand to get a slice of the pie?' Nikita added.

Schleicher shrugged. He was sweating now from the exertion of talking through blood loss and pain, and he started mumbling.

'What was that?' Nikita said, getting close to Schleicher. Schleicher looked up at him and spat in his face.

'I told Maxim it was a mistake to entrust a nigger to get a job done,' he said through bloody teeth. Nikita stood up and mopped his face calmly with a hanky in Schleicher's breast pocket. Then he reached down, picked the knife off the floor and stabbed it downwards into the top of Schleicher's shoulder. It drove two inches down through his shoulder blade, and he left it in as Schleicher released a cry that would have echoed down the hallway had Nikita not shoved the hanky deep into his mouth. Once the muffled wailing had stopped, he yanked the soggy, bloody rag out.

Tears of pain were dribbling down his cheeks as he fumbled in vain to reach the handle of the knife to pull it out.

'I wouldn't recommend pulling it out,' Nikita said coldly. 'The serrations are clawed, and it's dangerously close to your brachial artery. Rupture that, and your time will be very short.'

Schleicher's hand froze where it was and then fell back to his side, and he began to sob. If Nikita hadn't known what the man had done, he would have pitied him. But he did, and so he didn't.

'Let us continue,' Nikita said. He could clearly hear the sound of people on the floor below, working against the blaze, and smoke was beginning to make its way under the door in earnest. 'Why did you break into Walter Kielhorn's apartment?'

'The man was a traitor to the cause,' grunted the Stasi chief, coughing a little as the smoke began to rise around his head.

'Was?' Nikita asked nervously. Schleicher grinned toothily in response before his eyes fluttered and began to close. Nikita gave the knife a small nudge, like changing gear in the car, and Schleicher's eyes shot back open, a silent scream on his lips.

'Why did you ransack his apartment? What were you looking for?'

'Looking for?' Schleicher replied, looking surprised. 'We are the Stasi. We do not have to look for anything. We already know everything. We are not blunt instruments like you. We practice more sophisticated art forms.'

'Subtle but no less brutal,' Nikita replied, thinking of Heidi's story of her husband. 'Then why make it so obvious you had been there?'

'You have so much to learn, but then perhaps a sub-Saharan mind is not capable of subtleties,' he said, poking the beast.

Nikita gave the knife another yank, harder this time, withdrawing it a couple of centimetres and causing a small spurt of blood to leak out around the blade. 'By all means, keep it up with the racism, Schleicher. It's no problem for me,' he said.

'Destroying the apartment has nothing to do with looking for anything. It is a message to all others who might question the regime. We *want* people to know when someone has been taken by the Stasi. We want them to know without it ever having to be said. That builds respect for the party, respect for our society and respect for the rules,' wheezed Schleicher, visibly weakening now. 'Please, I have a heart condition. I need my medication,' he pleaded, and Nikita noticed the sweat was flooding down his face now.

'Soon, Ernst, soon,' Nikita said, 'because there's one more thing you haven't answered for me. The bomb. Who is the bomber, and where will it go off,' Nikita asked firmly.

'The bomb,' said Schleicher with a soft giggle, 'it will destroy the very essence of the West and the East and forge a glorious new world,' and his eyes closed.

'The bomber; case 511312, it is one of my finer plans,' he said, and his entire body fell forward.

CHAPTER 18

Nikita leaned down and slapped him hard on the face, but to no avail. He tugged the knife out of the wound, bringing small globules of flesh with it. But as the knife left the hole, a spray of blood followed it, and blood began pumping out of the hole. Nikita cursed. He must have hit the brachial artery, after all. His teachers in Slutsk would be appalled at his imprecise work. He pressed his fingers to the slick neck of the man and felt an incredibly weak pulse. He would be dead in a matter of minutes, and the chances of revival seemed slim. Smoke was filling the room now and making Nikita's throat burn. Allowing Schleicher to die in his sleep seemed a kindness he did not deserve, but a crash in the hallway outside made his mind up for him. He lifted the broken door from the frame and peeked out into the hallway. It was billowing with smoke, and he couldn't see more than a few feet in front of him, but the sounds coming from within the smoke told him that the firefighters were heading in his direction. With a last look at the curled-up form of Schleicher on the floor, now just looking every bit like a harmless, broken old man, Nikita darted down the hall and into a glass-fronted office, closing the door behind him. He pulled the blinds just as he saw the surge of firemen charge past, hunting for Schleicher's office. Once he had seen them all go past and into Schleicher's office, he covered his face with a jacket hanging on the back of the door and ran out into the smoky hallway.

As he entered the stairwell, the smoke was even thicker and full of ash. When he looked down, he saw flames licking through the doorway of the floor below, with firefighters working to contain them. He instead ran upwards and took to the now familiar sights of the East Berlin rooftops, bursting out of the security door and breathing in the fresh air. The rooftop was deserted, with nothing upon it other than a large flagpole rising from the centre of it and the East German flag flapping in the wind. He cast his eye around for a way out or down. The central building in the complex that he stood upon was flanked by lower white-painted buildings on either side, but the drop-down to both of them was at least five metres. Normally, he would back himself to make such a jump, but with one wounded and padded foot, another sprained ankle, and the seeping wound in his back, the thought of a drop and roll filled him with dread. He squatted low, not wanting to be seen by the crowds gathered outside the building and considered his options.

Making his mind up, he made his way over to the flagpole and slowly lowered it down, hoping people on the ground were too distracted by the inferno below to notice what was happening on the rooftop. Once lowered, Nikita removed the enormous tri-colour flag of black, red and gold, with the communist hammer, compass and wreath of wheat in the centre. He bundled up the flag, which was more than two metres across and made from what felt like silky parachute nylon, and stalked his way back to the left edge of the building. He tied one end of the flag around the metal rung holding a drainpipe in place and tossed the rest over the side of the building. With barely a pause, he eased himself over the edge, gave the fabric a tug to check that the knot would hold, and abseiled his way slowly down, allowing himself to dangle there, clinging to the edge of the material. His back was protesting against being stretched out so much, but he'd more than halved the distance of the drop. He took a deep breath and let go, landing as much as he could on his sprained ankle rather than his wounded foot, and tensed it to prevent it from rolling. He landed as catlike as it was possible to, all things considered, but more importantly, he landed without any significant pain. He chanced a glance out towards the front of the building and didn't immediately notice anyone pointing or staring up at him. He moved at a squat across the lower building he was now on. It was completely flat and stretched about 200 yards in front of him before the building took a sharp right turn where it worked its way around, forming a half-square. It contained a large outdoor area hidden from the world outside that was currently full of disgruntled and chilly Stasi workers waiting for the fire to be put out. Again, Nikita found it difficult to pity any of the secret police for having to live with a little cold for an hour or two.

He moved along the building, continuing to crouch down, keeping as out of sight as possible, and looking for a way off the roof. He could see right across the long tail of the building's rooftop and could not see any door at all, but as he reached the first corner, he spotted a trapdoor built into the felt of the roof. He pulled on the rusty metal ring and eased open the hatch, peering inside. It opened into a panelled-off ceiling, which Nikita imagined would run above a large, open office. There were metal struts laid across, one of which he landed softly on top of. He dug his fingernails under one of the ceiling panels, prised it up a fraction, and saw that his suspicions had been correct; it was a long but narrow, open-plan office. It was currently empty, with all of the staff having been vacated by the fire alarm, but the fire had not yet reached this far, and Nikita wasted no time in dropping down to the floor. He found an umbrella leaning against someone's desk and used it to nudge the panel back into place, but was more than happy to leave the trap door on the roof open and wondered how cold and damp the office would get before someone figured it out.

The office was dingy and sterile looking, with strip lighting and metal filing cabinets, and had succeeded in bringing the uniform greyness of the Soviet Bloc inside. He hurried through the office, searching for an exit, but as he left the room and found himself in another corridor, he looked behind him and saw there was a sign next to the door labelling it the 'Arbeitsgruppe S- Politische Spionageabwehr und Personalverwaltung'. *Work Group S – Political Counterintelligence and Personnel Administration.*' Nikita paused and looked around him quickly. There was no one around, but he couldn't have long; this building was unlikely to be affected by the blaze in the adjacent one. He darted back in and, searching around, found a filing cabinet marked 'Verhaftungen'. *Arrests.* He yanked it open and began rifling through but did not find anything in there for Kielhorn. He was about to close it but then had another thought and flicked through the letter L this time. He found what he was looking for, pulled out the thin envelope of papers and pocketed it. Then the fire alarm suddenly stopped, and he clearly heard the sounds of doors opening and the trudge of hundreds of footsteps as they hurried indoors from the cold. He grabbed a notepad and pen from a desk and jogged as best as he could on his foot, which was increasingly complaining as the padding gradually lost its cushioning, and hid in a toilet cubicle. He took the opportunity to rest his legs and back as he heard men coming and going in the bathroom, many of them discussing how cold they were and how they hoped whoever had caused the fire would be punished. Forgiveness did not seem to enter the lexicon of the Ministry for State Security.

Once he was confident that the building was busy and everyone was back at work, Nikita tucked in his shirt, did up the button on his suit jacket and walked back out into the corridor. People were too distracted to pay him much heed as he walked through the building, but he held his notepad in front of him, jotting down nothing in particular as he walked, and looked as busy as he could. He continued this way until he was out through an exit and onto the street outside. He pulled his coat tightly around him as the sky started to darken, and the sun sat low above the surrounding buildings. There was no way he could return to his own apartment now, and it was impossible to know if Rosin could be trusted, but it seemed unlikely given that he reported to Denisov.

Denisov.

Nikita wanted to punch a wall in frustration and fury at the man who had cost him so much, using him only as a pawn in a great game. He almost wished Colonel Klitchkov, Denisov's crazy predecessor who had forced him to join the KGB as a fifteen-year-old, was still alive; he would tear Denisov limb from limb for such treachery against his beloved Mother Russia.

Mother Russia, the empire that had taken his own mother from him despite promising to protect her.

The KGB, the agency he had sworn allegiance to, but that now worked to betray him.

Denisov, the leader who had gained his trust, was Nikita's only constant, a traitor only invested in his own pockets and a lust for power.

It all seemed so far-fetched, so unlikely. But the world of slim chances, outrageous espionage and backstabbing was the one Nikita had lived in for years. Yet again, Nikita desperately wanted a drink; he just wanted to forget it all and switch his mind off for a little while.

'Not yet, Niki,' he muttered to himself as the streetlights flickered on overhead. The only thing that mattered now, for the very first time in his life, was what *he* wanted. There could be no going back to the Soviet Union, at least not while Denisov remained as head of the KGB and as such an important member of the Politburo. Nikita felt a momentary pang at the thought that he might never set foot in the only country he had ever called home. It had been a cruel place for him, but the only one he had ever known, the only place to speak his first language. *Where do I belong?* he thought to himself as he trudged back towards the centre of East Berlin, keen to avoid the tram now.

The blaze at the Stasi HQ and the death of Ernst Schleicher would have everyone on high alert, and he attracted enough attention on public transport at the best of times, let alone coming from the direction of such an incident.

Eventually, after walking for over an hour, he found that he had walked straight through the city and to the Brandenburg Gate. The great sandstone arch, which stood within the restricted area between the two realms, could be truly visited by no one, standing now as a symbol of a mighty nation fallen, a country divided. East German military guarded the area, marching back and forth, posturing to any who might dare to try and cross, to join the untold number who had died trying. It caused Nikita to think of Kielhorn, of the family he had lost to the wall. Nikita found now that he wanted the wall to come down, wanted an end to communism and everything it had asked of him, but whatever life might look like for him now, whatever the future held, he would not do it with the blood of thousands on his hands.

The bomb had to be stopped.

It was dark now, but as Nikita looked up at the Brandenburg gate, he knew what he had to do but had no idea how to do it.

***

Nikita walked that night until his foot was bleeding, and his ankle was swollen as he followed the entire twenty-seven miles of the Berlin Wall. As the night wore on, he encountered more and more angry youths, heads covered with balaclavas and scarves, throwing bottles at the wall and the guards on top of them. More than once, Nikita heard the sound of gunfire echoing from the restricted zone as people were drawn to the wall and the sense that they were on the cusp of freedom. There was talk that the borders of East Germany were becoming looser, with people finding their way through to Hungary, Czechoslovakia and beyond, and people in East Berlin were beginning to believe that they may, one day soon, find their way back to families, friends and loved ones from whom they had been separated for almost thirty years. But during his time in Berlin, Nikita had never seen the wall so heavily armed, and he could not imagine that Soviet General Secretary Petrenko would allow the wall to tumble as easily as the people dreamt. But for all of his inspection of the wall, he saw no signs of any bomb, no Afghans or noticeably suspicious people. Nothing was triggering his trusted sixth sense, and that in itself made him very nervous.

As false dawn lightened the skies a fraction, Nikita entered a worker's café already full of tradesmen and ordered a large pot of coffee and a fried egg sandwich, which was the only food they had available. A distant clock was chiming 6 a.m., and a TV in the corner crackled into life with the first programme of the day; the morning news. The headline story was the breaking news of Ernst Schleicher's death and the fire at the Ministry of State Security. At first, nobody in the café was paying much attention, but a wave of shushing spread through the room, and all eyes turned on the small television mounted on a bracket in the top corner of the room alongside the counter. Then, starting with a low rumble, a crescendo of noise began to build throughout the room into a roar, a roar that Nikita felt like he could hear spreading across the city as people woke up. Nikita followed the news as best he could over the din and saw that the death was being described as 'suspicious' but that no further details had yet been released. The jubilation on the faces of the men in the café was unfiltered, and many started throwing their fried eggs at the ceiling like Frisbees and grabbing each other into bear hugs. Nikita just sat and drank his coffee, feeling the warmth and strength return to his limbs. He chewed his way through the egg, and he could not condone the others for throwing theirs away. It was hard and thick with grease but nonetheless gave him some sustenance.

Over the next hour, the gloomy skies were lit up by fireworks, and the grey morning was brightened by the sounds of cheering as giddy East Berliners celebrated the death of the tyrant who had controlled their lives with an iron fist, the man who had invented zersetzung torture, the man who had turned the people of East Germany against each other. Nikita wanted to urge them to be cautious, to remind them that no doubt an equally evil replacement would quickly step in to fill Schleicher's shoes, but in a city where little joy had been felt for decades, he couldn't bring himself to do anything to disturb that. But Schleicher still could disturb it from beyond the grave with his plans for a bomb which, as far as Nikita was aware, remained in place. The bomb that would, as Schleicher had described it, 'destroy the very essence of the West and the East.'

Was Bedar Al-Zalmay still in the country? The questions became riddles as he wrestled with them and made his head hurt. He shook with frustration at how impotent he felt with nothing to go on and a growing sense of urgency building within him. With so much change and uncertainty, the day of the bombing had to be imminent. It was the match that could set fire to an entire nation.

The day was wearing on, and with no other ideas, Nikita decided to return to Kielhorn's apartment and see if there was any other information on Schleicher or any other Afghan movements that he had there, though he knew the likelihood was slim to nought.

Although it seemed unlikely that the apartment would still be monitored now that Kielhorn was gone and Schleicher dead, Nikita felt compelled to be cautious and entered via his initial route from the rooftop.

He slid open the balcony door and was about to slide it shut behind him when he froze. Something was very wrong.

CHAPTER 19

Nikita stepped inside but did not pull the balcony door behind him and stood completely still, listening and taking everything in. The apartment remained in the same upturned state that he had left it in, but there was one key difference; the sound of voices coming from the direction of the study.

Nikita strained his ears but couldn't hear anything clearly, just the rumble and murmur of indistinct voices. He moved noiselessly into the kitchen area, his head cocked and his breathing silent. He continued and paused with his back to the wall next to the doorway, which was parallel to the room where the voices were coming from. He could hear them clearly now and stifled a gasp in shock as it became clear who they were.

The voices were talking in rapid Pashto, a language Nikita was all too familiar with from his time in Afghanistan. But while he was conversational, he stood no chance of interpreting it at the speed the two men were firing back and forth. There was a sharp word from the voice of a woman, and both of the men suddenly fell silent. The chatter was replaced by the tinkling sound of metal, like nails bouncing off one another.

Nikita hurried back into the kitchen and silently opened drawers, looking for something reflective to help him spy on the occupants of the room. He found an old pocket watch that was broken, but on one side was a small mirror. It would have to do.

He padded back to the door and, moving tentatively, lifted the mirror in front of him and slanted it slightly to try and see around the door frame and back down the other side of the wall. As he eased it forward, the room next to him came partially into focus, half blocked by the door frame. He moved the mirror back and forth to take in the room. He saw Bedar Al-Zalmay standing there, along with his bodyguard and the woman Rapa, who was lounging in the office chair and had removed the full-body niqab in favour of a hijab which just covered her hair and was wearing the baggy trousers typical of Afghan women. These were of a bright turquoise colour, but she had succumbed to a German winter cardigan on her top half, and Nikita noticed now that the heat had been turned up full in the apartment. He couldn't blame them. After a life spent in the scorching heat of Eastern Afghanistan, Berlin in November must feel akin to the Arctic for them. Nikita continued his scan of the room and then suddenly froze and whipped his hand back, breathing heavily.

No, it couldn't be.

He pushed his hand back out to take another look and make sure he had seen another man in the room. Surely not. He had to be sure.

As he did, the Afghan warlord's henchman looked directly at the glass. He shouted out in Pashto, and a gunshot hit the doorframe where Nikita's hand had been just a split second before.

Nikita rolled back along the wall and withdrew his Walther pistol, but shots then started firing through the wall itself. One bullet missed Nikita's head by inches as the wall revealed itself to be nothing more than a plasterboard dividing wall, and Nikita leapt forward into the entrance hall, rolling up and turning to fire himself. The people in the study all jumped out of sight, but potshots continued to fire out towards Nikita, keeping him at bay. He heard the muffled sounds of shouts between them as they began to organise themselves, and Nikita knew he needed to move quickly before they devised a plan. He ran across the doorway, dodging more loosely fired shots, and into the bathroom adjacent to the study. Without pausing, he began firing through the wall there, but this time, he was unlucky, as this wall proved to be a brick supporting wall, and the bullets that didn't lodge themselves in the wall dangerously ricocheted back, causing him to fall to the floor. This was all the chance that the Afghans needed, as sensing his hesitation, the bodyguard and, to his surprise, Bedar Al-Zalmay himself charged out of the room, guns aloft. Nikita rolled himself into the bath and shoved the door closed as holes began to appear in the door. He was trapped.

He knew he was low on bullets and frantically looked around for something to use as a weapon and found nothing. Some plastic disposable razors were the only thing with a sharp edge, and he was certain he would die with them laughing at him if he brandished one of those. Nikita could feel his heart racing in his chest, frantically trying to get in a lifetime of beats before it would all inevitably end once they came through the door. His eyes fell upon a medicine cabinet, and with nothing left to lose, he jumped out of the bath, risking a bullet finding him, and ripped open the cabinet. Inside, there was an array of soaps and shaving foams and a half-used bottle of disinfectant. Whoever had tidied up the apartment had also put the lighter and cigarettes that Kielhorn had been enjoying when they had taken him into the cabinet. Nikita grabbed them and jumped back into the bath. He unscrewed the cap of the disinfectant and shoved a wad of toilet paper into the top, dousing it well with the toxic liquid. Then he fired the lighter, and it didn't work. He tried it again and had no success. He shook it furiously and rolled his thumb across it over and over, and finally, with a sigh of relief, he saw a flame flicker into life. He pressed it against the toilet paper, and it immediately caught fire. The flames jumped up as the fire met the disinfectant. At that moment, the door burst open as it was kicked down by a strong heel. Without looking at who was coming, Nikita threw the bottle as forcefully as he could in their direction. There was a cry of surprise and then a roar as the bottle erupted into a mini firebomb. Nikita did not wait to see if the men had been incapacitated, intent on using his one small window of opportunity to make his escape.

He ripped away the shower curtain, using it to protect him from the blaze, and charged out of the bathroom. The plastic shower curtain immediately began to melt from the wall of heat, and he was forced to discard it as an Afghan Pulwar Sword came swinging down and the needle-sharp blade would have beheaded Nikita had he not allowed himself to fall backwards. He felt pain lance through his back as he landed heavily on his wound, but he didn't stop to think about it, instead rolling sideways and propelling himself at the legs of the man wielding the sword. The man stumbled backwards, which gave Nikita the chance to climb to his feet, but no sooner had he done so than the man, who Nikita saw now was Al-Zalmay, swiped out with the slender, curved Afghan sword. Nikita swayed to avoid it, but then the bodyguard crashed into him sideways, crunching him against the wall. Nikita felt the impact radiate through his shoulder and drive the wind out of him, forcing his mouth open in a silent scream of agony. Then the bodyguard was above him, holding two Khyber knives, twelve and a half inches of long, sharpened steel which tapered down to a needle-like tip, designed to pierce armour and plunge deeply beyond.

He waved the knives in a fighting stance Nikita had seen first-hand from the Mujahideen in the mountains of Afghanistan and had also seen first-hand the gruesome results of those who had tried to take them on. And then he struck. But Nikita was no novice fighter and had spent long years of KGB training perfecting the art of Combat Sambo Spetsnaz, or Systema, the Soviet martial art that focuses on hand-to-hand combat, weapon disarmament and, more than anything, maintaining a zen-like calm to turn an attacker's strike against him, coolly and ruthlessly. Nikita recalled Denisov teaching it to him, spittle flying from his lips as he roared at Nikita and his comrades. *'Discard ego, fear and tension. They can only become weapons of the enemy. Feel nothing, make them feel everything.'* Nikita took a deep breath, releasing any emotion, and allowed the Afghan warrior to come at him. As he entered Nikita's reach, Nikita sidestepped a swing of one knife, swiped with the other, and used his opponent's momentum against him, stepping swiftly behind him before he knew what had happened and then smashing his face into the wall. Al-Zalmay stepped forward and swung his sword, and Nikita held firmly onto the dazed bodyguard and allowed him to take the lash of the blade into his arm. He cried out as Al-Zalmay's eyes opened in alarm, and he stepped back. Nikita swung the bodyguard at him with a clench and release of his muscles, throwing him with all his might at Al-Zalmay. Out of the corner of his eye, he could see movement in the study to his left, but he kept his mind focused on the battle before him. Success did not lie in fighting a battle on two fronts. *Do what is logical*, his dead-eyed mind told him. For the first time in days, he felt KGB, he felt Soviet, he felt like the unstoppable weapon he had been trained to be.

As the two men untangled themselves, Nikita marched forward towards them. He picked up a Khyber knife that had fallen to the floor and threw it with all his might at Al-Zalmay, but his wounded bodyguard managed to parry it away with the remaining knife that he held, and he pulled Al-Zalmay to his feet. They behaved less like master and bodyguard and more like friends, Nikita noticed curiously but did not stop to question their relationship as he plunged mercilessly onwards. A roundhouse kick quickly disarmed the bodyguard of his remaining knife, and then Nikita landed a sweeping punch heavily on the arm wound the bodyguard's leader had given him. Blood was already soaking the bodyguard's hessian shirt, and he cried out in pain, falling into Al-Zalmay. Nikita heard movement behind him and flicked a glance behind him to see the woman looking terrified at what was unfolding before her. But Nikita's glance away was all the time that Al-Zalmay needed as he darted forward to make a killer blow, which would have run Nikita right through if it had landed true. But Nikita twisted just enough that it only cut his side. He grimaced but pushed his arm to his side, holding the sword in place and pulling Al-Zalmay towards him. The curved weapon cut in just above his hip, and he could feel it squeezing droplets of blood down his belly and back, but he ignored the pain and stared into the eyes of the man who had taken control of the Afghan resistance. Up close, he could see his hair was greying, both from the strands of hair showing beneath his turban and in his beard, while underneath the beard, his skin was pockmarked with the scars of long-gone teenage acne. He glared at Nikita with hatred in his eyes.

'You cannot undo what has already been done,' he grunted in English. Nikita was aware of the sound of the front door opening and closing and knew with certainty that the other person who had been in the room, the person he could still not believe was there, had just left but could not take his eyes away from Al-Zalmay. From behind Al-Zalmay rose the bodyguard, holding his knife aloft and his eyes glowing with the bloodthirst of battle.

Nikita closed his eyes, trying to detach himself from the pain of the metal grinding into his side. He opened them as the bodyguard stabbed down at Nikita's neck with the knife, and Nikita, with a roar of pain that he could not pretend he did not feel, pulled Al-Zalmay and the sword further into him. Unable to stop the momentum of his powerful attack, the bodyguard could not prevent himself from driving the knife straight down into the shoulder blade of his leader. Al-Zalmay screamed, and Nikita threw him to the floor, the sword sliding out of his side with him. Then, in one fluid motion, Nikita drew his Walther and shot the bodyguard, who was looking at Al-Zalmay in horror, in the heart. He tried to empty the magazine into the bodyguard to, as he had been trained, make absolutely sure but found that it had been his last bullet. He reprimanded himself for the rare mistake of losing count of his bullets, another error that would have earned him a severe punishment during his training.

The bodyguard staggered for a moment, looking up at the woman behind Nikita and reaching out for her before falling back. Nikita heard him gurgling slightly from the floor, repeating the word, 'Rahbar, rahbar.' *Leader, leader.* Loyal to Al-Zalmay to his final breath.

Al-Zalmay groaned on the floor, pulling the long knife out of his shoulder, and with a spit to the floor, stood up to face Nikita, fury in his eyes. Nikita readied himself in a fighting stance.

'Tell me your plan for the bomb,' Nikita shouted at him. Al-Zalmay only spat at the ground again.

'I would sooner die than tell a Russian dog anything,' he cried. 'You killed my mother, my father, and,' his voice caught for a moment with emotion, 'my children, my little children,' he cried, tears in his eyes. 'For what? Another country trying and failing to invade Afghanistan and failing but leaving behind a trail of ruin and destruction. We will have our revenge,' he finished.

'I do not deny it. I have the blood of many Afghans on my hands,' Nikita said. 'But I have never harmed a child, never ordered such war crimes. I am no longer a Russian. I have left them, I think, forever. But I will not stand by and allow a bomb to kill more innocent people, more children,' Nikita said.

'Once a Russian cockroach, always a Russian cockroach,' the man said, spitting once more.

'Let us save them all, save the innocents, and then we can work together,' Nikita pleaded. He noticed Al-Zalmay's eyes begin to soften, and he took half a step backwards. He nodded gently and looked over at the woman. And then his eyes widened in shock. There was there was a sharp crack of gunfire, and Al-Zalmay fell to the floor, dead with a bullet wound through his temple.

Nikita raised his hands in surrender as the woman, shaking, held a gun out in front of her. Her eyes were wide in terror as she kept looking from Nikita and down at the body of Al-Zalmay below her.

'It's okay,' Nikita said gently in Pashto, 'just lower the gun.'

'You'll kill me!' she stuttered.

'I need to see if I can get any answers from the bodyguard if he still lives,' Nikita said, 'and I can't do that if you might shoot me at any moment.'

The woman fired the gun again, this time hitting the bodyguard on the floor, who choked slightly and fell silent. She then proceeded to empty her entire magazine into the two dead men, and Nikita leapt out of the way, as her terror seemed to turn into fury as she fired at her two companions again and again.

The silence was total when the relentless explosions of the pistol were replaced by the empty click of the chamber, and the room reeked of cordite and blood. Nikita walked over to the woman now and moved to lift the gun from her hands, but instead, she threw it with all her might at Al-Zalmay and yelled something in Pashto that Nikita did not recognise but was left in no doubt that it was an insult. Then she fell sobbing into Nikita's arms.

Nikita had no time for sensitivity. 'Why did you kill them?' he asked sharply, pushing her back and holding her in place with his hands on her shoulders. 'Why did you kill your friends?'

'Friends!' she exclaimed and spat in the direction of her fallen comrades. 'I am just his silent wife, just required to follow him everywhere. And the other one? He was just an idiot who would belittle me and talk to me like I was not even human.'

'I needed at least one of them alive,' Nikita said, wanting to shake her. He marched into the study where they had been only minutes ago before the fight began. There were all the equipment and makings for a bomb there, but any sign of a bomb was conspicuously absent. Nikita's heart began to race, and he charged back to the woman, who was shaking.

'Where did he go?' Nikita said, grabbing the woman by the shoulders once more, as much to keep her standing as anything as she looked on the point of collapse. When she didn't respond, he forced her face up to look at him. He saw now how striking her face was, with pale grey eyes and unblemished skin, albeit with a mouth that seemed to rest in a scowl, like she'd smelled something unpleasant. She was young, much younger than the two men she had accompanied, not much older than Nikita himself. He repeated his question, and when she looked nonplussed, he took a deep breath and asked the question he had been avoiding.

'Where did Walther Kielhorn go with the bomb?'

CHAPTER 20

The woman looked like she was going into shock, and her mouth was opening and closing, but no sound was coming out. Nikita felt panic rising inside him now and was struggling to contain his frustration with the woman.

'Listen, it's Rapa, isn't it?' Nikita said gently, remembering the name he had heard her say when meeting Schleicher in Rostock.

She looked up at him but didn't say anything. 'Rapa, that man who was here with you, the man who owns this apartment, he has a bomb that is going to kill maybe thousands of people. I must stop it, but I need to know where Kielhorn is going?'

'I... I do not know of such things,' she stammered, 'they never told me their plans.'

'But you were here with them. You saw them making the bomb. You must know something!' Nikita exclaimed. *You can't be a total idiot*, was what he wanted to scream at her, finding it impossible to understand how she could have paid so little attention to what was going on in front of her. But then he saw the fear on her face, the fear she had lived with. She had learned only to be silent, only to do as she was told.

'He... the white man... he was very quiet. I do not think he is well,' she said.

'But you don't know where he went?' Nikita said.

She shrugged, calming down slightly. 'All I know is that the plans were very thorough. If he is fortunate, he will go through the gate to paradise,' she said. She walked into the study and collapsed in the office chair, looking small and lost. She leant forward onto the desk and began sobbing.

Nikita almost howled in frustration but had no time to lose. He picked up the Khyber knives and pushed them into his inside pocket. He searched through the drawers in Kielhorn's office and found a spare magazine for his Walther PPK. He rammed it in, sliding it back to click the first bullet into place so that it would be ready to fire. KGB weapons were always ready to fire.

He looked up at Rapa. 'Stay here. I will be back,' he said curtly. She lifted her head up from the table, but Nikita was already gone.

Nikita hurtled down the steps of the old building, through the lobby and past the alarmed security guard. The time to worry about being seen was past. He could hear the sirens of approaching police cars who had come to investigate the reports of gunfire, but he would be long gone by the time they arrived, and the authorities were already more than aware of who he was by this point.

He ran along the street, looking everywhere for some sign of Kielhorn, but knowing that his chances of finding him were unlikely. With no other option, he headed in the direction of the closest point of the Berlin Wall, which was only a mile or so away. Instead of taking the most direct route, he constantly diverted down side streets to give him eyes as far ahead on any possible route Kielhorn could have taken, but still could not see him.

Kielhorn.

He still couldn't believe it; the man he had considered the closest thing he had to a friend in Berlin, or anywhere else for that matter, had been standing with the bomb, with Al-Zalmay. Despite his misgivings and suspicions, he had come to trust the man, believed he had been taken by the Stasi, and believed his story of cutting old ties with Schleicher and Denisov. Now, Nikita felt like a fool. He had been trained to detect lies, but Kielhorn had proven to be a better opponent than he could ever have imagined possible. He had played the game better than any of them.

Nikita reached the wall just as the sun dropped behind the horizon. Within minutes, the gloom of twilight would sink into full darkness, which would make spotting Kielhorn even harder. He cast his eyes side to side, debating which way to go. He was on Leipziger Strasse, just north of Checkpoint Charlie, and with little else in the way of ideas, he quickly decided to run south to the American crossing point. It would be one of the perfect places for a bomb that was aimed at creating the maximum amount of havoc and international fallout possible. He turned off Leipziger Strasse, his attempts at running on his bleeding foot being more akin to a quick hobble. His foot was beginning to slip around inside the sodden bandages, as he pushed himself harder down the side street which ran parallel to the wall.

There were a lot of people milling around the checkpoint when he got there, with a number of agitated East Germans gesticulating with the officers manning it on the East Berlin side, demanding entry. There seemed to be a degree of confusion among the officers, but the crowd were being urged backwards at gunpoint.

Nikita didn't know what was going on, but he knew that a crowd was the very last thing he wanted right now. He frantically began wading through the people gathered there, pulling off hats and scarves at will to check their faces, despite loud objections and more than one punch or shove, but he ignored them. He had spent a lifetime being punched, kicked and called names by people he was trying to save. *Why should East Berlin be any different*, he thought to himself.

He cast his eyes all around, searching for any obvious hiding places where a bomb could be secreted. But in a street dividing East and West Berlin around Checkpoint Charlie, there was a very deliberate absence of places for bombs to be hidden. He reached the other side of the crowd and found himself no closer to finding the one-time polizeidirektor. He leant against the wall of what had once been someone's house right on the border before it was cleared following the erection of the wall on that dark night in 1961, his breathing ragged. His body felt tired. Tired and weak. He wasn't used to it, and he didn't like it. He had always been able to relentlessly rely on his body to perform, to feel strong and powerful, but now he felt only a fraction of his former self. He shook his head, clearing his mind of such thoughts. *Doubt is the domain of the weak* was another mantra that Denisov had flayed them with whenever he saw a look of fear, reluctance, or, God forbid, mercy in the eyes of any of his protégés.

Nikita again lowered himself into an emotionless state of logic, disregarding his panic and sifting through only the facts. He thought of Schleicher, of his plan, *'it will destroy the very essence of the West and the East,'* he had said in the seconds before his death. In Rostock, *'I have found just the man to carry out this operation... Berlin will burn.'* He had not spoken only of

East Berlin but of Berlin as a whole, something that was the essence of both the East and the West. Checkpoint Charlie made sense for that, yet here he was at the checkpoint with no sign of either Kielhorn or a bomb.

'What else, Niki. What aren't you seeing,' he urged himself, forcing the weary neurons in his brain to fire and connect the scattered dots.

He thought of Kielhorn and his reappearance and apparent willingness to carry out the bomb plan. It seemed so far removed from the character he had come to know, which didn't make it not possible but did suggest the possibility of coercion. He remembered Schleicher's dying words, referring to *'case 511312.'* That must have been Kielhorn he was referring to. He thought again of the meeting in Rostock. *'We will need to take some precautions to ensure some leverage,'* Al-Zalmay had said just moments before Nikita had been taken out, a memory that still smarted. Precautions with Schleicher's man, thought Nikita, what precautions could they take out against Kielhorn? He thought back to his conversations with him; Kielhorn had spoken about a father and sister on the other side of the wall that he had longed to see ever since the wall went up. The perfect leverage. Now, he had a motive for Kielhorn, but still not a location.

His mind filtered through the events of the past few days, of conversations he'd had, things he'd overheard and places he'd been. There must be some clue. He thought back to the Afghans, to Al-Zalmay and the fight. If they were using leverage against Kielhorn, it made sense that they monitored him right to the end to ensure the bomb was built correctly and that he was reminded of his duty to his family, as well as the repercussions if he strayed from his task. But there was something else about the apartment nagging at him, something that had seemed amiss.

The bodyguard's last words had been Rahbar, had been a cry to his commander, the man he had followed across the world. But Al-Zalmay had died at the hand of his wife, a woman who had also followed him all the way from the Tora Bora caves of Afghanistan. Why would he have brought her along for the journey when he apparently treated her with such disdain? There was something amiss about Rapa.

'Rapa,' he said the name out loud and a cold, icy feeling began to trickle down his spine. Rapa. It sounded an awful lot... like Rahbar. *The leader.* Nikita could almost feel the uncomfortable click of several things falling into place as he realised he had misheard her name in the Rostock barn.

Bedar Al-Zalmay wasn't the man who had died.

Bedar Al-Zalmay was a woman.

It all made sense. A sick kind of sense. She had killed the man Nikita believed to be the leader of Kulu Alqasas at the moment he was softening, the moment he was ready to tell Nikita the plan for the bomb. She'd killed the bodyguard when he uttered the word Rahbar. He hadn't been reaching for the man. He had been reaching for her, his leader. In Rostock, when she had cleared her throat during the meeting with Schleicher, her companion wasn't looking at her to be quiet. He was looking at her for instruction. He cast his mind back to his interrogation of the prisoner in the Tora Bora caves and realised he had never said it was a man, only that they had a new leader named Bedar Al-Zalmay.

Nikita did not allow himself any time to berate himself for not seeing what was right in front of him, for the prejudice he did not know he had, and to assume it could only be a man who led the Mujahideen. For that to happen, he reasoned, he must be dealing with a quite extraordinary woman. She had played her part exceptionally back at the apartment. He began running back towards it, hoping she might not yet have sloped away.

He was halfway back there when he remembered what she had said to him. *If he is fortunate, he will go through the gate to paradise.* Not through the *gates*, as would be the normal Islamic expression, but through the *gate*. Singular. He added that to what Schleicher had told him of it destroying the very essence of the East and the West, and the answer came to Nikita like a hammer blow to the head. A gate that could hurt both the East and the West, the most recognisable gate in the world. The Brandenburg Gate, the very spot Nikita had stood only hours before.

He changed direction, pushing his bleeding body as hard as he could not towards Kielhorn's apartment but towards the famous monument which sat in the no man's land between the two sides of the Berlin Wall.

CHAPTER 21

The going became frustrating slow as Nikita hurried towards the gate, through a combination of his failing body and the thickening crowds. People were singing and chanting. Something was happening. Eventually, the road opened up onto the broad clearing ahead of the Brandenburg Gate and the wall in front of it, and Nikita could move a little more freely. He cast his eyes everywhere, trying to process everything he could see as quickly as possible and identify suspicious behaviour, targets and potential bomb locations.

He trotted towards the wall and looked up and down it as far as possible, for it ran in a sweeping curve that cut out into the square. Armed soldiers were walking along the top of the wall menacingly, but people were openly insulting them now, presumably emboldened by the death of Schleicher earlier that day. Nikita marched back and forth, but there was no sign of Kielhorn. Nikita thought hopefully for a moment; perhaps Kielhorn had decided not to carry out the plan now that he was away from the Afghans and Schleicher was dead. But he shook off the notion. If there was one thing he had learned, it was to not underestimate Al-Zalmay. *All I know is the plans were very thorough,* she had said to him. Thorough enough to be certain that the leverage was strong enough to ensure success in the mission, no matter who fell along the way.

As Nikita took his second sweep of the wall next to the gate, he stumbled slightly and walked over a manhole. The sewers. The perfect place to discreetly plant a bomb directly under the wall and the gateway to the West. They didn't mean to open the Brandenburg Gate to everyone. They meant to destroy it. Nikita could see why Denisov had approved of the plan; the symbolism was undeniably powerful.

With the guards parading across the wall and the gathered crowds, there was no way Nikita could enter through the manhole he had tripped on, so he hurried back away from the square and searched a quieter street for another manhole.

He found one a few hundred yards away to the side of a road, between two parked cars. He ducked down and used the Khyber knife to help prise open the metal cover. The reeking smell of sewerage immediately greeted him, but he climbed down the iron rungs and sunk into the wall below nonetheless.

Behind him, a woman stepped out of the shadows of a building and turned off the power button on a video camera. She smiled to herself, removed the tape from the camera, pocketed it, and tossed the camera into a gutter as she walked away.

Below ground, Nikita landed in a passageway, took a moment to get his bearings and then set off in the direction of the Brandenburg Gate. He kept close to the wall to the side of the passageway and away from the pungent water flowing sluggishly along the channel beside him.

Feeling his way in the dark, his hearing felt heightened, sensitive to every drip of water, the pattering feet of rats as they fled from this new intruder. More than anything, though, he was desperately trying to hear any sign of Kielhorn or a bomb. Gradually, his eyes began to become more accustomed to the darkness, and he could more clearly make out the brickwork that domed overhead and see the stinking canal running down the middle, and he began to move quicker and with greater confidence.

He soon came to a fork in the tunnel and, with no subterranean signposts to point him in the right direction, grappled with the decision of which way to turn. He cocked his head to one side, trying to listen for any sign of noise from either passageway, but all he could hear were the sound of dozens of feet marching on the streets above. He opted to follow the tunnel to the left, which echoed the most with the sounds from above, reasoning that it was more likely they were headed in the direction of the Brandenburg monument than anywhere else. He knew he couldn't be far away now and quickened his pace while continuing to move completely soundlessly.

Down the conduits of the sewers he journeyed, his senses pushing out into the darkness. The tunnel curved around in a wide arc, and Nikita moved hesitantly, aware of more muffled sounds from above and less traffic noise. The air was completely motionless, heavy with the stench of human detritus and stagnant water. Occasional shafts of light shone down from road drains, but they were heavily clogged with leaves, which gave Nikita no indication of where he was. Instead, they stole any night vision he had built up away from him. His pace slowed, and he felt the curve of the brick wall flatten out and the tunnel narrow. Up ahead, he saw the briefest flash of light from a torch or lantern, but it was gone so quickly he could almost have convinced himself he had imagined it had it not been for the fact that the brief light had illuminated the face of a man. The face of Walter Kielhorn.

Nikita froze. Slowly, he shrank down into the darkness of a low overhanging of brickwork and listened carefully, wondering if he had been seen. He thought not.

From up ahead, there was a grinding sound, like a timer being turned into position, and a tiny red light began to flash. In the total blackness of the sewer, the tiny dot of light seemed dazzlingly bright, and as it flickered in and out, it allowed Nikita to see the outline of Kielhorn, bent over an alarmingly large contraption on the floor. Beside him were iron rungs leading up to a manhole and the square beyond. Nikita was in little doubt that it was the manhole he had seen next to the wall in front of the Brandenburg Gate.

A bomb that big would not only blow a hole through the wall, but it would destroy the Brandenburg Gate, the wall on the western side, blasting a pathway from east to west and killing a huge number of people in the process. He remembered now his first conversation with Barker, who had told him that the bomb would save countless lives if it brought about the fall of the Iron Curtain. But Nikita was no politician; he had no belief in the greater good, only what was right in the here and now. He was done killing at will for powerful, traitorous white men, done with the blood-soaked chess board of Cold War espionage and done letting some people die so that others may live. There was no big picture, only the right picture.

He eased himself out of his hidden nook and moved with absolute silence towards the polizeidirektor, who was bent over the bomb with a small screwdriver, tampering with some final piece of the explosive device. The tiny light from the bomb was enough to illuminate Kielhorn's face, in and out, but it did not stretch further than a couple of yards, so Nikita, cloaked in his thick, dark coat, was able to approach unseen out of the inky darkness. The bomb was next to a wall that was newer than the rest of those in the sewer, made out of concrete blocks rather than brick, and it blocked the tunnel, preventing anyone from using it to cross to the West. The wall had been built down into the sewer here to prevent people from escaping to the west via the subterranean channels.

He weighed his options; should he engage Kielhorn or simply take him out to then diffuse the bomb?

All of a sudden, Kielhorn straightened, and the flashing red light turned to a green bead of light, which Nikita knew could only mean one thing. The bomb had been armed.

That made Nikita's decision for him, and he withdrew the Khyber knife from his belt and crouched down, readying himself to pounce.

'I would not recommend it, Allochka,' Kielhorn said, startling Nikita and making his heart skip a beat. Kielhorn turned to look at Nikita, his face a flashing silhouette from the green light flickering in and out behind him. Nikita paused, tightening his hold on the long, slender handle of the knife but holding his crouched pose, warily watching Kielhorn. He said nothing.

'There is no point pretending you are not there, Allochka, I saw you by the flash of my torch a moment ago. It is too late now for you to do anything. You are here exactly as you should be, to watch,' he said, but his voice sounded different from before, slurred and more rasping, like someone who had just had a tooth removed at the dentist and was still feeling the effects of the local anaesthetic.

'What have they done to you?' Nikita asked, his voice appearing unseen out of the darkness.

'Only helped me to see that which had been hidden from me,' Kielhorn replied dumbly. 'I was a reluctant student, but through much pain and suffering, they taught me the way of the future.'

'They have brainwashed you, and a mind such as yours is too strong to give in to it,' Nikita urged. 'Disarm the bomb, and I can get you to safety. Schleicher is dead—'

'What?' said Kielhorn sharply.

'He died last night,' Nikita said.

'By your hand?'

'Yes.'

Kielhorn paused, his rewired brain trying to make sense of the new information. Nikita shifted forward a few feet, staying in the darkness but close enough now to act.

Eventually, Kielhorn sighed. 'Die nase voll haben,' he replied with a German saying. *To have a nose full.* 'I weary of this conversation,' he continued. 'Schleicher may be dead, but I can finish what he started. I can open the way to the West and a new world.'

'But so many will die!' exclaimed Nikita. 'Innocent people, women and children.'

'You do not grasp the bigger picture,' dismissed Kielhorn. 'Come, let us get away from here. This thing will go off in only fifteen minutes. We can drink beer and eat wurst and celebrate the New World.'

'You know I cannot let the bomb go off,' Nikita said calmly.

'Then you must die,' Kielhorn said emotionlessly, and a bright torchlight flashed out of nowhere into Nikita's eyes, blinding him.

A foot connected with Nikita's jaw, knocking him over and into the canal of sewerage with a great splash. Nikita's face burnt with the frigid coldness of the water and the scum floating across the top of it. He stood up in it, the water coming up to his knees, and wiped his face with his sleeve, trying not to think of the lumpy contents of the slime. But no sooner had he stood up than the shadow of Kielhorn appeared in front of the torchlight again and kicked him hard in the chest, forcing him onto his back and into the water again. Before Nikita was able to push himself up, the boot stood on his chest, forcing him under the water and pinning him down.

Nikita kept his mouth firmly closed and tried to grasp the leg, but the slime of detritus and excrement and the increasing numbness of his fingers in the cold made it impossible to gain a hold. The foot pressed down harder, driving the wind out of Nikita's lungs, which started screaming for him to breathe in.

Nikita forced himself to remain calm but found his strength waning, his body failing him, perhaps for the final time. His mind drifted back to the freezing Shelekhivske Lake in Northern Ukraine years before, during his training, when his so-called KGB comrades had tried to murder him by a thousand cuts, leaving him for dead at the bottom of the lake. Just as it had then, his mind filled with thoughts of his little sister Milena, of his father Gabriel, and even now, even after everything that had happened, he thought of Elysia. And, just as he had at the bottom of that god-forsaken lake, his mind filled with a roaring as he screamed to himself, 'NOT LIKE THIS!' and with a final surge of strength, he lifted his head and threw his fist with all his might straight into the groin of Kielhorn. It was a move he recalled his father instructing him as a child to only use in an emergency, and Nikita was quite sure this situation fit the bill.

Kielhorn may have been tortured beyond the normal realms of pain to a senseless place of feeling nothing, but even he could not fail to be impacted by the powerful muscled arm of one of the KGB's finest ever recruits smashing into his genitals, and he cried out a high-pitched scream. He fell to one side, his hands instinctively clutching his crotch and his foot leaving Nikita's chest.

With a final push, Nikita rolled himself out of the sewer channel and onto the narrow ledge next to it. He allowed the stagnant air into his grateful lungs with huge, heaving breaths. Kielhorn was keening slightly, like a crying kitten, lying on his side a few yards away from Nikita. Nikita climbed slowly to his feet and gave Kielhorn a powerful kick to the temple, which rendered him immediately unconscious, and the keening stopped.

Nikita staggered over to the bomb, turning the torch onto it and trying to understand what he was looking at. It was a large contraption with a multitude of different colours of wires looping in and out around a large metal casing. Above it was a small radio transmitter that was blinking the green light and a countdown timer that Kielhorn had activated. Unlike in the movies, it wasn't an enormous luminous dial but instead was a cheap plastic Casio watch that was ticking downwards, currently standing at fifteen minutes and counting.

***

LENINGRAD, USSR. 1986

'You fail, you die,' said Major Analtoli Tsaryov, his face impassive, almost to the point of ambivalence.

'You cut the wrong wire, you will also die,' he continued. 'If you misdiagnose the nature of the explosive, you will die. There are many ways in which you can die, but only one which will allow you to live. The odds are never in your favour when disarming a bomb. If you die, then it is because you are not worthy of a position in the KGB, the greatest security organisation in the world and the gem of our great empire.'

'Why bother teaching us if we're just going to die anyway,' grumbled Vladimir Popov, a fellow recruit that Nikita had long found to be irritating. But he did have a point.

The major looked long and hard at Popov. Then he walked back to his desk, pulled out a ball-bearing gun, and in one smooth motion, shot at the student, hitting him square in the forehead. Popov let out a squeal and fell backwards in his chair, causing the other students to laugh. When he got back up, there was an open, bloody wound on his forehead. He lifted a hanky from his pocket to wipe it, but Tsaryov shook his head slowly, his eyes unblinking. Popov falteringly lowered his hand and sat there glowering, blood dribbling down his nose and dripping off the end.

'Every bomb will be different. Bomb-makers will not use a standardised colour of wire to make your life easier,' continued Tsaryov as if nothing had happened. 'They will not always use the same explosive, and even the methods of arming and triggering the bomb will differ.'

Nikita found himself increasingly agreeing with Popov's assessment but chose to keep the opinion to himself.

'But,' the major said, 'there are some things that will always be consistent, and it is these that give us a small opportunity for success,' he finished flatly, cueing a collective exhale of relief. 'Follow me,' he ordered.

He led the class through a series of once grand corridors in a house that had been, in the Russian Revolution of 1917, either stolen from the nobility or reclaimed for the people, depending on who you asked. On the walls were squares of brighter paint where paintings had once hung, but now the house was gloomy and more than a little forbidding. The cream walls were occasionally interrupted by the blood-red Soviet flag emblazoned with the golden sickle and hammer, and the only portraits that hung on the walls were of various Soviet leaders from the past seventy years; Vladimir Lenin, the Bolshevik who had started it all, the man for whom the city had been renamed, Joseph Stalin, the revolutionary Georgian who had murdered more of his own countryman than even Hitler, Nikita Khrushchev the reformer, but it stopped at Leonid Brezhnev. There was no place for the current incumbent, Misho Petrenko, whose policies of Glasnost and perestroika, aimed to make the Soviet Union and its constituent states freer and more open, both policies that were deeply unpopular within the KGB.

The class of burly KGB trainees followed the major through sizeable French doors, which were thrown open to the bright summer's day on the northwest coast of the USSR and into an enormous garden. A vast lawn stretched for acres before them, and various gardens were spread around to either side. Tsaryov showed little interest in the landscaping of the once proud gardens and trudged sharply across the lawn, his heavy boots digging into the soft grass. He walked at pace and led them through to a wood which lined the bottom corner of the grounds. It was a dense woodland of beech, birch and oak, and the men followed their superior silently, all well-trained in walking through broken ground without making a sound.

Tsaryov rounded a dense copse of hornbeam and maple trees and stopped. Without a word or a signal, his followers stopped in unison, unquestioning. He turned to them.

'In the trees ahead is a bomb. It is a fairly standard bomb, as far as it goes, and you will select one from within your ranks to attempt to disarm it. If he fails, his death will be instant and messy. If he fails, the rest of you will also face a terrible punishment, although you will live to tell the tale, but I suggest you choose wisely.'

Nikita's heart simultaneously sank and began to race as he knew without question that he would be the lamb to the slaughter. It was always the way, always the one forced to be the punching bag. But normally, the outcome was a beating or some other painful experience, never being blown up. Right on cue, he received a shove in the back from one of his comrades and staggered forward.

If Tsaryov was surprised, he didn't show it, his face continuing to show the near-braindead expression he always maintained as Nikita stood at attention before him, awaiting orders. He instructed Nikita to stand at ease and handed him a pair of reinforced gloves and a small toolbox. He nodded in the direction of the bomb.

'You should be grateful for my kindness, Allochka. It is unlikely that in the field, you would be armed with a toolbox of equipment.'

Nikita didn't bother to thank him. Instead, he set his shoulders and walked in the direction of the explosive device. Something hard suddenly struck him on the shoulder, and he stopped to look down and saw a stone fall to the ground.

'You must learn to disarm a bomb under heavy fire and in stressful conditions,' said the major, with the slightest hint of a smirk playing upon his rubbery lips, and he waved to Nikita's fellows to follow suit. Projectiles from around the woodland began to rain down on Nikita as his comrades eagerly took the task of being openly allowed to throw things at him. A heavy stick jabbed him sharply in the tricep, drawing blood, but Nikita kept his focus only on what was ahead of him. 'Sticks and stones may break my bones,' he muttered to himself, deliberately omitting the second part of the rhyme.

Then, the bomb swam into view. It was only small but had enough dynamite taped to it to destroy a house, let alone Nikita. His heart rate gathered pace, and sweat began to gather on his top lip, which had little to do with the balmy July day. He looked down at the bomb and wondered how or why Tsaryov would force one of his students to do something that almost guaranteed his death with so little instruction.

He gazed down at the device. There was very little to it; no timer, no obvious trigger. It appeared that it would remain completely dormant unless someone was foolish enough to tamper with it. There were three wires, one green, one red and one black. Nikita looked closely, lying flat on the ground beside it, to see if there was anything else he was missing, but it really was a very simple bomb. With a deep breath, he lifted it, and it was then that he saw a trigger. There was a small radio device that the wires were passing through, and when he looked behind him, he saw Tsaryov holding something that he had no doubt was the device that would trigger the bomb.

'I forgot to mention, Allochka. You have two minutes, and then I will press the button. I suggest you make some fast decisions.'

Nikita stepped behind a thick oak tree, which at least took him out of the line of fire for the things being thrown at him, and gazed down at the bomb. The three wires went below a metal rim and into an enormous tangle, making it impossible to identify, within two minutes, which might be the lead that stopped the bomb from being detonated if it was cut. It was, as Nikita had feared it would be, a set-up to destroy him. He was left facing the first bomb he had ever encountered and had a 33 per cent chance of survival.

He took a deep breath, slowing his heart rate and ignoring the sweat that was now streaming down his face, his clothes sodden. If this is what it came down to, he had survived worse odds than 33 per cent before now. He could only hope that luck was on his side.

He looked at the wires. Red, green and black. Tsaryov had told them that the colours of wires in bombs were rarely what you expected them to be and rarely made sense. As such, Nikita, aware that it was a flimsy reason to discount, pushed the green wire to one side, convincing himself that green probably didn't mean a positive outcome on this occasion. That left him with just the black and the red to pick from.

'Tick tock, Allochka,' Tsaryov called callously as the other students jeered and catcalled insults at Nikita.

'But words will never harm me,' Nikita said, finishing the rhyme. 'Black or red, Niki, black or red. It's time to decide,' he muttered.

He deliberately blocked thoughts of his family from his mind. There was no use in dwelling on them now. He would live or die on the cutting of a wire. He thought of the major, the expressionless man with pockmarked cheeks, fat lips and greasy white hair. There was much about him that reminded him of Denisov. Both gave nothing away, both had the capacity for unusually extreme levels of cruelty, and both were even more patriotic to the Soviet empire than the average KGB agent.

Red flags adorned the halls. For them, red was the colour of triumph, of victory and power. But black... well, Nikita knew only too well what they thought of black. He was reminded every day. Tsaryov was no fool. He would have known beyond any doubt that Nikita would be selected for the suicide mission by his classmates, would know that his death would be the example to set for the real Soviets, the blond-haired, blue-eyed, white Soviet young men, to never be complacent with their bomb lessons. Picking black as the wire he must cut to save himself? It was exactly the sort of twisted joke the major would enjoy.

'Desiat, deviat, vosem,' Tsaryov began counting down from ten, and the other men joyfully joined in. 'Sem! Shest'! They roared. Nikita lifted the wire cutters from the toolbox, which was the only item that was in there he absently noticed.

'Piat!'

'Chityri!'

Nikita placed the cutters around the black wire, unable now to stop his heart from pounding, closing his eyes to prevent any hint of tears.

He would not die crying in front of these people. He would die thinking of his family, of his mother, father and sister, and allowed images of them to flood his mind.

'Tri!'

'Dva!'

Nikita cut the wire.

'ADIN!' shouted Tsaryov and gleefully pressed the button.

Nothing happened, and the woodland erupted with the sound of laughter as Nikita collapsed to the floor, alive but never quite the same again.

***

Nikita's face was grim as he remembered his experience in the Leningrad woodland. It had taught him very little other than he would like one day to kill Major Tsaryov, but the mantra of *you fail, you die,* was a hard one to push out of his mind.

He inspected the bomb in front of him, and it was noticeably more complicated than Tsaryov's device, not least because of the small countdown timer. The metal casing around the bomb made it impossible to see the inside, but from the size of it, Nikita was confident there was a huge amount of explosives in there. The clock had ticked down to ten minutes now, and Nikita began to get nervous. He could not see a way of detonating it without any tools. He flashed the torch around and found the screwdriver that Kielhorn had been using when he arrived.

He furiously began to unscrew a metal panel at the side of the device, and once all the screws had been removed, pried it off incredibly delicately and laid it softly on the stone floor. He flashed the light inside and gasped.

He had been right; the inside was packed with dynamite, enough to blow an enormous hole in the centre of Berlin.

CHAPTER 22

Bedar Al-Zalmay walked into Berlin Schönefeld Airport and checked in for her flight. She made her way through to the departure lounge and ordered a coffee from the small kiosk. She carried it over to a seat, which gave her both a view of the runway and also of a television. She hoped it would all show on the news before she boarded her flight, but that depended on whether Kielhorn finished the job or not.

Her hand absently sat in her pocket, stroking the small device that had only one button. The button that, when pressed, would send a radio signal all the way to the sewers of East Berlin, all the way to the bomb, if Kielhorn did not detonate it first.

She gazed up at the television, where the news anchor was discussing a press conference that was about to take place involving a government official.

Rumours were beginning to swirl that the contents of the conference could also be quite explosive, but the details were still unclear.

Out of her handbag, Al-Zalmay pulled the small videotape that she had removed from the video camera with which she had filmed Nikita's entrance into the sewers. She slid it into a small padded envelope and stuck down the flap but did not write anything on the front. An announcement was made that her flight to Belgrade in the communist-ruled Yugoslavia, from where she would change and fly to Islamabad in Pakistan, was ready to begin boarding at Gate 39. Her smile faltered slightly, for Afghans feared the number thirty-nine, a curse said to be upon it, but her smile returned as she reminded herself it was just a superstition, nonsense thought up by those who feared that which they did not understand. She understood everything, and it was going like clockwork.

She drank the last of her coffee, stood and began walking at a relaxed pace in the direction of her gate. As she passed Gate 17, she stopped at one of the plastic seats next to a thin, nondescript-looking man with a pencil moustache, small spectacles and Brylcreamed pale brown hair. She bent down to check something in her bag and took out the package with the tape, placing it on the chair while she continued to rifle through her bag. With a look of relief, she pulled out her ticket, stood up, hoisted the bag back over her shoulder, and continued towards the gate. Behind her, Rosin picked up the padded envelope without so much as a glance at Al-Zalmay and walked off in the opposite direction to the woman.

He pushed the envelope inside his thin brown jacket and, with a nod to a security guard barring a door at the end of the departure lounge, was let through and into the bowels of the airport, where he could slip away without going back through security. As he climbed the stairs, he rubbed his chin nervously. He was not comfortable with what he was being asked to do. For all of the challenges Allochka brought with him, he had served Mother Russia loyally and did not deserve to be branded a traitor. The KGB station chief wrestled with it; it was an order direct from Denisov. The tape must be released to the news outlets shortly after the bomb went off, with the world to be told that a known CIA agent had killed thousands and destroyed the Brandenburg Gate. With all fingers pointing at the destructive capitalist Americans, it was a move sure to revive confidence in communist rule and restore the Soviet Union to its former glory. Rosin loved his country, but he did not love this plan. Allochka would burn.

He continued wrestling with it as he turned into a long, deserted corridor that stretched far ahead of him and would lead him back through to the main entrance of the airport. By the time he got halfway along the corridor, he had made a decision. He would destroy the tape and tell Denisov that the tape had been lost in transit. He couldn't stop the bomb, but he could save Allochka's life, at least for the time being.

He was so lost in thought that he didn't notice someone slip silently out of a side door behind him, and he didn't notice as they rapidly approached him from behind.

The last thing he would ever know was the smell of delicate perfume and the brush of long, golden brown curls as a syringe was pressed into his neck, and he was dragged into a broom cupboard as all went dark.

Elysia looked down at Rosin sadly. She did not like killing, but this was the only way to protect Jake, though he would never know. He would never know he was the reason she had rejected the request from her Greek employers to return from her MI6 secondment. He would never know they had asked for her back at all.

She took the envelope out of Rosin's jacket and tore it open, letting the tape slide out and fall to the floor. She stamped on it with the heavy heel of her boot several times, ensuring it was entirely destroyed, before scooping up the pieces and sliding them back into the envelope. Then, she pulled a small bundle of clothes from a shelf of the cupboard that had been left there for her and hastily got changed, feeling uncomfortable doing so in front of Rosin even though she knew he was dead.

***

Al-Zalmay sank into her chair in first class on the flight to Istanbul as passengers filtered past. She couldn't help but smile. The Western infidels would feel the wrath of God, the Russian barbarians would be crushed by heroin addiction spreading across the Eastern Bloc, and Afghanistan would finally be free of invaders to write their own history at last. As the flight taxied to the runway, Al-Zalmay removed the radio device from her pocket and stroked it with her long, manicured nails. The plane gathered pace, speeding along the runway and, with a fierce smile, she pushed down her thumb and pressed the button that would wreak untold havoc on the city. It was exactly five minutes ahead of the scheduled time, but she could no longer wait. Maybe Kielhorn had already detonated it, maybe not. Maybe he had escaped in time, maybe not. She did not care; he had been nothing more than a useful pawn whose mind Schleicher had bent to their will.

It was time for Berlin to burn.

***

Nikita's hands were wet with sweat and slime as he struggled to keep them from shaking. He had worked all of the sides of the bomb and could now see everything within. It was unlike any bomb he had ever encountered in any of his training or since; dynamite sticks were stacked upon one another, taped together with wires and leads laced throughout them, the plastic sheaths all changing colours throughout to make it impossible to disarm.

Nikita was almost grateful at its complexity; it made his decision for him. He could not dismantle the bomb, only disconnect it from the countdown timer and radio receiver. This, however, was hardly any more straightforward with such a complicated device.

He shone the torch underneath the top of it to look at the wiring that connected with the Casio watch. Three wires had been linked to it, with a switch that would be activated when the countdown timer hit zero. The wires were sheathed in green, red and black coating, just as with Tsaryov's device, but unlike his experience in the Leningrad woods, there was no clear politics behind the choice of colours and no indication of which would disconnect the timer and which would bypass it to trigger the switch immediately.

All three of the wires led to the switch, where they became lost in a tangle that Nikita could not interpret in the time he had, before all changing to different colours and descending into the bowels of the dynamite. Nikita tried to trace the leads down and found that one of them reached a dynamite stick at the bottom, but it was sheathed in blue and could not clearly be associated with any of those at the top. He was preparing to make a snap decision and hoped for the best when the torchlight crossed his hands, and he noticed blue paint had rubbed off on his sweaty fingertips. He shone the torch back on the blue wire at the bottom and saw that someone had painted over the wire to add to the confusion within it, but as it had been painted on plastic, his wet fingers had easily rubbed it off. He spat on his fingertips, rubbed away at the coating some more, and found that the paint came off easily and revealed a red coating underneath.

He returned to the top of the bomb and rubbed at the coating of the leads under the switch with incredibly delicate movements. He found the colouring also came off there to show the original colours from the top of the bomb, green, red and black. The moist air was so warm and humid that sweat was dripping down across Nikita's face, stinging his eyes. His heart was racing at full throttle, and he was convinced that at any moment, he would accidentally activate the bomb, killing him and thousands of others in the blink of an eye. The timer was racing downwards at what seemed like a ridiculous pace, now down to six minutes and counting.

Tracing the wires tenderly, Nikita began to grow in confidence that the red wire would deactivate the timer.

'What are your chances?' he said to himself, ignoring the tremble in his voice as he raised the Khyber knife. 'A solid 33 per cent chance of success again,' he added with a hollow laugh.

He lifted the knife carefully, holding it against the red wire, preparing himself to cut it. He thought once more of his family and how he longed to see their faces again. He thought of Elysia and saw it all so clearly now. How much time he had wasted by staying distant, by never saying the right thing, by pushing her away so much that she stayed away. What a waste of precious time.

No longer sure if the water in his eyes was sweat, sewage or tears, he took a huge breath, savouring it as his last, and cut.

CHAPTER 23

Time seemed to freeze as Nikita instinctively shielded his face, his eyes screwed up in anticipation. There was a small ripping sound and a clatter that echoed through the sewers. Then, when nothing further happened, Nikita slowly lowered his arms and looked back at the bomb. It stood exactly as it had, except for the watch, which had rolled off to the side, hanging limply from the two remaining wires. Nikita reached for it, careful not to tug on either of the other wires and cautiously hit the stop button on the watch timer. It froze at five minutes and five seconds.

He shone the torch over the rest of the bomb and was delighted to see that the cut wire had also deactivated the radio transmitter, which had stopped blinking. He was confident now that the bomb had been deactivated, but it still remained enormously dangerous—one match could bring down the Brandenburg Gate.

Then, a gunshot hit the wall behind Nikita and sent a shower of sparks over the bomb. He threw himself over the device, trying to protect the dynamite from the sparks and ignoring the peril it put him in. Once the sparks had faded, he rolled off and to the ground, falling with a splash back into the sewage.

'I will kill you!' Kielhorn cried out of the darkness as Nikita rose from the water. It was an exercise in terror as both men flailed in the pitch darkness, throwing heavy punches blindly at one another, some connecting, others missing completely.

'Walter, stop!' Nikita cried, hearing a rush of air as a blow narrowly missed his cheek. Nikita returned with an uppercut and felt his fist connect with Kielhorn's jaws. There was a furious grunt as Kielhorn fell backwards and crashed into the water.

'I have disarmed the bomb. People do not need to die. Remember who you were before they tortured you! Remember your father and sister!'

'First, you will die, and then Berlin!' cried Kielhorn as another shot fired out, widely missing Nikita, but the flash of the pistol burnt his eyes and momentarily lit up the tunnel around them. It gave Nikita enough time to see where Kielhorn was, and after throwing a quick glance behind him to check that the bullet had not lit a spark near the bomb in any way, he plunged at where Kielhorn had been holding the gun.

He crunched into the German, missing the gun and crashing them back down into the sewage water. Nikita pushed the hand holding the gun away, but Kielhorn hooked a finger into Nikita's mouth and pulled, fish-hooking and almost tearing his cheek, the foul taste of the water permeating through his entire mouth. Nikita yanked it out, feeling the nail scrape away layers of skin from his gums and headbutted Kielhorn as hard as he could. There was a loud splash as Kielhorn fell backwards, but then his free hand rose up out of the water to gouge at Nikita's eye. Nikita cried out in pain as it felt like his eye was going to be ripped from its socket, and he thrashed his head from side to side, trying to force Kielhorn to loosen his grip, which gave Kielhorn the chance to raise himself out of the water. Meanwhile, their other hands were locked in a battle over the gun as Kielhorn tried to force his arm up to aim the weapon at Nikita while Nikita tried to lean his weight into holding it down. He ripped at Kielhorn's eye-gouging hand and punched him in the face several times in a rapid-fire combo that sent Kielhorn gurgling back below the surface.

He could not be allowed to fire the gun again anywhere near the bomb.

Nikita used both arms now, trying to tear the weapon out of Kielhorn's grasp as the polizeidirektor brought his head back above the water with a gasp. Nikita bent back Kielhorn's fingers one by one, feeling one finger snap as he forced it back, causing the German to roar in pain. With a final surge of strength, Kielhorn yanked at the gun, and there was an enormous bang of noise.

For a dumbfounded moment, Nikita thought the bomb had gone off, but then, shaking his head, which was ringing from the noise, realised the gun had fired. He could not feel any pain and felt his body blindly in the darkness.

It was then he heard the laboured breathing from Kielhorn below him.

'You win, Allochka,' he groaned, falling backwards with a splash.

Nikita tossed the gun to one side and grabbed the man, pulling him out of the water and, with a heave, rolled him onto the walkway next to the sewage channel. He staggered his way back to the bomb and fumbled around until he found the torch. He switched it on and ran back to where Kielhorn lay, his breath rattling in his chest.

Nikita looked down and saw that the bullet had gone through his chest. He tore open the man's shirt, which revealed that he had punctured his right lung, and bloody air was spurting out of it with every breath. On his chest was a fresh brand, with the number 511312, that had been given to him by the Stasi torturers. Nikita ripped off a strip of shirt and tried to plug the wound, knowing that doing so could simultaneously save the man and kill him with infection, but he had no other choice.

Kielhorn grabbed Nikita's wrist and looked up at him. Nikita saw him properly now; his eyes were wild and red-rimmed, with one of the eyelids completely cut away. His hands were nail-less, much like two of Nikita's, from the methods of the Stasi torturers.

'Stop, Allochka,' he gasped, more bloody air bubbling from his chest. 'It is too late for me.'

'I will save you. You will live. You will live to see your family once more.'

'My family.' Kielhorn sighed, lying back with a beatific expression on his face. 'What I would give to see them one last time. But it is only a dream. The powers that move us like their pawns will not let this plan fail,' he grabbed Nikita by the collar now and looked at him intently, his red eyes wild. 'You were meant to be here, Allochka, and the bomb will start the Cold War anew,' he finished, falling back and gasping for breath.

'The bomb has been stopped, and so will Denisov and Al-Zalmay,' Nikita said softly. 'Your family dream is not dead yet, Walter, and neither are you,' Nikita said and hefted the man over his shoulder. Kielhorn was too weak now to protest, and Nikita moved back to the ladder up to the manhole next to the bomb. With an effort that threatened to cripple his ruined body, he climbed with the added weight of Kielhorn up the iron rungs and forced open the manhole cover. There were several screams as the two excrement-covered men appeared like monsters of the deep out of the sewers. Nikita swayed under the weight of Kielhorn and was forced to lay him down on the ground. A space formed around them in what appeared to be a now packed-out square in front of the wall and the gate. Nikita was faintly aware of chanting and cheering coming from around them.

'Arzt,' he grunted at a young woman who was looking on in horror as Nikita fell to one knee. He looked up at her again. 'Er braucht jetzt einen Arzt.' *He needs a doctor, now.*

The woman nodded slowly, her eyes wide, and ran over to a nearby phone box. When she returned, Nikita had gone.

***

Nikita crashed through the door of an apartment block and staggered along the ground-floor corridor. Many of the doors had been left open as people seemed to have left their homes en masse in a mad rush that evening. He picked one at random and walked inside. The apartment appeared to be empty, but the television was blaring loudly.

Nikita walked past it but then froze as the news reporter's words filtered slowly into his sluggish awareness. He took a few steps backwards and stared down at the screen, sewage dripping off him onto the tiled floor.

'...citizens will be able to cross the inner German border immediately,' stated the Zweites Deutsches Fernsehen reporter. 'To repeat, from now on, citizens of the German Democratic Republic can exit directly via all border posts between the GDR and the Federal Republic of Germany. This was announced by Politburo member Günter Schabowski at a press conference in East Berlin just moments ago. The press conference was fraught with confusion,' continued the news reader, and it cut to a clip from the conference where a journalist asked Schabowski when the new regulations would take effect, and he replied, 'As far as I know, it takes effect immediately, without delay.'

It reverted back to the reporter, who continued talking about the new travel law, but Nikita zoned out as the realisation of what it all meant slowly dawned upon him. It explained the crowds and the chanting that he had only vaguely been aware of when depositing Kielhorn.

He hastily stripped off the suit Curbishley had provided him with, saving anything from the pockets that had survived, and shoved the clothes into the rubbish bin in the apartment bathroom. He stepped under the shower, digging the soap deep into his flesh to rid it of any vestiges of the sewers and trying to ignore the pain that lanced through his back, foot and myriad of other injuries as the water splashed against the open wounds. His foot was in particularly bad shape, looking puffy and possibly infected. He couldn't see it, so he convinced himself that his back was faring better. He finished his shower and raided the meagre contents of the homeowner's medicine cabinet for bandages and antiseptic. It wasn't much, but it would do for now, and he felt significantly better about it, though he knew his foot needed proper medical treatment.

Nikita was desperate to get out of the apartment and see what was happening for himself. He took clothes from the bottom of the drawers that he was confident were old and wouldn't be missed, pulling on a pair of jeans with holes in the knees, a patched jumper and an anorak hanging by the door. He grabbed a bottle of schnapps from the sideboard that would probably be missed rather more and took a long swig, allowing himself to enjoy the warmth as it cascaded down his throat and into his stomach.

He picked up the phone on a small table next to the front door and dialled the number that Curbishley had given him.

'Yes?' said a slurred voice that sounded in a similar condition to the one Nikita hoped to be in very soon.

'It's Marshall,' Nikita said.

'I'd ask if the line is secure, but I don't suppose it matters anymore, old boy,' the Englishman said jovially.

'The bomb, it is beneath the Brandenburg Gate,' Nikita said.

'What? You're sure?' said Curbishley sharply, any sign of the drunken slur instantly gone.

'Very sure, being as I disarmed it,' Nikita said. There was a loud exhale from the other end.

'Perhaps lead with that part next time, Marshall,' Curbishley said with a wry chuckle.

'The bomb isn't armed, but it's still very dangerous,' Nikita said. There's enough dynamite to blow the Brandenburg Gate sky high. It's in the sewer next to the wall on the east side. It will need to be dealt with urgently,' Nikita urged.

'Very well, I will see it done,' Curbishley said. 'You did your job well, agent. I would love to discuss some further opportunities for gainful employment...'

'No thanks,' Nikita interrupted. 'I'm getting out of the game.'

'Ah, but the game will always be played,' Curbishley said sagely.

'I think it was you who told me that when it comes to the game, one must write one's own rules.'

'Did I really? Gosh, that's awfully profound. Well, you know where we are, tally ho,' Curbishley said and hung up the phone.

Nikita allowed himself a small smile at the Englishman's whimsy, then wrapped a scarf around his neck and headed out into the tumultuous Berlin night.

***

Bedar Al-Zalmay gazed out the window and wondered if the pilot would make an announcement during the flight of the bomb in Berlin. There had been no noticeable sign of unrest amongst the flight attendants, but Al-Zalmay wasn't worried. The plan had been watertight. She knew, without doubt, that right now, the West had been thrown into a state of turmoil. Moscow would burn next, just as they had burnt the land and children of her homeland.

A flight attendant with long, curly hair smiled warmly at her as she pushed the trolley along the aisle and passed her the in-flight meal. The food was some sort of unrecognisable chicken-in-a-sauce dish, and alongside it was a cupcake with edible purple and yellow flowers. She picked one up and chewed it. It was sweet, and ignoring the chicken, she continued to nibble on the cake and sugary flowers while gazing out the window.

The need to clear her throat interrupted her musings on the destruction of Berlin, and she signalled to the air hostess for more water, noticing that her mouth was very dry from the plane's air conditioning. Pain began to grow in her temples, which was not surprising, she reasoned, with the amount of focus and planning that had been required in recent weeks. She lit a cigarette and pressed the button above her to call for more water. But the cigarette was making her feel woozy and dizzy, and her vision began to flash and blur.

At the front of the plane, Elysia opened the door to the pilot.

'We're good to go,' she said, and the MI6 pilot nodded. Elysia closed the door, holding onto a chair as the plane banked hard to the left and began to turn back towards Berlin. She looked up and saw that foam was oozing out of the corner of Al-Zalmay's mouth, and she was convulsing. She walked over to her and put out the cigarette that had fallen into her lap and was singeing a hole through her clothes. She put on a pair of latex gloves and, using a pair of tweezers, picked up the remaining flower petals and put them in a sealed container.

'Nightshade petals are definitely not for eating,' she whispered to Al-Zalmay, who was still now. Elysia gently closed the Afghan's staring eyes and turned back to the front of the plane, her face set.

CHAPTER 24

The city was alive, more energised than Nikita had ever seen East Berlin. For almost thirty years, the people had been silent, but now they had found their voices, and the world would hear them.

He fought against the throng, working his way back into the city and away from the wall. There was one more thing he had to do.

Public transport had ground to a halt, and with his ruined foot, his pace was slow, and he feared he would already be too late. When he finally arrived at the glass and chrome building that he had come to know well, he was unsurprised to find the security door propped open. He made his way upstairs and knocked on the door.

His hand had barely dropped when the door was yanked open, and there stood Heidi in the process of pulling on her coat.

She saw Nikita, and her face broke into an enormous grin.

'Niki!' she cried and threw her arms around him, pulling him into a fierce hug, which caused Nikita's back excruciating pain that he worked hard to hide. 'Didn't I tell you! Change has come!' she said, stepping back and holding his hands.

He stepped with her into the apartment. 'You were right, Heidi. I'm so happy you were right,' he said, but he didn't smile. Her own smile faltered.

'What is it? What's happened?' she asked. 'Tell me.'

Nikita closed the door behind him and pulled from inside his coat the file he had taken from the Ministry of State Security and handed it over to Heidi.

She looked down at it, and her eyes filled with tears. On the front, it said only 'Joachim Liebers'.

'What is this?' she gasped.

'It is your husband's file. I took it from the counterintelligence department at Stasi HQ,' Nikita said.

'What? How?'

'That is not important,' Nikita said softly.

'What does it say?' she asked in a small voice, barely above a whisper.

'I do not know; it is not mine to read. But I hope it gives you the closure you are searching for,' he said. He gave her a gentle kiss on the cheek and turned to leave.

He heard the tear of the envelope behind him as he turned the doorknob and walked back down the corridor.

But seconds later, he heard running footsteps as Heidi charged after him.

'He lives!' she sobbed with joy, 'Joachim is alive!' and she fell into Nikita, sobbing uncontrollably, the build-up of years of fear, uncertainty and pain catching up with her in one bittersweet moment of untold relief.

Nikita pushed her back, his hands on her shoulder. 'I am so happy for you,' he said, his face breaking into a smile of warmth and compassion.

Heidi pushed his hands out of the way, kissed him roughly on the cheek, lingering for a moment, and then pulled him into another bone-crushing hug.

'Thank you,' she whispered into his ear through sobs.

'Perhaps one day I'll see you when I'm not fleeing the authorities.' He winked at her, and she laughed, wiping tears from her cheeks and watching him as he walked away.

***

Nikita stood on top of the Berlin Wall and stared at the Brandenburg Gate. He'd gone there to check that Curbishley had been good to his word and saw undercover British agents descending the manhole, which was enough for Nikita.

The square was full of people sharing drinks, kisses and unbridled joy. All kinds of music were blasting out from both sides of the wall. The best party in the world was in Berlin tonight. Nikita tried to listen to the different types of music, feeling an interest in it after reading at the library. He thought of having a hobby and laughed to himself. Men like him didn't have hobbies... or maybe they could? He considered it, the laugh falling from his lips as he imagined the interests he might now try to pursue, of the music he might learn to make.

Others sat on the wall near him, some dancing a jig upon it, and many hammering at it with chisels; some to keep fragments of the wall as a keepsake, others to bash a way through it.

But Nikita didn't feel like celebrating. Instead, he looked across the no man's land between the two sides of the wall and to the mighty monument that stood between it and thought of his future. He took a long swig of the now half-empty bottle of schnapps and sat down, his feet dangling off the edge.

'Of all the walls in all the world, you just had to be on this one,' a voice said to one side.

Nikita did not turn and instead continued looking out across the wall.

'What are you doing here, Agent Nightshade?' he said, more coldly than he'd intended.

'A little thing like the Berlin Wall coming down isn't something I wanted to miss,' she said, sitting down next to him. Nikita did not respond.

'Al-Zalmay won't be a problem anymore,' Elysia said, a bitter look on her face.

Nikita looked over at her and raised his eyebrows. 'That is good, but I suspect it is not the last we will hear of Kula Alqasas. The Afghans, more than anyone in this whole mess, have the greatest reason to want revenge,' he said. He thought of the desire for revenge against Denisov that had been simmering in his belly ever since Schleicher had told him of the KGB leader's complicity in the death of his mother and put it to one side as something to think of another time, in another place.

For a long time, Nikita and Elysia sat in silence, drinking in the scene as holes began to appear in the walls. People raced through, brushing aside the confused and overwhelmed border guards. For the first time in decades, people from the East and the West came together as one, meeting under the Brandenburg Gate. People wept and hugged as families that had been torn apart caressed the long-forgotten faces of their loved ones with disbelieving eyes.

'They never gave up hope, despite everything Schleicher and the Soviets put them through,' Elysia said.

'Hope is sustenance for the soul,' Nikita replied.

Elysia laughed, a light, tinkling sound that touched something inside Nikita. 'I never thought I would hear you talk of hope,' she said. 'Mr There-Can-Be-No-Future-For-Us, blah, blah, blah,' she said.

'I believe it was you that last said we could have no future, Elysia,' Nikita said, swallowing his pain at the memory and taking another swig of schnapps.

Elysia took the bottle from him, took a long drink herself, and breathed out heavily.

'Maybe you were right. Maybe this life is not good for the soul,' she said and turned to look at him.

He glanced across at her. 'Why are you dressed as an air hostess?' he asked curiously.

Her eyes burnt into his, fixing him with a deeply intense stare.

'Tell me your name,' she whispered.

Nikita swallowed again and shook his head. Tears stung at his eyes.

'I can't,' he said.

'Tell me your name, and maybe there is a future for us. Maybe we can forget the past and cross our own wall,' she said. 'There will never be a better time than this to escape this life, to forge a future together like normal people.'

Nikita shook his head, hurting inside.

Elysia slumped and looked forward. She took a long drink of the schnapps and stood up.

'Goodbye, Agent,' she said sadly and kissed the top of his head before turning and walking along the wall.

Nikita rolled his shoulders and clenched his jaw in frustration, anger rising like bile within him.

'My name is Nikita,' he whispered through his tightened lips. He clenched his fits and jumped to his feet.

'MY NAME IS NIKITA,' he roared along the wall to Elysia, who froze.

Slowly, she turned as Nikita limped towards her purposefully. He reached her and grabbed her hands.

'My name,' he said breathlessly, 'is Nikita.'

Her face went through a myriad of emotions as she registered it all. From surprise, to fear, to angst and relief before finally settling on a smile of absolute warmth.

'Well, Nikita, it's a real pleasure to meet you,' she said, squeezing his hands. He moved his hands up to her cheeks and pulled her face gently towards his. He kissed her more deeply than ever before. Then, pulling apart, they both, without a word, dropped down from the wall and into the space between the East and the West.

They passed under the Brandenburg Gate, stepped into a large hole that had been knocked through on the western side of the wall, and disappeared into the jubilant crowds beyond.

ACKNOWLEDGEMENTS

This book has been a labour of love for a multitude of reasons, and it simply would not have been possible without the support of an awful lot of people. Above all else I want to thank my wife, Anne, who is always my first editor, my biggest fan, and an incredibly tolerant woman to put up with my writing trips, exhaustion (and grumpiness) from late nights and early mornings of writing, and is all round just the most wonderful person I know. I am also indebted to my parents Baden Smith & Deborah Williams for their proof reading & feedback, and to Nicola Smith for her help with the German translations. My thanks must also go to my editor, Imogen Evans, for ironing out the many wrinkles in my writing. Kieran Mace designed the cover, as he did for Where Giants Walk, and I am eternally grateful to him, not only for his infinite patience with my endless tweaks and changes, but also for producing such fantastic covers.

Finally I want to thank you, the readers. Publishing The Soviet Comeback was a dream come true, but it's only because of your support that I was able to see my way to diving back into Nikita's world. I'm constantly astonished that anyone would want to read anything I've written. Thank you so much!

Stay up to date with all the latest news from Jamie Smith!

Instagram @theexhaustedwriter

Facebook @jamiesmithbooks

TikTok @theexhaustedwriter

Printed in Dunstable, United Kingdom